THE LOW ROAD

The
LOW
ROAD

Katharine Quarmby

unbound

First published in 2023

Unbound
c/o TC Group, 6th Floor Kings House, 9–10 Haymarket,
London, United Kingdom, SW1Y 4BP
www.unbound.com

This book is a fictional account based on historical sources. In some
cases, names of people, places and sequences have been changed.
See the acknowledgements on pages 315–8 for more detail.

Typeset by Jouve (UK), Milton Keynes

A CIP record for this book is available from the British Library

ISBN 978-1-80018-239-4 (hardback)
ISBN 978-1-80018-240-0 (ebook)

Printed in Great Britain by CPI Group (UK)

1 3 5 7 9 8 6 4 2

With thanks to the patrons of this book:

Mary Quarmby
Josie Tindale
Raffy Tindale

*For my family, and in memory of Michael Quarmby,
1935–2017; Stephen Tindale, 1963–2017 and
Ingrid Abrell, 1966–2017*

Ye'll take the high road
And I'll take the low road

Part One
Waveney Valley, Norfolk

Chapter One

The sound of it in the darkness, a thudding; the fracturing next, then silence before a screaming fills the air till it is full. I am clenched in a grip that defeats me.

The man on the black horse is quite still. The constable looks at him. He nods. The stake descends again.

I must be the one who is screaming and I am wet with tears, or is it sweat, and I am held so tightly that I cannot break free.

The clutch releases. I open my eyes and they are on each side of me and their voices are low, reassuring. I look at them in the candlelight and slowly come back to here, to now. He helps me up for a moment, I rest against him. She makes the bed and I lie down on cool cotton. Between the two of them.

I wasn't always like this. I think if I tell the truth it will help me, and so, as the light moves across the swept wooden floor, I make a start. There will be gaps, I don't doubt. I will tell what I can when I can.

For a moment I remember how it felt, holding that dear dying hand, so worn down and rough with honest labour. How she fixed me with her eyes and told me: *write down what you cannot say out loud.* I wasn't sure then how much I could reveal.

It's different now. I cannot get through this if I do not talk true, tell the whole of my story now. So I make a start. This is not just for me any more.

The worst comes first. If I could stand with the child I was, and take her by the hand, if I could pull that poor little girl to my breast so she could not see what is about to unfold I would, a thousand times. Too late for that, so instead I'll tell our tale, the child, the girl and woman that I was and am, and I'll mend our story so that it becomes a whole for the first time.

This is a story about love, honestly. About the three people I have loved with everything I have in me, and how I've loved them miles and miles and years and years apart and I won't be told by anyone, any more, that my love is wrong. I take the words that have been thrown at me and I cast them away. I will not be judged. I am not unnatural or vicious. Let me explain.

Here I am where it started then, as dusk falls on a late spring day. It has not chilled yet, and my window is open. I hear the thud and scuffling of many footsteps on the dusty road outside the doctor's house. I stand on my tippy toes and peer out of the attic window and as far as I can see there are people, a great crowd of them, processing slowly down the Thoroughfare. As they come closer, I see that Matthew Wypond is at the front.

Then I see my mama lying on a cart. The sacking that should have covered her nakedness has slipped. The great concourse moves on and my eyes are scarred with this, as if a hot knife has seared my eyeballs.

The birds do not sing even as they roost for the night so that the only sound is the trundling of the wheels, for the people are quite silent, their heads bowed.

4

I tear my sheet from my bed and I run down the back stairs. I am clad in the linen shift I won on that fine day when I ran the length of the town and could not be beaten. I keep my head down, join the back of the concourse. The street is dry beneath my bare feet.

The light has nearly left the sky when we arrive at Lush Bush, where our parish ends and another begins. Everyone halts, and I creep between their legs. They are spattered with mud, blood on the butcher's long apron, the reek of unwashed people at the end of a long day's work.

I must get to my mama for I have her shroud. I see a great deep hole, hard by the willow tree. I hear the sound of a horse, trotting, and there is the archdeacon, Tom Olderhall, astride Black Bessie. He pulls on her bit and she walks through the crowd to the centre. To the hole.

Two men lift my mama from the cart. I see now that she is dead then, the archdeacon spoke true. And then I am whirled upwards, and Jem Summers is smiling at me with the two teeth missing that means that he whistles as he talks and he hoists me to his shoulders and fixes me there so I cannot move. Olderhall nods, once.

The men tip my mama in the hole and it is then that I scream and try to throw my bed sheet in to shroud her, but I cannot reach her. Summers laughs but then the silence falls. Although Olderhall gives no blessing, all at once the people kneel, but Summers does not let me go so I sway, sickened, as the people remove their hats. Olderhall sits high and straight above us on Black Bessie, frowning.

He nods again.

The parish constable takes a stake and places it between my mama's breasts and then another man drives it home. A long sigh comes out from all of us, and then he nods once more. The stake makes sure. My mama will wander no longer on the parish boundary. She is fixed for ever more.

The screaming is all around us and it comes from me, a child of just ten years, and then it cuts off with a gulp of air and at last I am silent.

Chapter Two

Before then. I was a girl living with my mama on Wypond's Farm, in the village of Weybread, in the Waveney Valley, right near the market town of Harleston, in the Earsham Hundred, in the fine English county of Norfolk. My mama, Mary, named me Hannah Tyrell. The farmer, Joseph Wypond, grazed his cows and sheep on the water meadows and I could see them, moving slowly from spot to spot, if I stood right straight and peeped out of the small bedroom window. If I looked the other way, stretching out as far as I could until my neck ached with it, there was nothing but fields, flat and far, until they met the big old sky. Joseph Wypond and the good wife, Martha, grew barley for the brewery, oats, wheat and some smaller fields of rye and sugar beet. But the good wife loved her milk cows most of all.

I begged to help Mama and the good wife with the milking, and so when I turned five or six, they put me to it. We washed our hands under the pump with a sliver of soap so thin I could see through it, and then we took the clean buckets into the barn. We had a stool each, and I remember how it felt to sit down by the warm flank of a cow, and take the teats in each hand, holding them between my thumb and forefinger and pulling gently down as the milk spurted into the pail. Sometimes the cows moved, restive. The good wife said, "Stroke them on their flank, girl, talk to them gentle," and so I did and learned how to still them. As I grew accustomed to them, I could milk with my eyes half closed. At the end of milking, when our work was done, the good wife took up her scoop and filled up three small wooden cups with warm milk. That was my dawn and my dusk until I turned eleven.

By evening I was so tired that Mama would push me up the stairs, step by step and round the corner till we were in our room. If lift up my arms even today, as I undress, sometimes it comes back to me, how I would stand there as she slid my garments up and over, fold them neatly on the chair and then do the same till we were naked together and shivering as we put on our nightgowns and knelt down. The rag rug was soft beneath my knees as she prayed that the Good Lord would keep us safe from the perils and dangers of the night, then a sigh as she added, without fail, "on land and sea". Then last of all, a prayer for my dear dead father, and then we climbed into bed for the best moment in our day.

The tales told in bed, I try to remember all of them, but they come back in snatches for I must have slept and missed so many endings, so what I have is in fragments. Tales of the sea, up Great Yarmouth way, where the Tyrells came from, they were my favourite, as I lay curled up like a teaspoon inside a soup spoon, breath on my neck as she talked. Those tales, she told me, which were sometimes bad, sometimes happy and sometimes sad. Sometimes I have woken since and a piece has matched up with what I knew, so it makes sense at last. Sometimes, though, a patch has torn off from the whole. I wish I could summon her, ask her how I should stitch my tale together.

See I can conjure her up even now, her voice with the grey North Sea in it, a washing and pulling over Yarmouth Sands. "I was born a week before Christmas, in the year 1785, within sight and sound of the sea, and if I close my eyes, girl, I find myself there again."

Her voice was sometimes steady and sometimes warmed with remembered happiness, a chuckle in the back of the throat, a rough hand gently stroking my head.

"I can even smell the herring that Father hauled home at the end of a good day's fishing. We had our two lighthouses, to guide the fleet in, and there was the fine old church of St Nicholas, which rose so high that you could see it wherever you were and follow it home. I was christened there in the bitter February of 1786, and then our Henry after me, three years on. Our house was in the third row, counting back from the marketplace, and we would run up and down the rows, back and forth to school or to get provisions, dodging the troll carts. They would come rumbling along after you, and you would hear a man or woman shouting for you to 'git out the way, bor' and we would squeeze ourselves against the wall so that they could rumble past and look at what they were carrying. Once we were through the rows and out on the quay there were ships, as far as our eyes could see, so close that there was scarcely a gap between them, so that even a child could jump from one to one. If they dared. If I dared."

Her voice breaks on the shore and I fall asleep.

I can see the farm table, where we ate together and worked side by side. The great brown teapot and the sugar bowl next to it, the bread that we proved and kneaded every day, the churned butter, salted and melting on the crust I was given every time the loaf came out of the oven so that my tongue fair popped with flavour when I bit down. My favourite food was a Sunday best, dumplings with salted pork, green beans from the kitchen garden if it was summer, or a braised dish of rooted vegetables from the sacks in the barn, herbs sprinkled on top with a flick of Mama's fingers. In the hungry gap, when the harvest was eaten and our stores ran low, we rode up to market in Harleston and shopped for heavy baskets of provisions until I thought my arm would break. I did not know what hunger was then.

Even now, when I open the door to the big barn and the waiting animals, as I breathe in, it takes me back to that other barn I knew then, the cows and the sheep, the horses that farmer Joseph kept to hitch to his cart, and then his sturdy young stots he raised for the market. I breathe in and I am home, or sometimes, when I am near running water, I swim back upriver, through the years to the beck, which joined the Waveney and ran slow and quiet through the water meadows. On the spring and summer evenings, once the men had finished their working day, they took up their rods and went down there and cast into the clear water. I can remember the great day that old Mr Snowling hauled out a pike that weighed in at a full ten pounds and he brought us a piece. I pulled out the bones from my mouth and never ate it again.

I was sent to the parish school in a village nearby, whose name I have somehow forgotten. I remember walking there after milking, over the fields with Mama, to join the other boys and girls. The Reverend Smith, who taught us at first, was very kind to us. He was a tall, well-built man, although deaf so we had to speak up loudly when we sang our letters out. He taught us to ring the handbells as well, for he told us that he missed the bells he had rung as a young churchman, and so we rang out a chime for him quite heartily for we loved him. He even taught us to knit and sew, although Mama had raised me already to do both, so he would pat my head as I knitted a row in front of him, quick as anything. I was always sorry on the days that I had to miss school, when all of us were put to sowing crops or bringing in the harvest, for I loved it there so much.

I recall one fine warm day when Mama was not in a bustle to get back to the farm, on the way home from school. She led me off the cart track and down to the river, to a place she knew where the bank sloped gently into the water. We sat down and she fumbled in her pocket, brought out a bread roll to share, still warm from the oven, wrapped in cloth.

The taste of the salt butter on the warm bread stays with me, as we gazed out on the river and ate until every crumb was gone and all that was left was a lick of salt on my lips. Then Mama lay down on her stomach, and so did I. "Look, Hannah," and she showed me how to float my fingers into the water so that the little fishes could swim under and over. "Close your eyes now," she said, and I did. There was a tickle over my hands, and I opened my eyes to see how the fishes moved across them; I laughed to feel them, and so did she.

In the winters it was different, and we went at a brisk trot to and from the school. Two years running the river froze over and all who had boots skated the length of it between Redenhall and Barber's Sluice. That second year, when I turned seven, or eight was it, Robert Threlford ducked too late as he skated under the bridge and laid himself out quite flat on the ice. He woke up to find the whole village laughing, as he swore out loud that there were stars in the sky though it was still daytime.

There was a place in the river where Mama and the other villagers always pulled us children past, fast as they could. It was just as we walked up the hill into Harleston, over the Shotford Bridge, where the river curves right round like a bent pin and is deep and fronded so that the water runs over the waving weeds. If any folk were on a cart the man would whip the horses hard to trot over the bridge, fast as they could. I asked Mama why one day, but she pinched her lips together and said not one word. Then I went behind Mama's back, for I was quite eaten up with curiosity.

I was in the kitchen with the good wife, when she was dropping off one afternoon and I was sewing up a rent in a skirt. She opened one eye, drowsy and looked at me sleepily. "I remember my grandmama telling me that the witches were ducked there, and if they floated, they were condemned. Look around when we cross, my lovely, for if you see magpies, the witches will be nearby. You be careful now, my girl." I gasped, but she had fallen fast asleep now, and I dared not tell Mama what she had said.

Every time we crossed the bridge I looked down into the water where the weeds floated and then up into the air in case there were magpies above us, with their blue-black plumage glinting as they flew.

Sometimes, when I dreamed, the witches visited me, asking me to free them from the green fronds that grew in the depths and had entangled them. I would wake up and Mama, stirring, would ask me thickly what ailed me. But I did not tell her and instead waited, safe in her arms but quite stiffened, until the witches freed themselves and flew up and vanished into the night air. Then at last I could sleep.

I think I knew even then that I was lucky to live with my mama on Wypond's Farm, for I never wanted for a thing and that was not true of everyone in the village. From time to time Mama and the good wife would hunt out everything that was spare in the great larder and pack it up, and then Mama and I would fill a basket each and take it out to families who had less than ourselves.

One of them I remember well, for her husband had died and when we got to her cottage at the end of the village, I could hardly believe what I saw when we went in. Everything had been sold from under them, so they slept in their clothes on the floor and the children sat in a row on the dry soil as I went along and fed them.

When we left them, shaking her head, Mama said that the poor man had been in despair, for he had lost his employment, and been driven to an awful death. Now the family had no money.

"Still," she said, with a shake and a shiver, "I will pay our respects when he is buried at the church, but you will stay behind to milk on your own."

She came back from the funeral with the good wife, and I saw how they were both crying, and then Mama wiped her eyes on her apron and joined me for the last of the milking.

"Was it terrible, Mama?" I asked, once we were in bed.

"They have been sent to the workhouse now and their cottage is empty," she said. We hardly knew them, but she was so sad.

"Can we visit them there, Mama?" I asked. I felt how her arm tightened around me.

"No," she said, between her sobs, and when we were next walking by the workhouse she pulled me to her and away from the gates and hurried me on. I never knew why she hated and feared the buildings that locked the poor like us in, until much later.

On Sundays we walked along the lane and the Low Road, and I watched where the sky joined the land until at last, I spied it, the church tower soaring out of the flat lands, the four turrets glinting gold in the sun. There was a good half hour walk after that sight, for the church sat like a squat toad amongst the fields, with only the tower soaring up into the skies. As we got nearer, we could hear the old bells ringing out that were lifted into the tower when old Queen Elizabeth reigned, summoning all to prayer. When we got to the church, I would count the white and brown cattle out loud for Mama – one, two, up to thirty at times – as they grazed quiet on the meadowlands. Then Mama would open the lych gate, and walk past the gravestones. In the spring violets and primroses burst out with colour in the green hedges, and the birds sang their hearts out. We would always stop at one particular grave with a wooden cross, and lay flowers we had gathered, or winter berries. This was where my papa lay, from before I was even born.

For Mama was a widow, she said. The man she had been betrothed to, my papa, her George, had died. His family, the Lings, did not know us, even in church.

I knew this tale off by heart, and when I remember it now, I can hear how she told me, with her voice rising and falling like the sea, and how she held me closer and closer as she talked until I could hardly breathe.

"We had saved for many months so that we could marry. I had no dowry and George's family had set themselves against the marriage." A deep sigh, and then she continued. "The good wife had given me a grey dress, in a soft cotton, and I had hand sewn our favourite flowers around the hem, cornflowers for me, and poppies for George. I had put by a small trousseau, too, and hand sewn it, in the summer evenings when there was enough light. You know the dress." Her voice wavered. Then she brought her tale to an end, with a kiss on my head. "He would have loved you with all his heart, my dear one, but he was taken from us too early."

She never told me how, but I knew, right enough, for she had cried in the kitchen with the good wife on the day that marked his death, and the good wife had held her and told Mama that she would never be alone, as long as she lived, and that the farm was our home. I sat at the top of the winding stair and listened as Mama recounted what had happened, as if she could not believe how he had been taken from her so sudden, as if by talking she could wind back time and win my papa back.

"I'll never forget what you did for me," said Mama.

A rumble from the good wife, kindly as always, then she spoke up clear.

"His was the first accident with a threshing machine, but not the last. I can still hear your screams when they came running to tell you that his hand got stuck."

I wanted to go to Mama and comfort her, but I needed to know the truth about my papa. I held my breath to hear the last of it.

"I cannot tell you how it was to sit with him on the cart as we jogged up to Dr White, and how he winced over every jolt but even tried to smile at me. And then they carried him in to Dr White and I was sent out and I could hear this awful sawing sound and one sharp cry from George."

"They had cut off his finger for it was so badly crushed," Mama added.

The good wife spoke then, and said, "I still cannot understand why the Lings have been so cruel to you, for Hannah is their only granddaughter."

"They never acknowledged me, even when he was dying, for they blamed me. They said I had forced him to take the work on the machine, and that it was my job to check it and if I had done so it would not have jammed. But that was never true and when Mrs Ling came to the doctor's house she cursed me and has never spoken to me since."

I heard how the good wife comforted Mama as she sobbed her way through the last few hours of Papa's life. "Dr White came to me and I knew straight away from his face and I flew down to George and kissed him. He jerked one last time, then he was still, and I saw how the whiteness crept up from his fingers and the colour left his dear face and my poor George was gone."

I shuddered at that, and crept away, when I had heard more than enough, about how the magistrate had called for an inquest at the Swan Inn, and how Mama was spared any blame, but she had to give evidence all the same, pregnant with me.

Mama went through a hard labour with me on the farm. Just before she pushed me out from safety into the wide world, the parish midwife, Mercy Gunton, came in to inquire upon the father. Mama cried out in her pain and told Wife Gunton it was her George, her true love, but that he was dead.

Just moments later there I was and I had dark hair like my mama and papa, and the good wife Martha cleaned me as best she could, and swaddled me, and laid Mama down gently after washing her, and put me at her breast. I had been right easy to feed and had latched on straightway, then fallen asleep on the breast. That was always the point in the story when Mama would say, as she stroked my hair, "You are all I have ever wanted, my girl." But then her voice would tremble, as she added, "If only your papa had held you, just the once."

Then the parish, armed with the information from Mrs Gunton, went to the Lings for relief. But they denied the betrothal, and denied that they would have been married and said Mama had ill-used Papa by not minding the machine well enough.

"They never owned who you were to them," said Mama, and if it was not for the good wife, where would we be? "She kept my place here, and promised that no cost would ever fall on the parish." And so the Lings were not pressed for relief, and some even called me a bastard, and my mama worse words still.

The Reverend Smith christened me, although some people said it was wrong to do so. Mama said I hardly cried when he took me in his arms, and poured water on my head, and said the blessed words: "She will be kept safe, and turned away from Satan." Mama took the pen she was given, and wrote my name into the register. "No dead man could be named as father, so I was not allowed to write Papa's name in, and so the reverend entered you as base born. But we know the truth." This said by Mama with a brave look on her face.

So Mama always laid flowers at his grave and then looked me up and down, from my shoes to my bonnet, before we went into the church. She would tie my hat closer and flick dust off my clothes and shoes and tell me to put my shoulders back and walk straight into the church, and make her proud.

We sat at the back of the church, in the free seats, on the nearest side to the carved oak door where all entered. The working men sat on the other side. If we were kept working too long, and had to hurry to get to the service, we had to climb upwards, where a few old stools jostled for space before you took the winding stairs to the bell tower. That was my favourite seat, looking down on the people of the town, for I could be quiet there, and gaze down on the whole crowd of them. I would try not to laugh as I saw one scratch his head and then another person did the same, as the lice jumped from pate to pate, and I saw a child pinch his sister, and nobody looked up to see how I watched.

Once the poor were in their places, I would hear a trotting and then a flurry of voices outside, as the carriages came up the track to the church. The archdeacon and the great people of the parish came in, two at a time, to sit at the front in their private pews, processing down the aisle towards the nave. There went the squire from the Gawdy Hall estate, and the other squires from further afield if they were visiting, the doctor and his wife, and the overseer, Mr Wypond, the farmer's brother. He would turn and nod to his brother and his wife somewhat grandly, as if he was better than them, but everyone knew who he was just the same, and some wondered quite openly why the overseer was not married, with him nearing some forty years in age.

Then came the pews for the postmaster and the draper, then Mr Henry Fox, the town's attorney, then the butcher and the other tradespeople. Then came the churchwarden to shut the collarmaker, the watchmaker and the grocers into their pews, with bowing and bowing, and I would count them all in as the pew doors closed with a snap. The farmer and his wife sat near to us, and the good wife would always turn and wave at me. Sometimes we walked back together, and sometimes she even found room for us in the cart, if it was raining.

One day, in the February when I turned eight years of age, on Valentine's Day, the Archdeacon Tom Olderhall, our new reverend, came calling at the schoolroom for the first time. Silence fell as he entered, for he was now the big man of the parish, and then we rose as one to honour him. I had heard about him, for the farmer's brother had visited and told the good wife all about the honour of the great man arriving. He had met him and welcomed him to the town, and had an audience with him. The archdeacon had not chosen to come here, he told Wypond, but it was his Christian duty. He had wanted to pursue his studies in algebra, for he had won prizes for his superior knowledge. But instead his father had told him that he would represent his alma mater in the county of Norfolk. He might even become the Dean of Norwich, and this would be an even greater honour for the parish.

He had ridden over from Cambridge on his horse, Black Bessie. He had told Wypond that he had taken advice from the Reverend Walton, and he would reduce the number of base-born children in the parish, and there would be no more baptisms of such children as Reverend Smith had done.

After he had gone Mama brought the dough from the larder and slapped it against the table, as she spoke with the good wife. "Hannah, you must go upstairs," the good wife said, and shut the door against me. But I put my ear to it, and heard snatches of what she said to Mama.

"You must be careful, Mary, for he has an eye on women without husbands. On children who are base born."

Mama spoke then and I heard how angry she was, as she thumped the bread.

"It is not our fault. Does it count for nothing that we were going to marry before he died?"

The good wife murmured something back, comforting at first, but Mama spoke up and at last Martha said sharply, "I have told you, stay out of his way. For Hannah's sake, if not your own."

And then I heard the kitchen door slam and the good wife sigh impatiently, and I tiptoed upstairs as the dough slapped on the board, more violently than before, until at last there was silence, and a smell of baking.

The archdeacon's wife, Elizabeth, the daughter of the warden at his college, came four weeks later to open up the rectory at Starston. The good wife visited her and told Mama how beautiful she was, with dimples in her cheeks, golden hair and blue eyes. She gazed up at her husband in church, I noticed, as if he was God himself. But she looked away in his first sermon when he thundered about fallen women and I saw how her gaze faltered, before she put her head down and her bonnet hid her from view.

Her husband visited my school two or three times a week. And on that day, as he swept into the classroom, I was instructed to stand up straight and say to him, "Good morrow, Valentine." And I remember that I spoke so well that his stern face softened briefly and he fumbled in his cassock and he gave me a penny, a whole penny, for speaking up so clearly.

At Easter that same year the whole town assembled for the races down the Thoroughfare. Mama put me in for the eight years and under and Jem Summers and the overseer held the ribbon on each side of the children to mark our starting line. Then the archdeacon blew the whistle, the ribbon fell away and we were off. I knew I could run, but not like that. I left the girls behind me, then the boys. The twins to Jem Summers were just in front of me. I could beat them, I thought, and I ran between them and to the finish line and it was only when we were walking back, and one of the two kicked me, that I saw they were quite dark with anger that a girl had beaten them. But as we came to the square there was my mama, a great grin on her face, and the archdeacon Olderhall holding a packet for me, and two smaller packets for the twins.

I unwrapped it later, with Mama. "It is quite beautiful," she said, stroking down the embroidered shift. "Almost too pretty to wear." And then, with a shake of her head, "Your papa ran as you did. Like the wind. You did us proud, girl." A little pause, then she added, "I saw how the archdeacon smiled on you. Perhaps things will turn out well, after all."

Chapter Three

O n May Day there was a furious flurry at the farm. We roused ourselves and the milking was done right early and the cows led out with a slap on their rumps to the meadows. The farmer was outside brushing the horses down and he had brought a man to the farm for the evening milking, for we were going out for the day. I helped the good wife and Mama pick flowers and wind them around the sides of the cart and to garland the two fine horses. The three of us went into the house then, to dress in our Sunday best, but still Mama would tell me nothing about where we were going, as I heard the horses being readied for a day out. Instead she plaited my hair with two pink ribbons and bade me shush so we could hurry. We ran back outside. The farmer stepped back and his face cracked open to see the three of us. "Pretty as a picture, all of you," he said, as he helped the good wife up first, her round cheeks shining, then Mama, along with a great basket and an earthenware jug, both covered over with muslin, with Mama holding tight for safety. Last of all me, with a rough bow.

I piped up, "Where are we going?" and all of them looked at each other before Mama put a finger on her lip and said,

"Just you wait and see." With a jolt we were off, and before long had turned off the farm track, into the village and beyond.

When I woke from Mama's shoulder, for it had been an early start, I found that we were by the river, in a spot where I had never been before. All around me there were market stalls and everyone was dancing and there was a long pole in the middle with ribbons. I clapped my hands and I saw how all of them were smiling at me, and one after one the farmer whirled us off the cart. Mama undid the basket and the farmer and his wife handed round large hunks of bread and cheese and we stood there in a row, eating. Then she poured out a sweet drink for each of us, and I could taste the honey and lemon in it, though I was allowed no more than a few sips, and then the farmer took his wife's hand and they went off to the dance.

We packed up the food and then Mama took my hand. First, we danced up and down and across and around and she told me this was called strip the willow. I can feel her hands on my arms, my waist, even now, how she guided me through the steps that all the dancers knew but me, and how she held me tight and let me loose, and then off I spun in the dance as we moved up and down. I saw how the good wife beamed as the farmer stumbled over his feet, and how the whole great party laughed and danced. My feet were fair smarting, but as that dance reached its end, we all then stood in a circle and took a ribbon; Mama and I shared one. The music started again and we wove in and out as my feet burned hotter and hotter, and at the end, I looked at the pole and the ribbons were woven together and now everyone was smiling and clapping their hands and the farmer and his wife held each other tight and he was stroking her hair.

Mama took me to sit on the cart, and I leaned on her

shoulder and looked out. The musicians were up higher, on a stage, and I saw how they were dark and the men wore scarves around their necks, rings through their ears and how their feet tapped as they played. There was one young man whose hair curled over his collar, and at the end of a song they all ceased except him; he put his violin to rest on his shoulder and then his bow sang a song that I knew was sad and happy at the same time, and I saw how all the faces turned up to him and then to the ones they loved as they held them tighter.

Mama must have carried me up the stairs asleep that night because I woke to find her shaking me and smiling, and it was milking time again. As I leaned against my cow, half asleep, I asked Mama, "Can we do that every May Day?"

She laughed and said the farmer would decide, but she hoped so. "After May Day comes the summer, and then the harvest, so there is plenty to look forward to," she said, passing me my mug of milk. We drank them together and I saw how she had a moustache of white froth, before she wiped it on her apron.

We had a good harvest that year, and Joseph and Martha gathered everyone together in September to celebrate, with a table groaning with food, and he sat at one end, and his wife at the other.

Before we ate, the farmer gave a prayer of thanks for the plentiful food, the hard work, the good weather, and the plentiful harvest. The workers were thanked as we ate, and Mama was given an extra shilling for setting out the table, for to produce such a feast was a right enterprise. The farmer himself took the knife and great ladle, saying it was his turn to serve, and heaped fine red meat on the plates, in a thick stew with carrots, turnips and potatoes.

Usually the farmer dealt with rabbits and hares himself,

hanging them for a full seven days for he liked his game rich. This time he had no occasion to skin the hare himself, so Mama herself had to cut the fur, then get her hand in and pull the skin off. "Like flaying," she muttered, and looked fair green with disgust.

I could not look away from the hare's head, cut loose from its body, staring at me all the while as Mama took his jacket off, as the farmer called it. "You've undressed him well," he said, passing through. "Can you paunch him yourself?" Mama nodded reluctantly, and pulled out the hare's entrails, cleaned the body of its waste. When he was clean inside, she held him up and poured his blood into a bucket, threw the innards in.

"Here, Hannah, for the dog," she said, handing me the bucket. The old dog came out to the end of his chain eagerly, as I went over. I tipped the mass into his dish and walked away so I did not hear his jaws working.

We jugged the hare with carrots, turnips and potatoes, and I ate heartily as the men did, for I relished the taste. But I cast an eye sideways, saw how Mama hid her portion underneath a turnip, then scraped it away hurriedly into the waste when she cleared the plates. I wondered why she did that, but all of a sudden the men took out their clay pipes and lit them, and the bowls smoked so much that I could not even see my mama's face.

I coughed and heard a man laugh, and felt my mama put an arm around me; then the farmer opened the kitchen door and the smoke cleared.

The men put the table to one side and I was set to work, putting out more candles until the whole room was alight and the smoke drifted up and away. Mama took me in her arms and a fiddle scraped, then we all started to dance. Mama handed me on to the good wife and we danced strip the willow and I laughed out loud to hear the clogs and boots all about us, clicking and galloping on the hard stone floor, as Mama watched on smiling. A pause then, before the next dance struck up, and Jem Summers came towards me, begging for my hand. Mama shook her head.

"If she will not dance then you must," he said, with a hoarse guffaw, and dragged her to the middle of the room. She looked back at me for a moment and tried to smile. I watched how she danced with him, and how he passed her to the overseer, and then my eyes must have closed for the next thing I knew, it was morning time and we were in bed together, her arm curled around me.

Chapter Four

The good wife was stricken, a month after Harvest Supper. She lost a child, who would have been their first-born, and the poor tiny body was buried in the churchyard. He had not been christened, so the archdeacon said there could be no funeral, but he would say a blessing as he was laid to rest, and the farmer and the good wife came back in tears.

She was in pain all over and she asked Mama to go to the dispensary for opium or laudanum, anything that would ease her sorrow. I begged to go with her, for I loved the town and I had never been in the dispensary. We walked up the hill in silence, and there was no pointing out of fruits in the hedgerows, or birds in the sky, or playing a counting game with me. This I knew meant that taking me was against her better judgement, her mouth shut like a trap and her eyes set forward, walking so fast that I had to run and then walk so as to keep up with her.

I was excited all the same as I had never entered the shop before, and it was a mysterious place from the outside; I ran to the door and opened it for my mama as the bell tinkled overhead. It was not a big place, from the inside, but quite dark and resplendent with wooden panels from floor to ceiling. Mrs Spurgeon stood behind a high counter, in a starched white apron. Above her were glass bottles in different colours – clear, blue, brown and green. The brown ones were set high on a shelf behind her. White pottery measuring jugs sat on the counter, below which there were more bottles, and the dark panels slid open so that the apothecary, Mr Spurgeon, also quite resplendent, could select his items. Mama asked for "Mrs Wypond's medicine" and before handing it over, the apothecary asked, earnestly, how she was faring. Mama nodded and said she was recovering, with God's grace.

Then the apothecary handed over a brown paper bag, with four packets inside, and wished us a good morning. Mama handed over the money, and then we walked back. I was not so happy to go again, more than once a week, as the year turned and the road up to Harleston grew mired and icy. The good wife had become so desperate that she would be watching for us at the farm gate and walk with us to the kitchen. She would have a jug of water on the table, and swallow her packet down in one gulp, she was so eager to recover.

But she grew no better and could no longer milk. She was so quiet now, so tired. Mama pleaded with her to rise early, to get back to the old ways, before the sorrow, but the good wife could not find a way out of her sickness. Mama brewed her poppy tea to still the pain, and she sat by the window, sipping it, until she put it down and asked for her powders instead. Mama asked the chemist if there was anything weaker she could give the good wife, and he offered her Godfrey's Cordial instead, in a dark brown bottle, and Mama put the powders away. As the good wife got even weaker, she took to sipping this instead, off a teaspoon, until her hands shook so much that Mama took the spoon and fed her off it like a baby. I smelt it once, and it was sweet and sickly. I put out my tongue to lick what was left but Mama caught me, slapped my hand away and the spoon clattered onto the floor.

The farmer said little, as his wife wasted away before his eyes. But our household changed, and there was no more singing as he came in after working, and he could not whirl the good wife round when he saw her, but instead dropped a kiss on her poor head. Where once the good wife had held sway at the table, now it was he. We had taken over the milking, but now Mama also helped the good wife to dress, whilst I mucked out with one of the men, and at night there were no more stories, for we were both so tired. Mama then helped the good wife down to the parlour, and she only spoke to ask for her Godfrey's, like a child begging for a sweetmeat. She would sit by the open window and go into a kind of dreamland.

I can see the farmer now, standing at the open door, looking at his wife, as she looked out and away from him. As if he had lost her, but she was still there.

I asked Mama when she would get better, and Mama just shook her head and looked down at me. "She lost her child, Hannah; a woman finds it hard to recover from such a loss," and she stroked my hair. I ran to the good wife then and tried to rouse her, amuse her with a game of cat's cradle. But she just sat there, quite still, the wool falling from her limp fingers, and in the end, Mama took me away and put me to work.

Towards the end of that year the good wife seemed to grow smaller; sometimes I wondered if she would just disappear altogether. She shrivelled and shrank, and Mama took in her dresses for her, tightening the seams so they fitted again, on a Sunday afternoon before the light faded.

Towards the end, as the pain got worse, she could take as many as a hundred drops of laudanum in one night, and still moan with pain. And in the day, she was so stupefied she hardly knew me at all, but she knew Mama, and followed her with her eyes, slowly, like a dying dog.

She died just two weeks before Christmas, a hop and skip before my mama's birthday. She was to be buried in the churchyard at Redenhall, and when they came to measure her for her coffin, it was almost as small as that of a child; four men were enough to carry her out to the cart and on to the churchyard. We followed after, crying. I loved her, and so did Mama, and nobody I knew had ever died in my born days.

Not even a week after she passed, Archdeacon Olderhall came to the farm on Black Bessie, looped her reins over the farm post and knocked and entered the kitchen without waiting. I was chopping apples at the table, as the farmer sat there, still and silent, as he had done every day since the good wife passed. Mama had told me, "Just stay with him, when I cannot."

Olderhall sat down. The farmer scarcely stirred, and so Olderhall reached over, tapped him on the shoulder. "Your brother sends his regards, Wypond."

A pause, and then to business. "Boney is threatening trouble." He spoke grimly and my knife shook in my hand.

Mama had told me about the emperor, Napoleon Bonaparte, and the sea battles that brought the wounded to shore up on the coast, round Yarmouth way. "There were men who lost limbs, my girl, yet they kept Boney from our shores," she said proudly, although others had lost their lives. Yet he was threatening us still, from over the seas.

"I will be training the men to defend themselves if he invades. I can count on you, Wypond?" A question in his voice and the farmer looked up at last. Olderhall continued. "If Boney comes ashore, I will send the children and wives to the workhouse for safety." At that I shivered with fear and saw how the farmer started, and tears rounded in his eyes, for he had no wife or child, but Olderhall talked on, ignorant of the pain he was causing.

Come rain or shine he forced the men out to drill, after their labouring day was over, the mud and blood and sweat on them. On market day, when she went among the other women with her basket, Mama always stopped and bade Elizabeth good morning, for other people pulled away from her and conversations broke off when she pulled open the door of a shop and the bell tinkled overhead. Mama said that she should not be blamed for her husband, for what did she know of how resentment was building against him throughout the parish, and she was powerless to stop him anyway.

Farmer Wypond had kept us on, and for that Mama told me that we should be grateful, for we had a roof over our heads and food to eat. But he was a broken man, and he would sit for hours, brooding, in the candlelight. His brother, Matthew, the overseer, came to the farm often, to assist, or so he said. He would stay there at night, instead of riding his horse back to Harleston, and he would call on Mama, quite sharply, to make up a bed for him. I noticed that she slid past him, her arms full of sheets, flattened to the wall. I did not understand why her face was blank, but I felt quite sick inside, to see her shrink away like that.

Mama had taken to coming to bed later, and sometimes I woke when she came in. I would feel behind me, for Mama would shake, silently, and once her face was damp and salty and she struck my hand away roughly and turned away from me. I cried out, and it was only then that she said she was sorry, and that her head hurt, and then she kissed me and I fell asleep.

*

Harvest Supper came round again, the first without Martha presiding. The farmer had brought in a hare again, and his brother had brought some rabbits, shot over Redenhall way. Mama skinned them, paunched them and dressed them but when we were alone in the kitchen, she told me that I was to go upstairs when the men came from the town.

"The overseer is bringing a party of them from the town. On no account are you to come down. They are disorderly, and I will serve them alone."

She slammed the cleaver into the rabbits, and a part flew off into a corner. Mama did not heed it, and continued to hack the rabbits into rough chunks, and then threw them into the pot. Once I had finished with the vegetables and the pot was on the simmer, she sent me up with bread and cheese and her face was quite black and stern.

The light left my room and still I could not sleep, for Mama was down there with the disorderly men and the smoke was drifting up the stairs and I hated the reek of the pipes. I could hear the clash of tankards clattering onto the table, and then the singing started, then the oaths.

There was fighting then, and jeers and whistles, and then a silence. I thought I heard my mama cry out, but it was muffled. I could not sleep but at last I heard her footsteps on the stairs, slow and tired. She said not a word to me, and I dared not tell her I was still awake.

A while after that harvest, as we were dressing for milking, I noticed Mama smooth down her stomach with both hands, and then sigh sharply. When she stood up, I saw that her stomach was sticking out and I asked her what she had eaten the day before to make her so fat. And before she could help herself her hand came out towards me and slapped me on the face. And then she gathered me to her, and cried out, "I am sorry, Hannah, so very sorry, please

31

forgive me," and it was as if she was the child and I her mama, for she sobbed until I thought she would soak the bed through.

It was a few days later that Mama told me that she would have another baby. I asked who the papa was, for I thought for one exciting moment that I would now have a father like others did, but she said there was none. She shook me then and said fiercely, "You must keep your silence about my state, you hear me now, my girl?" I was frightened but nodded.

The winter came and Mama swathed herself in layers and kept herself on the farm. She sent me up to the town on market day in her stead, as often as she could. I watched her stomach grow, and how Mama dressed so carefully so that it was hidden from view.

Chapter Five

I remember the night when my sister was born. It takes so little to travel back there; a woman's cry, a barking dog and the memory pulls and tugs, like a puckered scar.

It is just a few days before Easter, and Mama is not expecting it. She is mopping the kitchen floor, slowly, and I turn away from her to throw some scraps to the dog outside the door. She cries out suddenly, and I turn back to see her holding fast to the kitchen table as the water slops over the stones. It comes from Mama, and at last it stops. I run to her and she pants out, "Help me upstairs, my girl."

I hope the farmer will not notice that she is gone, but I recall that he is out in the fields. I can stay with her. She crouches and holds onto the bedstead at last and tells me to put a rag in her mouth. Between the pains she stops, pants out words. She tells me to go downstairs and come back with hot water, towels and a clean, whetted knife. "Hold the knife in the fire once you have sharpened it on the stone. Then wipe it clean and bring it straight up," she says, urgently.

I see with a jolt that the farmer has come back to the yard, and is washing himself at the pump. I tell him, stumbling over my words, that we are both unwell and need to sleep till milking. He shrugs, nods and walks back to the fields and at last I have time to hold the knife in the fire, wipe it clean, gather the items she asked for and run upstairs.

She sweats as she rocks back and forth. I bathe her neck, her forehead, as she labours. She cannot die, not my mama, and leave me here. "Please, Mama, please," I beg her and she makes an effort; she pushes one more time and it is just as it is in the barn, with the cows, and then our baby is there, followed by the dark red of the afterbirth.

The bells are ringing out for early service.

Mama whispers to me, as she holds the baby on her breast, that I must take the knife and cut the cord, close to my sister's stomach. I sob then, and ask her, "Will it hurt you?" and she gasps out that it will not. I take the knife. When I have cut it, she rasps out, "Tie a knot in it," and I do, though the tears are brimming in my eyes.

When it is done, I slop everything into the bucket, help Mama up so I can change the linen. "You must take the afterbirth with you, and you must milk, child. Tell the farmer nothing, Hannah, you cannot." I hear how she speaks, as if our lives depend on what I do now.

She falls asleep, with the baby curled into her arm. I look down at them. I take the linen with me and pick up the bucket. The whole room reeks of blood and soil, sharp scents to my nose. I must milk as if nothing is wrong, as if Mama has caught a chill and is ailing.

I tiptoe down the stairs, and take the bucket with me, linen over my arm. My head swims. I must conceal everything and clear and wash before the milking. I hear the dog bark as I creep outside, the bucket slopping. I tip the contents out – blood, afterbirth, cord – and the old dog rouses himself, whimpers. I watch him gulp it down, and turn away as the sickness rises in me. I have work to do. I walk over to the pump, wash out the linen. My hands are red and raw by the time I throw the wet bedding and clothes on the line. I wash them again until the blood has gone and the water runs clear.

By the time I am back from milking, Mama has stirred slightly. I see that the baby is feeding, her dark head close to Mama. I put out my hand, stroke the baby's head, feel how it pulses underneath my palm. She stirs, then falls off the breast, sleeping.

There was a tale that the good wife had told me when I was young myself, of the helpful folk who charmed away maladies and put the unwanted out of the way. She had told me that the good fairies that flew around and were ever present, even if they could not be seen, would rock an empty cradle, take away your trouble.

I look over at the cradle, pick up my sister and swaddle her. She makes no sound as I place her in the cradle, cover her warmly with blankets. The cradle rocks as I climb into bed, next to my mama.

Her eyes open briefly and move across to the baby in the cradle. A smile as faint as a breath crosses her face. Then she sings. A lullaby she sang for me when I was younger, from up on the coast, with the sound of the sea in it. I take a breath, join her song for the sleeping baby.

As my eyes close, I wonder if the good fairies will find the open window, take away our trouble, for what can we do with her?

I wake with a start, for a cold breeze shoots in and across my skin, and then the sun comes out in a clear blue sky. The old dog is barking, and the birds are calling.

Mama asks me to bring the baby over, and I swing out of bed, walk over to pick her up.

My sister is silent, cold and stiff. She will warm up, once she has fed. Mama struggles up to sit, holds out her arms. I carry the baby over, and for a moment she looks expectant, and then as she takes her she screams, then pushes the sheet into her mouth and screams again, in complete silence.

She weeps for hours and I do not know what to do but be busy as the horrible day goes on. My poor mama. I have placed the baby back in her cradle and sit on the bed, next to Mama. I give her water, but she will take nothing else. The light fades at the end of the day and I change Mama's rags, place her swollen leg on clean bedding, kiss her. "Kiss baby, one more time," I plead. She turns her head away, to the wall.

"Too cold," she says, but she holds out her hand to me and I take strength from her for what I must do now.

I wrap the baby tight in the blanket, then the sacking from the barn, and I wrap my shawl around me. I have only been out in the evening twice, when Mama took a fancy to walk to evensong so that we could be blessed against the week to follow, as she told me. I must find somewhere quiet for the baby, where she can lie and never be found. I open the door and walk down the stairs, with the baby tied to me beneath my shawl. I am shaking with fear, or is it cold, but I must do this, I must help my mama.

I go straight out and walk down the farm track. A bird flies out of the hedge in front of me, clatters and wheels away. I walk on, clutching my burden. I cannot lay her in the graveyard, for the earth is hard and besides, the grave-digger Sam Cook keeps a sharp eye on his domain.

There is a deep pond, by the windmill, near the work-house in Harleston. The pond belongs to the Wypond family and is called after them. I recall that the mamas drag their children away from it and even smack them hard if they venture in, for it is right deep and they might drown. The mill there is five storeys high and its sails turn whip, whip, whip in the wind.

The baby can go in there, and never be found. My baby sister deserves better, but what else can I do?

I must turn left and walk up the hill before all the light is gone. But I think that my sister may float, and so I bend down and grope until I find two stones near the farm gate and fold them into the baby's blanket. I tuck her head close to me, for it has nodded, and it chills me, the dead weight of it moving against me. I shiver at the awfulness of this; I have to go on all the same.

I dare not look down into the dark waters as I cross the bridge, for what if the witches fly upwards and catch us as we walk? There is a swoop over my head and a caw. I start, hold tight to my sister as the black birds wheel round, land together in great numbers on a fir tree, caw and then are silent.

I could leave her here instead, walk back home and try to sleep. I would be back with Mama in no time at all.

But I cannot lay her to rest with the witches, where the crows and the magpies fly; it isn't right that she should lie underneath the weeds.

I stand for a while, and then I see a waggoner, jolting home. I press myself into the hedge and hear as he clatters over the bridge, the reins slack in his hand. He does not see me but he has frightened me and so as soon as he has gone, I move on and fork right, into the back road that leads to the town. It hugs the fields and there is nobody there, and at last I see the workhouse, closed shut against the night. I stand there, quite still, pressed into the side of a house where a candle burns in the window against the darkening. Nobody would see if I peeped, one last time.

I crouch down on my heels and open up the sacking. My sister's eyes are closed and, in the dusk, as I stroke her hair, I remember Mama telling me that my hair had felt like newly spun silk when I was born. I wish that she had been born at a different time and a different place, for I had wanted a sister so much, to play with and raise up to be my friend.

If she was here now, in this warmth I live in now, I would hold her against me and care for her. But I cannot go back and change what I did. So the child that I was wraps her up tightly against the cold and I walk towards the pond and I lower her in. At first my sister floats, and then the bundle sinks from view and I cannot help myself; I feel how the warm tears spurt on my face, then sting in the cold. Then she is gone.

I do not know how I found my way back, except that I held my arms outstretched in front of me as I stumbled forward, and at length I heard the old dog and found the wall of the house and then the handle of the back door, then the tread of the stairs.

I found my mama, lying quite still, crying in the dark. But she was there, and I had kept her safe. Us safe. She asked, "Is it done?" and I squeezed her hand, undressed and heard how she whispered, "Thank you, my girl."

As I took off my socks, I felt how they stuck to my feet, but I pulled them off all the same and lay down, held my mama close, curled around her. As I finally drifted off, I came to with a jerk. I felt my sister in my arms again, and how she had looked, with that whorl of hair at the top of her scalp. Then she flew up in the air, and I was alone again, with my mama, as I had always been. I had held my sister, and I had carried her and now I never would again. My baby sister was gone.

Chapter Six

I dressed at dawn, as quiet as I could, for the cows could not milk themselves. I glanced at Mama. She had huddled into herself. Not again, I thought, not like the good wife, who had shrunk until her clothes hung on bones. I could not lose my mama, not like this; I had nobody. It must not happen again. I could not be alone in this world.

I pulled on my woollen socks last, feeling my way in, pushing past the flakes of powdered blood. One stuck fast to the wound on my foot, but I was too cold to do without them. I hobbled down to the pump in the farmyard and splashed my face, so that I woke up. Nobody else had stirred. I unstuck the sock from my foot and ran it underneath the pump, so that water ran red first, then clear again, and then brown with mud from the other. I dried each on my apron, put the socks on again. I opened up the barn, and when I sat down, the tears came as I milked the first cow, then the next. I took the cup and drank the warm milk down, salted as it was.

Finally I had just one cow left. My hands sore after yesterday, as I milked her. I laid my head against her, and at last the buckets were full. I stood up and my head swirled, but there was no time for this. I went to the kitchen. The farmer was there, staring out again, blankly, at the fields. "Mama is still sick," I said.

He looked at me then as he used to and pity flitted across his face, then a frown.

Had he heard anything? An image of Mama, rag clamped between her teeth, to avoid sound.

"Take her bread and milk," he said, finally. "But tomorrow is market day."

"She will be better by then." My voice firmer than my thoughts. Nobody must suspect. Our lives depended on this.

I roused Mama and we went together the next morning, although I carried the basket for her. She walked, head down, and forced herself to speak in the baker's, and her voice was strong. But as we left, I saw how she was leaking blood into the road, drop by drop. I scuffed it away, kicking up the dirt, following on behind as closely as I could, until we returned to the cart. On the way back, I whispered what I had seen and done, and Mama clutched at me and said that she would change her rags, and that I should unpack the items for the kitchen and put them away.

I had nearly finished when I heard knocking, hard and heavy, on the farm door. The archdeacon was there, and behind him Black Bessie, her bridle looped over the farm gates, grazing quietly, although her sides were gleaming with sweat as if she had come at a fast trot.

He looked at me but he did not speak, and strode past me, calling out for the farmer. They found each other in the kitchen. Beyond, I could see that the first shoots, green and bright, had forced their way through the hard earth.

Olderhall came to a stop in front of him. The farmer looked up.

"I must talk to you. The girl must leave." My heart flew up then into my mouth.

The farmer looked at me, jerked his head upward, without a word.

I left the room. The stones I had carried weighted me down still, felt in every ache of my body. I closed the door, sat on the stairs, so that I could hear. I had to, for both of us.

"I need to take Tyrell away with me."

Then it was as if he could not stop talking; the words poured out of him: how he had eaten his luncheon and gone to pray but was disturbed by a furious knocking at the door, that it was the parish constable and he was told that he must go to Wypond's Pond, on Jay's Green, and how he had ridden over on Black Bessie.

A group of his parishioners had stood around the pond, in a huddle, the parish constable in the middle of them, next to Matthew Wypond, the overseer. They were all looking down at the edge of the pond.

"There was a bundle there, wet rags. They parted and I went to it, picked it up."

A silence, then, "The carpenter told me he found the baby this morning, when he was drawing water from the pond. She was swaddled, weighted down with stones, cold to the touch."

Another pause. "I've held many babes for christening, but this one, I picked her up and the water poured down from her. There are wives like mine that long for babes. How could anybody do this to her? She was so cold."

Still the farmer said nothing.

"I sent the baby to Mr Priest, to examine her. He will then send the child to Widow Beamish. The parish must pay for her to be wrapped in black baize."

At last the farmer spoke. "Why are you here?"

"I have come to fetch her." He spoke impatiently this time. "We discussed those who should be questioned. Your brother spoke up, said Tyrell had not been seen in town. She has dark hair, just like the child. I have asked the constable to summon two others."

Again, a silence. Why did the farmer not speak up for Mama, after all she had done for him and the good wife? He must help us now, surely.

"A cart is here to take her to the lock-up."

"And her daughter? What should happen to her?"

"The dead child must have justice. The other one can go to the workhouse, under your brother's care. Her mother may have done this, Wypond. You cannot defend such a woman, that has birthed two base-born children, killed one. She must face justice."

I could not go to the workhouse. Mama had forbidden it; I could not go there. Those poor children who had been there, separated at the door from their mama. And I, to go there alone? Where were they taking my mama?

The farmer started to talk, but Olderhall talked over him. "I buried your wife, Wypond, do you not remember? I gave you succour in your melancholy. And I recall that Tyrell brought us tea, and lingered in the doorway, until I bade her leave. You have given her too much freedom. She has taken advantage of you."

He paused, then added, "Or have you, perhaps, a hand in this, that you defend her?"

The farmer stammered, but spoke up then, to my surprise.

"What will you do with her? She has been ailing these last days," he said, uncertainly.

"I must lock her up, and then send to Cambridge for advice on the correct punishment. If she is found guilty."

I stood up, walked to the top of the stairs, and then round the curve. How could I save her, what could I do? She had done nothing wrong to deserve this.

Mama was standing by the attic window, and she had tied a bundle together.

42

"Hannah, I heard enough. Come here, sit with me."

She pulled me down to the bed, took my face in her hands. They were rough against my cheeks. I should have softened them with goose fat, rubbed it in to every sore finger, the cracked palms. I had no more time today but tomorrow I would bring a quantity up to the town, when I visited her there.

"The rags are in the bucket. You must wash them out and then hide them. Hannah, say nothing. Promise me you will not speak up."

I looked into her face, smiling sadly at me, pale in the light that trickled into the room.

I felt her arms around me, and breathed her in, and then we rose as one, and I took her bundle and we walked down together, to where the archdeacon stood waiting by Black Bessie. The farmer said nothing, nothing at all, as Mama was taken away on the cart, looking back at me all that way and smiling, until they turned off the farm track and were lost from view. Then he spoke to me quite gently, and told me what I must do that day. But I spoke up and asked him, "Why did you not save my mama?" and he could not meet my eyes and said nothing back.

I waited for her to return that evening, at the end of the track, as the light failed. The farmer came to find me, for the cows were not milked. He explained to me that the archdeacon had kept her in the lock-up and we rattled up there in the cart, after we had milked together. He had put together victuals for her, and a bottle of milk still warm from the milking.

We arrived at the market square as the light failed. I ran straight to the lock-up and peered in. There was a straw mattress in the corner and Mama, lying down. I could just make out dark stains on the straw. "Mama, I'm here." She did not stir. "I have food and drink, Mama. Please, take it."

My voice cracked on the words. Mama did not move at first, but then stirred, pushed herself upright. She hobbled over. Her hair, so clean and soft, had straw in it. "Here, Mama," I said, pushing the food through, then the bottle of milk.

The lock-up stank of urine, and of the iron that rises from blood. "Pie, Mama, and water, and a bottle of warm milk."

She took the food and sat down with it. She tried to eat. "How are you, child?"

All my words drowned in my throat.

Mama put the food down, carefully, and came back over. She took my hands between the bars and stroked them. "Remember, Hannah, I am always with you. Come and see me tomorrow. I cannot sleep well here. Bring the spills of opium for me, but do not let anyone see. I need all of it in case I am in here for a few more nights."

I kissed my mama as best I could, through the bars. Then the farmer put his hand on my shoulder, and I felt the weight of it as he guided me away. I turned back and we waved at each other, but both of us had tears in our eyes that streamed down like rivers in full spring spate.

The next day, I came again, with the paper packets. This time, Mama seemed more peaceful. She reached through the bars and touched my hair, gently.

"This is nobody's fault. Least of all yours, girl," she whispered. Then one more sentence cracked out.

"You go on now, my girl," she said, in her soft voice, something that the two of us had said often, as we pushed the cows out after milking, clapping each one on her flank as she moved into the yard and then beyond, to the pastureland. Mama's eyes were shut, and then she asked the Good Lord to keep me safe, as she had done so many times, as we knelt together on our old rag rug. The farmer clapped his hand on my shoulder. As the horse moved off, I looked back, and I could see Mama, waving through the bars, until, at last, we dropped down the hill and clattered over the bridge and she was gone from view. The farmer looked at me then, and tried to comfort me, but I shrank away from him, for he had never answered me or helped my mama and that night I lay quite cold and alone in the bed we shared and cried until I fell asleep from sheer fatigue.

I was milking the last cow when I heard a horse outside and the barn door opened. The Archdeacon Olderhall stood there. He filled the doorway, and then all light was gone. He spoke stiffly, as if from his pulpit.

"Your mother is dead."

My hands fell away from her teats. I sat quite still. I could not take in his words. They could not be true. There was no world without my mama.

He paused, then went on.

"She took poison, did away with herself. The watchman found her this morning."

I am not sure what happened next – the farmer said that I must have fallen off the stool and hit the bucket, for when he came running, he found me lying there with the milk spilt all around me and the cow breathing on my face. Olderhall was surveying the scene fair blankly, frozen. The farmer set the stool upright, got a rag and wiped me down, and then he told me to go to my room. But I could not move from the soft straw, the warmth. So he took me in his arms and carried me upstairs and laid me gently on my mattress, and then he left me all alone, for he had to talk to Olderhall.

I lay curled around my mama's shape, but she would never be there again, to hold me and to beam with pride to see me, to tell me her stories. Her voice had broken on the shore and she had been carried out to where I would never see her again.

Chapter Seven

I could hear their voices quite clearly, for some were raised and all were clear, as the door was slightly open. There was the farmer, his brother the overseer, Dr White and the archdeacon. They were deciding how to dispose of me and where. The overseer went first.

"She should be committed," he rasped. I knew what he meant, and how hard Mama had fought to keep us from the workhouse, from him. "She is of bad blood, and should be watched."

My cheeks flamed at that. The farmer cut across him, angry at last.

"She can stay here; she has done nothing wrong. Why should she lose her home?"

I was somewhere in the middle of this, being kicked around like a pig's bladder.

The archdeacon said that was wrongful, in the circumstances, and that I had been born of sin and should not be left alone with a man.

Then Dr White spoke up, and they all were quiet. "She may stay with my wife in the town, and we will seek for relatives in Yarmouth, where her mother came from. If there are none, we will look after her and train her up for service."

I had asked Mama to tell me, many a time, if we had family in Yarmouth, for I knew she had a brother once and had loved him, and I had wanted a sister or brother myself. So, one night, when she was tiring, and a little distracted, I asked her once again. And she looked at me sadly, but said at last, "You are old enough now to hear the tale. Why we are two and have no family to speak of."

Then with a sigh, she told me. The saddest tale, of how her brother and father were lost at sea. "I loved him with all my heart, my Henry. Lost on his first trip out at sea, and we only knew him and Papa by their ganseys, knitted by my mama."

There was more to that tale, I learned later. But for now, I knew only there would be no more stories told to me at night, or as we milked, one two, one two, as the buckets filled.

A thought floated to the top of everything, clear and sharp, the scum beneath. Mama had been wronged. One day I would have justice. Another thought followed on then. I had never rubbed the goose fat in and now her hands would be rough for ever more. The tears came then and the voices broke off.

There were footsteps outside the door, and then inside, walking towards me. This was Mrs White, sitting down next to me, stroking my hair until the tears came spurting out. "You're to come with me," she said gently. "I'm sorry for your loss." And then as I cried, she gathered me to her and held me, and she was scented with lavender water and roses and she felt like my mama but Mama was gone.

She helped me pack up my belongings, such as they were. There was the dress Mama had sewn for the wedding day that had never happened. I folded it carefully, and put it in the bundle. I took up our shawls, the hoop that the blacksmith had made. I paused at the doorway and looked back. I had lived here, prayed here, talked here, slept here, all with my mama close by. This was my fault. I had rocked the cradle and my sister had gone down into the weeds with the witches and Mama had refused to let me speak. She had thought she was cursed once, I remembered. Now it was my turn and I knew that I would think this forever, that I had brought this on the person I loved most. I am not sure it has left me since that awful day. I placed my hoop back on the bed. I would not have need of toys again.

Then we went down the stairs and out into the farm-yard, and got into the carriage and rattled away.

I went to live in Candler's House, in the middle of Harleston, on a Saturday. The doctor's wife had cleared out an attic room and furnished it so nicely for me, with her own things, such as she could spare. But however kind she was, she could not keep from me all the news in the town that gathered the people into the Thoroughfare, to talk and point.

Mrs White told me that Widow Beamish had wound the baby in black baize, ready for her burial. Sam Cook dug a grave at Redenhall church, hard by the hedge, in the unconsecrated ground to the south of the church, for those poor souls who died without a Christian baptism. I begged to go, so that I could pray for her soul to go to heaven, even if she had not been touched with the holy water, but Mrs White shook her head. "It is not permit-ted," she said, gently enough.

Sam Cook came to the house that evening, for he was sore all over from gravedigging. I hid myself away, so I could hear him talk, for he was a soft talker, that one, as if he was ever by the dead and should behave with sobriety. The cook asked him, of course, for she was avid for news, and offered him ale. He asked her for clean water first, and washed himself before I heard a kitchen chair being pulled out across the floor and then he must have sat down.

A pause as he drank, cleared his throat, thanked her.

"Nobody there for the poor baby, except the archdeacon himself. I laid her gently enough in the grave and waited for the blessing."

A silence. Cook broke it and asked, "So what did happen then, Sam?"

"The archdeacon said nothing and then at last he turned away and nodded to me to do my business. So when he had gone, I put the earth in, but gently mind, with my hands. I said a prayer for her myself, for who can be buried without one?" His voice shook. "I patted her down then with my shovel."

Then I heard a grown man cry and stuffed my apron into my mouth.

What I had started, when I rocked the cradle, in the cold light of a Sunday morning, was not over yet.

Chapter Eight

I could hear Cook talking as I polished the bannisters leading down to the kitchen.

"There'll be a coroner's inquest at the Swan. Poor soul, hasn't she suffered enough?"

I had worked my way down the stairs from the top to the bottom with my two rags, one for the beeswax, one for the shine. Mrs White had left me at my task, for I was doing so well.

Another voice spoke, but the cook spoke over, in spurts, as if she was working at the same time but could not stop herself from speech.

"I saw her body, on a cart. It was half covered in sacking, but you could see her arm, dangling. Henry Fox told the doctor that twenty-four good men had been called, and twelve chosen, to be paid a shilling to sit in judgement on Mary Tyrell."

I do not quite recollect what happened, as then Mrs White was holding me on the stairs, in a huddle, as the tin of beeswax rattled down to the bottom. Somehow, she took me into her bedroom, and I sat at her feet and wept again. "Hannah, you should not listen at doors," she said, but gently.

Then she said, with reluctance, "Hannah, are there any relatives with whom you could lodge, now that your mother is gone? I could take you up to Yarmouth this week if there is anyone there?" I heard an urgency in her voice. "It might go easier for you if you could leave this place soon, put the past behind you."

I looked at her but her gaze had settled somewhere outside, as if she dared not meet my eye. Nobody had ever wanted us, my mama and me, and now I belonged to nobody. We had only ever had each other – or so I had thought, until one Mothering Sunday, when Mama had, all of a sudden, taken me on the Accommodation, all the way to Yarmouth. Mr Salter the coachman had remembered my mama, and set us down at a great building, away from everything else in the town, and Mama had knocked on the door and it had opened with a weighty jangling of keys. We walked down a long dark corridor and then more jangling, and another door opened. I remember that my arm hurt, for Mama had packed up a basket with bread, sugar and butter and it was heavy.

There were, perhaps, some ten or so women in there. Light trickled into it through a window, quite high, and I noticed how it fell across the floor in bars, shadow and light, shadow and light.

One woman was knitting, a great long snake of a thing that trailed across the room and moved as her hands worked. I noticed how the end of it had landed near to the soil bucket. Mama put me behind her and said, "Mother, are you all right, for we have come to see you." I hear it now and know that there was love in her voice, but also hesitation. Fear, I know it now.

The woman raised her head and looked at Mama. Her fingers knitted on. Then she rose, still knitting, and pointed her needles at us and cursed Mama. The wardress pulled us both out of the room as Mama cried out for mercy and she dragged me out and to the market square.

She seemed to be in a kind of fever, for drops stood out on her face, but she did not stop and walked fast towards a church. "Come," she said, and her voice was brittle. So I ran after her as she fastened the gate, and we went through the churchyard. She did not falter until she reached a headstone, and then she sat back on her haunches and put her arms around it, and pulled me to her, and then the tears came. "Henry and Papa," I heard her say, through her tears, and she fumbled in her basket and laid the lavender sprigs on the stone before she hugged me close to the cold stone again and the tears fell into my hair. I knew then that if she could have raised them from the earth she would have done so, but there is no way of doing so, that I know of at least. Before we got on the coach, she had found a child, begging, and gifted her the provisions we had brought. I watched as the child's face cracked open, and she ran off into a row, whooping.

She did not speak as we travelled back to Harleston. It was that night, as we lay together for warmth, that Mama told me the woman we had seen was my grandmama. Mama said that she had never recovered from the wreck of their life, for sometimes things that were broken could not be mended, however much you wanted to make them whole again.

"I thought she would like to see you, her granddaughter, but she never forgave me, for she blamed me for Henry dying, for Papa too." An old superstition behind it, because Mama had jumped on and off the boat before it left, a wish to be the boy that sailed, not the girl left behind. The girl who would see the storm that wrecked her family. And the grief had left my grandmama quite mad, my mama sent away for the shame of what she had brought on our family, the town itself. She had started out here again, alone, and now it was turn and turnabout.

I shook my head. "There's nobody. Nobody left for me."

Mrs White stroked my hair. "You're safe here. You have me."

But she could not take away the pain that was lying in store for me, and Cook knew everything, and so did I, for I needed to hear what was to happen to my mama, and so the bannisters were polished to a sheen that week and if the great wings of the kitchen table were folded down, as Cook worked, I could even hide underneath. So I heard everything, muffled, but clear enough, and I made no sound, whatever was said.

The cook kneaded her bread and talked. The archdeacon had written to his superiors, to ask about the fit and proper sentence on a woman suspected of infanticide, who had then laid hands upon herself. He received his reply the next day. So then he told the jury, and they told the townsfolk, what their Christian duty would be, as that April day turned cold and dark inside the Swan Inn. There was a verdict, he told them, that was not often used, but it was the law in this case. Two of the jury gasped. Others turned pale. One raised his hand. "Is there no other verdict, archdeacon?"

One of the women who worked in the inn told the cook everything, as she put the bread aside to prove, and they pulled out chairs to sit down and drink tea, gossiping comfortably as I held my breath so I would not make a sound.

The jurymen processed into the Swan at ten o'clock in the morning and they sat in the big, dark room at the back of the inn, which was used for grand and awful occasions. The woman who told cook about it all, a good wife who was called Margaret Green, said she had gone in herself, lit candles all along the length of the table, then banked the fire as slowly as she could, so she could listen in. The coroner coughed, then spoke, looking downward, his finger following the script in front of him.

"You good men of this district, summoned to appear here this day to inquire for our Sovereign Lord the King when, how and by what means Mary Tyrell came to her death, answer your names as you shall be called, every man at the first call, upon the pain and peril that shall fall thereon."

The coroner continued, saying: "You shall now diligently inquire and true presentment make of all such matters and things as shall here be given you in charge, on behalf of our Sovereign Lord the King, touching the death of Mary Tyrell now lying dead, of whose body you shall have the view and shall, without fear or favour, affection or ill will, a true verdict give according to the evidence and to the best of your skill and knowledge, so help you God."

Having taken their oaths, the jurymen were given their instructions and the cook swore blind that they went pale to hear what they must do.

"We must now view the body of the said person, lying dead." Margaret Green moved away from the door, as the men rose and filed upstairs, into the small, dark room where her body had been laid on a plank upon the oak table. They all looked down at her, naked, and the coroner said, "I identify the body now lying dead as that of Mary Tyrell."

They peered at my mama, some looking intently, others passing through as swiftly as possible. Then they turned away, in silence, and walked back to the room where they were to pronounce on her. My mama's trial began, though how could she defend herself, for she was quite dead.

First the surgeon himself, Mr Priest, rose. He kissed the Bible and then the coroner examined him. Mr Priest had a deep voice, fine and strong, and it boomed throughout the room. The cook swore blind it could be heard in the Thoroughfare, where folk had gathered outside, looking up at the open window as the men deliberated within.

"A fine baby girl was found in the pond, wrapped in a cloak. Three women were taken up for questioning and one of them was Mary Tyrell, who had a base-born child already. I examined the infant, and in my opinion, she was alive when she was born."

The feel of her in my arms, warm and sleeping, as I laid her gently in the cradle. Opened the window, the cold air across her small body, heaped with blankets.

Then Tom Olderhall, who gave his occupation as arch-deacon, reverend and magistrate, gave evidence. "I took up Mary Tyrell myself, and the other women were brought to me for questioning. Tyrell was ill and weeping through the sessions, but said nothing to me. I gave instructions that she should be put back in the lock-up and that she should be fetched, this Saturday past."

There was a silence, then the coroner asked Olderhall to continue.

"I learned that she had taken poison and died by her own hand, a mortal sin that requires punishment in itself. But there is more. In my opinion, she was the most likely mother, as she already had one base-born child. She had loose morals. I made enquiries, and found that she must have obtained the laudanum she used from the farmer, in a mixture obtained from the chemist, called Browne's Chlorodyne; it had been left over from a store from the death of his wife, to assuage the pain of her sickness, and to help her sleep at night."

A juryman spoke up then, timidly, and asked how she

had got the baby into the pond. Nobody knew, and the archdeacon said it was not important and asked the coroner to sum up, so he did and the jury retired to another room to reach their verdict. They did not argue, the cook said, and signed the form or made a mark if they could not write. The attorney, Mr Henry Fox, bought each of them a tankard of ale at the bar, and thanked them, and they were paid their shilling; when they had drunk their ale, they went on their way.

Later that day Mr Priest came to the archdeacon, and closed the door to the study behind him, but the servant lingered there, and so the story got out – even I heard it, from my point on the stairs – for it was too good to keep locked up. "This is too cruel," said the surgeon. "The town will be known for this and this alone, for all of time."

But Olderhall shook his head, and said, right loud, "No. I must deliver justice on the dead, for the dead. I have taken advice, and it will be so."

So when I dragged myself to bed that night I felt sick inside, for I knew that something was planned, but had no idea what it was. Mrs White forbad me quite strictly from leaving the house, except to take turns with her about the garden, but she did not tell me why. I noted that she hovered around me and kept me busy so that I had no occasion to linger on the stairs or creep under the kitchen table for news. But I wanted to know where my mama would be buried, for I should be there, as her child, to speed her on her journey.

I recalled that when the working man had taken his life and his family ended in the workhouse, he had been judged mad and so the good archdeacon Olderhall had given him a Christian burial at Redenhall church. Then after a while his friends had found a position for his widow, and they had come out of the workhouse and lived again in the Pulhams, modestly enough. So why not my mama, who had helped them and others – why should she be laid to rest differently from that man, for she was a good and kind and Christian woman and I was her chief mourner, and so I must be there.

On the Friday a man came, on behalf of the parish over-seer, and knocked loudly on the door. He said that the property of Mary Tyrell was to be taken from her daughter and given to the parish. I heard the shouting and ran down the stairs towards him, but Mrs White held me back with one arm and shot back at him that the property the child had belonged to her and her alone, and then she slammed the heavy door shut in his face. The man had shouted, through the closed door, as Mrs White took me away, "We will have our judgement on her, all the same," as I shook with fear and rage at him.

Mrs White sat me down in the parlour and held me, until the shaking stopped. "Hannah, you must stop this. You must not listen to conversations that are not meant for you; no good will come out of such curiosity."

But I spoke back and asked her straight, "What is to happen to my mama?" She would not tell me and at last, she sent me to bed.

The memory of that evening when I ran after my mama; the great concourse, the dark hole, the staking. It is the second scar across my heart. It healed over for a while, but it catches still across the pucker.

The doctor's wife had caught me as I fell from Summers' grip, slapped him like a pistol crack across the face. She and the doctor had laid me in their carriage and she had looked back to see the earth levelled over my mama. It was done whilst I lay there, still and white, and no blessing said but the ones she gave as she watched Sam Cook pat the mound. The people walked away white-faced and shaking. The deed was done.

When my strength had come back to me, what was I left with? Mama was gone. Just Mama's words in my heart. *You go on now, girl.* Mrs White told me when I woke that I had called out for Mama many times, but that she was dead and buried now, and that I should make peace, and that I had a new life with her. Mama, dead at twenty-six, and my sister, dead before she had even turned one day old. My life as a child ended when Mama was buried, in wood and soil and blood, and now all that was left had turned to stone.

Chapter Nine

I held Mrs White's hand as we walked up Candler's Lane together, towards the school on Jay's Green. We came out near the workhouse, and the pond. I looked upwards instead, into the two willow trees that were in new bright leaf. They whispered "baby, baby" to me alone. We reached the door of the school. Mrs White asked me if I was ready, then we stepped in together. For a moment the room was quiet and all the children looked at me with knowledge in their shining morning faces, though they said not a word. Then my new teacher welcomed me in and found me a place to sit.

My new life lasted for some four years. I learned my letters and my numbers and I learned plain cooking and other home skills. Mrs White taught me fine sewing, and how to mend with a stitch that hardly showed.

I learned other lessons as well: that I was cast out from the town where I was born, and I was made to feel that most at school. The Archdeacon Olderhall came, two or three times a week, to inspect us. The first time he came the teacher sprang up as if he had been stung, and shouted at us to stand up straight, next to our desks. Then the archdeacon walked to the front of the class and his gaze swept over us but it stopped on me, as if it had snagged there. He stared at me, as if he could see right through me, to my base-born heart and the stones that weighted it. Did he know, could he know, that it was my fault that my sister had died? I turned my eyes down and trembled each time that he came.

The older children knew full well what had happened to Mama. Some said nothing, but Jem Summers' sons, who had lost the Easter race to me, were truly unkind. They told the others not to speak to me, and when I turned my back they would whisper together and laugh if I came near. I took no notice of them, and it must have irked them, for one day in the schoolyard, as I stood at the door looking out at them all, the two brothers spoke up in unison, and sang out my name, and then the whole class said my mother's name out loud and then shouted, "She is dead." I turned away so they could not see the tears that sprung out of me, and the teacher came running out. He saw my face and took me in the schoolroom but I would not tell him what had happened. He beat the boys all the same after school, so hard that they never did it again. Instead, the whole class left me completely alone between nine of the clock and one p.m., when at last I could take my items and walk back to the big house, where Mrs White waited for me, as often as she could if the doctor did not need her.

I never accustomed myself to the pond and the trees that whispered to me. Sometimes I saw Matthew Wypond there, outside the workhouse. He would look up and stare, then walk away, quite fast, as if I reminded him of something or someone he would rather forget.

There were nights when no dreams came, but often I would wake in tears to find Mrs White by my side, setting a candle down on the chair by my bed and sitting with me till I calmed. She held my hand and I saw how her hair was loose and long as she bent over me in her nightgown and shawl. However kind she was she could not drive forth what

I had seen or turn time back so that what had been done to Mama could be undone. I never told her what I had done, and what I had brought onto my mama, for underneath I knew it was my fault, as well as that of the men I hated.

There was the farmer, who had said nothing, and then there was his brother. There was his friend, who had held my legs tight on his shoulders so that I could not look away from the wrong that was done to Mama, and so I could never wash the image of what they had done to her from my mind. Whenever I saw the farmer, on market day, he looked away as if my gaze hurt him, then hurried back to his cart and whipped the horses as they turned. But all the same Mrs White told me that he sent for news of me, and offered to support me if ever I needed money. Yet he seemed ashamed, whether of me or of the past I did not know, just that my life I had lived until then had snapped shut like a trap. It had been set again and nobody would talk to me any more of it, lest it catch me with its sharp teeth.

I was sent to bed as the birds roosted and I heard how they called and then whirled into silence, and I was quite alone. How would we have lived together with my sister, if I had not rocked the cradle, set in rhythm everything that followed? I thought that we would have ended in the work-house, under the eye of the farmer's brother, for where else was there for us? We would have been together, but Mama had sworn that we would never enter such a place. The questions burned me, fell about me as if the letters had come loose from their words and were flying through the air all around me. Who had forced Mama, and why had she not told me what had happened? Had I killed the baby, had I killed my mama, by everything that I had done?

The Archdeacon Olderhall preached at me every Sunday. I had no grounds on which to refuse to attend church, a duty that could not be shirked unless illness came. So, as late spring softened into summer, the family would take up its prayer books and we would walk up the lane, past Jay's Green, and process, single file, along the narrow path to Redenhall, over the fields. The man who had watched Mama staked through the heart would preach of the love of God and I would have to pretend to pray but I hated him for taking my mama away on a cart, for sending away to Cambridge for the cruellest verdict.

Then there were the men, in the Swan Inn, who had sat in judgement on Mama and judged her guilty of *felo de se* and put her dear dead body on that cart and had it dragged through the town. No doubt they were there, scattered through the rows in the church, amongst the congregation that had assembled in silence to see Mama naked, dead, staked. I might kneel and say the prayers but none of it meant a thing to me, for I knew the difference between word and deed and how many had trespassed against us.

The thermometer dropped like a stone that first winter but the sky stayed blue and the earth clear, set in its neat plough lines, field after field frozen in rows. The doctor read of a momentous celebration that was to take place in Norwich to mark our victory over the French. Mrs White pleaded to take me with them, and so we wrapped up warm and the doctor himself drove the twenty miles to Norwich. At first, I huddled back in the coach seat but as we got near the city, I looked out to see the cathedral and the castle, for I had never been there before. We arrived around noon and walked around the marketplace. In the centre there was a great fire and a spit and a bullock was roasted whole on it. Mr Lowden the butcher flourished his two knives in the air as his men took the bullock from the fire. The sun caught them and the crowd cheered as he pushed them into the flesh.

I fainted straight away to hear how the bullock thudded onto the ground, for it took me right back to the hole, my mama's grave. When I woke up, I had been laid on the ground at the end of the market stalls, and Mrs White was peering down. "The crowd broke through," she said, "and the meat was torn and fully spoilt." I looked around and I saw dogs scuffling for the last shreds of flesh.

All around me were brightly coloured tents that covered the market stalls and they shone out in the winter sun. I held my hands over my ears, for all around was shouting, haggling and dealing, and with the trotting of the horses into the market and the bargains that were to be had I could not think straight. The bonfire burned on. As I stood up, I saw how an ugly lumpen cloth effigy of Boney was thrown on and twisted in the flames and I buried my head in Mrs White's shawl, for the straw inside burnt up and fizzed. All the same, as we travelled back I told Mrs White I was glad that they had taken me, for I had enjoyed the journey with her, and nobody knew me there and stopped and stared, or whispered behind my back.

After Christmas, as the year turned into 1814, the thermometer dropped further and I wondered about Mama, lying in the ground. All day long the ice stayed in its patterns across my window. Then the snow came, and the frost decorated the trees, and the fall was so deep that we could not leave the house for most of January and even into February. Dr White took a newspaper from London, which came up on the stagecoach once it could force its way through. He read aloud, as we huddled around the fire at night, of a great Frost Fair, held on the frozen Thames itself, and I wished that I could see the sight and I wondered what it would be like to skate on a river, free and flying on the thick ice. And then I wondered, did the water still flow underneath, and what would happen if the ice cracked and if the witches pulled such as me under, claimed me as their own? I shook my head and crept closer to Mrs White as the doctor folded the newspaper, put it down.

Another time he told us that Coachman Salter had relayed news of a great feast at Yarmouth for the victories, called the Triumph of Neptune. The coachmen wore laurel in their buttonholes and Boney was dressed in his uniform and fettered so that the effigy clanked with it and then set alight. They laid tables out on the frozen quay, and skaters served roast beef and plum pudding to those wrapped up warm to eat there as Boney burnt to a crisp, and the hungry bonfire was fed until all had eaten their fill.

Spring came at last. The snow melted, and even the Waveney was so full that the river welled all over the water meadows, and whenever we rode out, we saw that all around Harleston had turned into a great lake. It did not abate until the end of March but when it did the flowers pushed up in abundance, and cowslips and daffadowndillies decorated the gardens and the verges.

On Mama's death-day, I slipped down the back stairs and walked out. The lane that followed on from the Thoroughfare was quiet. The last time I had walked out, then run this way, was in my shift, a sheet on one arm, to bid farewell. This time the air was warm and a breeze ruffled the flowers at the edge of the track. I left Harleston behind and carried on walking. I reached the two cottages that sat on the fertile ground where the town ended. The willow leaves had burst forth and were a bright new green. The breeze lifted the light branches and let them fall again, and I stood there, near the tree, and then lowered myself down, so I could sit with my back to the trunk. I sat there, silently, watching the wind play with the new leaves. *You go on now*, Mama had told me, and I was trying to. But what should I do with such a wide and empty life ahead of me?

Chapter Ten

The next day we walked over the fields to church, on a late Easter Sunday. Poppies and cornflowers grew amongst the wheat, and the air was warming. Overhead, the swallows had arrived. I sat downstairs in a different place now. The Archdeacon Olderhall was taking the service and my mind drifted away, back to Mama and life only a year ago. Then I felt Mrs White sit upright, as if someone had stuck a pin in her, and the colour faded from her face. I looked around and noticed that some in the congregation had turned to look at me, and Mrs White put her arm around me, but she could not protect me from his harshness.

He could not leave it alone, me alone, even after everything had been taken from me. His gaze fixed on me as he spoke.

"On Easter Sunday we remember the Christ that died for us, so that all our sins were forgiven. But we must also remember those among us who sin and do not repent. Who are born of sin."

Mrs White clutched me against her then, even tighter. I saw how her cheeks burned red as she stared back at him defiantly, but I could not bear it, and put my head in her lap.

There was a great rustle then, and I peeked up and saw how Elizabeth had stood up from the front pew, her cheeks also quite red, and walked down the aisle and out of the church. I did not know what she meant by this. But I knew, as the sickness came over me, that this sin, such as it was, would follow me all the days of my life in this place, and that one day I must leave it all behind or else it would swallow me whole.

The price climbed high for bread in the town and the poor agitated for food and rioted against the tithes that Olderhall and other men of God imposed. Just twenty miles away a threshing machine was dragged from Winfarthing to Shelfanger, the doctor read in the newspaper, and then sunk in the water so that it was ruined. The cattle that grazed outside Redenhall church were maimed and sheep were stolen all over the county. There was a riot, in Diss, where an angry body of men and women assembled to complain about the dearness of provisions. I heard that the magistrates assembled there and called out the Yeomanry and I wondered what it would be like if the same happened in Harleston.

The archdeacon seemed to fear nobody but rode around on Black Bessie, at all times of day and night. I heard the cook say that he was never home, because Elizabeth could not bear to be in the same room as him. Some said that she had taken her clothes and set up a bedroom for herself, one fine morning, without asking his permission. Was it because of me, I wondered, or for my mama, at least, who had always been so kind to her? He had not resisted her, but that day he went out with his gun and he shot a magpie and hung it on the wall, outside her window. He told everyone who asked that it was the devil's bird, and he had cut its beak off for Satan should not answer back to him.

We heard some months later, when the bird had been

picked clean, that Elizabeth was with child, and then that she had delivered a daughter, called Isabella, with fair curly hair and bright blue eyes. We were there at her christening, when the archdeacon took his own child from the arms of his wife and christened her as the water ran down her face, and down his surplice, and she cried, lustily. She kicked out at him, the living weight of her, and then his wife stepped up and tore the baby from him as quick as she could, and held her tight to her bosom, head nestled in, tucked in away from her father, and then left the church before the service was ended. I saw how he looked after her, and how at first his face was raw and undressed. I thought I could see water gathering in his eyes and then he shook himself and his eyes hooded over like an owl out hunting, and he rose to the pulpit to deliver his sermon.

His mercy reached only those he favoured. I was polishing the furniture in the drawing room when I heard Cook's voice float up the stairs, and I tiptoed down for I recognised how she talked now, when an event excited both pity and horror in her. She was talking of Weybread, and then I heard her talk of Wypond's Farm.

"He must have been in despair, poor soul, to commit such a sin."

I heard how she paused then, as a murmur of agreement spread in her kitchen. "He was discovered when the cowman came, for he had not milked the cows and they were making a racket. He found that Wypond had hanged himself, in his own barn."

I heard another woman speak up, avid for news.

"Was there a note?"

Cook knew everything, it seemed, for she said that his brother came at a gallop and no note had been found, or so he said.

The other voice spoke again, keen with curiosity. "It

makes you wonder what had happened before. With the Tyrell woman, who was got with child."

Another murmur of agreement.

Cook protested at that. "He was a good man, from all accounts, and none of us should gossip."

She gossiped all the time, I thought, bitter. He would never have hurt my mama, he was too hurt himself. I did not believe it was him, but I knew now I could never ask him for the truth, for he was gone; everyone I knew from the farm had been snuffed out, except for me. Olderhall must have taken pity on him, and buried him at Redenhall, whilst my mama lay unmarked and unremembered.

More people entered the workhouse that year, nearly five hundred in all. Their belongings, such as they were, were sold at auction in the market square. Sometimes their friends bought them, to hold against their escape. But nobody had much money to spare, as the hunger took them. Mrs White said it was a blessing that I had not been forced to go to the workhouse, for it was full enough now. But the doctor looked angrily at me when he saw me, and I knew that I was there on sufferance; I could hear Mrs White's voice pleading and a rumble from Dr White, not once but often. I couldn't lose this, and so I did every task that was asked of me and kept away from him as much as I could, so as not to annoy him. I hated him for making me indebted to him.

He had enough work, for men had limped back from war with injuries, or with limbs hacked off hurriedly on the battlefield, but they had no money to pay him, and all over the Waveney Valley, the farmers were laying off their workers as the wheat price dropped. Labourers started to tramp the roads, looking for work. The soldiers, called Dragoons, rode into Diss and Norwich to quiet the atmosphere.

There were hangings in Norwich of men who were poor,

needed bread and who protested. In Diss, the good rector wanted to reduce the tithes, to assist them. The first threshing machines were broken. Fires were lit, night after night, and sometimes I could even see them, when the house was locked up tight but outside the fires flickered where once there had been a long stretch of dark fields. I was excited by what they did because they rose up when I could not. I might not dare to light a fire but I loved to see them burning.

In Harleston the first Dissenters came to visit, with radical sermons being preached on the common about the rights of men to organise. I heard Olderhall talk to Dr White about "the great pest in my parish" and how thoughtless and ignorant the labourers were. But I thought different, and how Mama had always tried to assist those poorer than ourselves and how these working men just wanted to feed their families and pray amongst folks like them. Matthew Wypond was accused of an impropriety with the parish accounts. There was an inquiry, and he was cleared. All the same, he spent more time on the farm now his brother was dead, and I was happy to go to school and not see his face catch sight of me then turn away like a rat, scuttling into the dark.

Mrs White had grown large and tired, as she was with child. Like Mama, she needed me to do her commissions. She had to buy ribbons for her bonnet one day at the draper's, in the market square. I entered, carrying Mrs White's straw basket. Such ribbons there were: velveteen, silk, satin and of all hues. I wanted to make Mrs White happy again. I was nearly full-grown – a girl rising up in age now, decked out in a brand new white pinafore with a crisp pocket at the front. The draper had another customer and walked forward to serve the gentleman. Whilst he was distracted, without thinking about it overmuch, I slipped a pink ribbon in my pocket, heart trembling, and pointed to two green ones for Mrs White and paid for them when he came to serve me. They were wrapped in tissue paper, and I walked out, just as the stagecoach arrived on the square with a whinny from the black horses. A ribbon for Mama, I thought, and walked slowly back to the house, happy.

The next day, emboldened, I stole a sweetmeat when I was buying the loaves of bread for the household that could not be baked that day as the cook was ill. It tasted soft and melting in my mouth, with those plump raisins. The moon rose high in the sky and the blackberries grew fat. When I walked down to see Mama at Lush Bush, the smell of burning leaves stayed with me as I tied the ribbon round the tree where I rested, Mama's tree.

Over the next few months, as Mrs White reclined on the velveteen sofa and her stomach swelled, I stole three more ribbons to tie on the tree at Lush Bush for Mama, four sweetmeats with raisins, some good straw to redo a bonnet, and some laundry off a hedge. That was blamed on the Gypsies, who travelled through on their way to the fair in Norwich, and to my shame I was relieved that none thought of me, for it was unkind of me to get others into trouble, yet I could not stop stealing. I wanted my own things, to put by, as my mama had, for I had so little. I had heard Dr White talking to Mrs White about the sailors coming home from the wars, and how times were hard and all must retrench; Mrs White looked at me protect-ively, even as my cheeks burned and his words hit home.

I was standing at the kitchen table, rolling out pastry with Cook, when I noticed that Mrs White gripped the table, then cried out. Around her spread water. I remem-bered. We helped her upward, to the bedroom, and brought clean water and fresh sheets. The doctor arrived back. He ran up the stairs, burst in.

"Hannah, you may wait downstairs. Cook, outside the door."

I heard Mrs White crying, then a silence, and then the sound of a baby, weak, insistent. But then came a shout for Cook. She ran inside and closed the door.

The newborn survived, a boy who would be christened James, and Archdeacon Olderhall, his godparent, came to the house to give succour to the doctor, and the house was dark and I had lost my only friend, for she had tried so hard to keep me safe, and now she was gone. I could do nothing to help her now, except to buy mourning ribbons for the house, with an extra one, which I slunk into my pocket for my dear mama, for she had been right fond of Mrs White. I would tie her tree round, to remember the kindness Mrs White had shown me.

I had just opened the door to walk out. Instead, I felt the heaviness of a male hand land on my shoulder. I twisted away from the feel of it, but he held me tightly and marched me out into the square. There was Bessie, drinking from the trough, and the archdeacon standing next to her. The shopman handed me over to him, for he was the magistrate. And so then we walked together back to Dr White and all the time he held me tight, as if I had somewhere to run. The door was opened and Olderhall bade me wait in the hallway, whilst he went into the dispensary. Then Henry Fox, the attorney, came, and he would not look at me but went straight in to the other men. As the door opened, I saw Dr White through the doorway, his head in his hands, and all the time a faint and desperate wailing, as if a baby could not find food. "Like mother, like daughter," Olderhall said, as I stood outside the door. "I am thankful my dear wife is not here to see this," Dr White's voice caught on the words. "Bad blood," I heard another other voice say – that must be

Mr Fox – who then added, "What's bred in the bone comes out in the flesh."

Other tradespeople came forward the next day, so many of them who I did not even know and where I had never shopped, with their suspicions of me and how I might have pilfered and put items I had not paid for into the basket. I was formally accused of pilfering, although I cared not what they thought, and then I was taken in the late afternoon away from the house that had been my home and walked down the street to the square, with the churchwarden on one side, and the constable on the other, both of them towering over me like great trees. The churchwarden said to the constable that I should be whipped, like the vagrants he paraded in the market square before the whip came down on them, and the labourers who missed a church service.

The constable drew himself up and spoke back. He said that no sentence had been passed on me, and that I was just a girl and too young to be locked away in this manner. They stood in the market square and talked to each other as I looked up at them. So I was not whipped in the end, and the churchwarden walked away, quite stiffly.

The constable looked down at me and sighed. Then he took out his keys and opened up the door to the lock-up. It was an enormous oak door and inside it was dark and cold, although it was still daylight. There was just one small grille in the door itself and a small window, high on a wall.

The last person who had been cast in the lock-up was the town drunk, and it smelt of vomit and of his sourness. There was an earth closet in one corner, covered with a plank of wood. He said that he would fetch me a clean blanket from his cottage, and fresh straw. He pointed to the straw mattress in the corner. "Sit there." He came back before long, and scattered fresh straw so that the place smelt like the dairy on the farm. He brought bread, cheese, two blankets and a mug of water. "From my well," he said. "It's clean to drink." Then at last, he turned the key in the lock with a thunk and a clud.

I was quite alone.

Mama had passed three nights here. Then, on the third night, she had taken poison. I say it out loud, as if she can hear me. "You left me alone, Mama."

There is no answer. Wherever she is, it is not here. I speak then. Perhaps she can find me here. "Mama!"

I try again. "I went on, Mama," and then I have no more words, for she does not answer, and I wrap myself in the blanket and look up at the window. The stars are up, for it is a clear night, and cold with it. I am so frozen I have no idea if I can sleep, and yet at last I lie down, as I did with my mama, and curl into her absence.

At some point in the night the weather turns, and it rains so vigorously that I hear the sound of it, dimly, through my sleep. It is so cold that I shake as I slumber and as dawn comes, I stand up and walk from one end of the cell to the other, to warm myself with my exertions. Did Mama do this when she woke? Did she leave that trail of blood, scuff it out on the floor? There is no sign of her here at all, and I walk towards the door and hold the metal grille in each hand, remember how I had passed her the paper spill, the food, and how our hands had met, one last time.

At last there is movement outside, footsteps. I step away as the door is unlocked and opened. The constable stands there, with a steaming mug of chocolate and a bun. An extra blanket.

"They have gathered at the sessions and have reached a verdict," he says, and my hand shakes as I drink.

There is the sound of horses next, a horn.

The constable turns and there is Mr Henry Fox, the attorney.

He addresses me directly, as if I were dirt on a fine shoe.

"You are going to London, to the refuge, and I hope you will mend your ways and become a grateful and most repentant object there. Mrs Thurlow, my housekeeper, will go with you and she has packed up your belongings from your room. Hurry now, for the accommodation waits for nobody."

The constable took back the cup and I thanked him. I had no idea what Mr Fox meant by the refuge, and me becoming an object.

"You should be right thankful," said Mr Fox, "for the good people of Harleston and all they have done for you. They have taken up a collection and been right kind. On your way now, for you take the stagecoach in just a few minutes."

The words washed over me, for I was numb. I heard only I was going to London, and away from the only place I had ever known, and where I had lost Mama.

Part Two

London

Chapter Eleven

S o, barely a day later, this is how I come to stand in front of a whole row of men, behind a long, dark oak table, all dressed in black coats, tightly buttoned against the cold, with gleaming white shirts and black ties. I hold on to Mrs Thurlow's hand; she squeezes it and stands aside and a tall man says to me,

"Your story, child."

He has greying whiskers and dark hair and as he talks, I see that a man next to him writes down every word in neat clear script in a heavy brown leather book, without a blot or a false step. This great man is Mr Charles Haskin, the superintendent of the refuge, and the most important personage.

"I, I . . ." I trail away. For where should I start? The man looks up, holds his pen at the ready.

Even when I look back now, I see how my life unspools, with a jump and a jerk, as if the bobbin was not set right, and catches on memories that I could not then say out loud. Yet I must try.

I stand up quite straight. I must sift my words, catch the heavy clods and tell them only the grains of truth. So, I do not tell them of how it felt to lie like a teaspoon, curled up inside my mama's arms, or how it felt to help my mama birth my sister, cut the cord that bound them. I cannot tell them of how it was to carry the dear dead burden and see her sink. I will not say what it was like to hear Olderhall tell me, as my hands grasped the teats of a cow, that I would never see my mama again. Or of how it was to see my mama, lifeless, unclothed, on a cart, or of the sounds that return in darkness. I must not tell them that at night my mama comes to me in my dreams and speaks to me and that when I wake, I am drowning in water because she flies up and leaves me all alone and I still do not understand why she has left me, or why we were so ill-used, I only know that I am lost if I do not beg these people to hold me, as best they can.

They do not want to hear these things, these men. Instead, with my head up, I look at them, one by one, and I tell them that I had given myself to pilfering, after my friend Mrs White had died, and that my mama had committed an iniquity – I speak this word louder and with emphasis, for they want to see my separation from the only person who ever loved me – and then destroyed herself. I tell them that I have repented of my own acts, and that I would be honest and hardworking if I was admitted. I tell them, and the tears that come are true, that I have nowhere else to go and no friends to whom I can turn. They listen in silence, and then they call upon Mrs Thurlow, and she comes to stand next to me but does not take my hand.

She speaks in a voice I do not recognise, a hard edge to it that cuts. "The girl has exhausted the patience of the town and so we took up a collection for her. If you admit her, she could be reformed, and be put into service when the time comes."

They nod at that, and write their notes and then we are sent out. I do not know what I hope for except not to be sent back to a place which hates me and which paid to send me away.

The house servant is waiting outside. She speaks slowly, as if the word is dragged out from her. "Come," she says, and gestures at the same time, as if she is not sure that her word is enough to set us moving. We follow her downstairs to the kitchen and this time she sits with us, and we eat together. I see now, as her cap slips for a moment, that her hair is mouse-brown and her eyes a dull grey, like two round stones pulled from the river to dry on the bank. She rolls her bread into pellets as she eats, and dips them into the broth, and after a pause I do the same. Mrs Thurlow watches us both, right kindly, but does not follow suit.

After she has finished her broth, and wiped her mouth on a rag, she is called again to take two other objects for their interviews. When she is gone, Cook says, in a confidential voice to Mrs Thurlow, "Maria is the maid in the house. Poor child, she stammers. Mr Haskin has said that she will not be placed for service." They both nod, and I see how she opens her mouth to say more, but then turns away and busies herself when Maria appears again in the doorway, as if she did not want to speak of her impediment in front of the object.

Such changes already, a new life unfolding, with new personages to understand; I was so confused by it all I could not think straight, though I knew that I need never bow and scrape to those who had hurt me ever again, if I could just be admitted.

I had been whirled to London on the Accommodation the day before this happened, with Mrs Thurlow to accompany me. Right from the start she had been kind to me, as I stumbled out of the lock-up, unable to bear the light. She wrapped a shawl around me, and from the smell I knew it had belonged to my mama. But there was no time for tears.

"Come, child, the coach waits for no man," she said, as she took the ladder carefully. I looked on as she patted the seat next to her, and so I too climbed the ladder. At the doorway I paused and looked out on the square.

"Sit down, child," I heard.

Mrs Thurlow had made a space between herself and a large man, whose girth lapped me as I sat down. I shrank away from him. She passed me a small bundle. "I packed up your room for you, child. Everything is there." Then she added, lowering her voice, "Your mama's items too, her dress." I felt the tears prickling, looked down at the bag and hugged it close, huddled into Mama's shawl. All I had left fitted into my lap or was wrapped around me. Opposite me sat an older woman and her husband. They were shivering, and the older woman wrapped a blanket around them both, smiling at us all the while.

"We've come down on the Mail coach with Mr Salter. He is the best coachman in the East of England. He keeps good time and waits for no man," she said, proudly. My eyes prickled, for she spoke as Mama had done, with her soft lilt and pride in the stagecoach. I marked that this time no children had run up to the horses to feed them. Instead, the square seemed cloaked in a waiting silence.

Mrs Thurlow bent down, packed straw around our feet, and I noticed that the fat man was straining to do the same, but could not reach over his stomach. She packed him in, and then, in that small space, everyone nodded to each other, got acquainted. "We have thirteen hours on the lonely road, before we get to London," the old woman said. I felt the coach sway slightly, as Coachman Salter climbed up. I shivered, shrank back into the seat.

"Be thankful that it is the winter. Mr Fox said if it had been the summer, the folk would only have paid for outside seats."

All eyes turned towards me and I rubbed my eyes, for they were prickling. Mrs Thurlow softened and spoke again, her arm around me. "This poor girl has been orphaned. I'm taking her to a refuge, poor soul."

They looked rightfully sorrowful at that and I was thankful to her that she had not shamed me, and indeed hugged me tight.

Then, with the horn sounding, Mr Salter whipped the horses, and off we went. The coach rumbled over the dirt roads and we crossed the bridge; I looked down briefly into the river, then up into the sky, and I saw five great birds, flying as if they formed an arrow between them, pointing onwards. A part of me said follow on, as I watched to see where they went, and ahead we travelled, until the birds flew up so high, I could no longer see them, past Scole, Diss, faster still, then I woke up to find myself shivering as we clattered into London.

"Leadenhall Market," Mrs Thurlow told me as we rode past a covered market, shut up tight. "We will be at the Spread Eagle soon."

We arrived at eight in the evening on Mr Salter's watch. Mrs Thurlow climbed out and down the ladder, and then reached out a hand as I followed, so stiff that I nearly fell. Then she turned away, to hand the old couple down. The coach stood there for a moment, as the rain fell on us, all together, and the old woman took me by the shoulders and embraced me; she folded me into her voluminous clothing. "God bless your poor soul," she said. Then both she and her husband kissed me and walked into the darkness. The large man tipped his hat to us, and then walked eagerly towards the open door of the inn across the cobblestones. Light was streaming from it, the sound of voices spilling out, laughter. Strange to me.

I looked up and around at the courtyard. The inn itself

was built around three sides, with stables on the remaining side. Above were rooms and a gallery, with men leaning on it and smoking. The horses were rubbed down and led away. London smelled different to Harleston. It was a mix of smoke, rotting vegetables and exciting vapours, coming from the inn. I realised then that I was hungry and swallowed, for my mouth had dried out on the long journey down. Men loitered at doorways, and others stood on the gallery, looking down, with tankards in their hands. The coachman came over to me, tapped me gently on my shoulder. "I remember you, Hannah Tyrell." He spoke kindly enough. "I recall how you and your mama visited Great Yarmouth." Such a pang, to hear her name, spoken with kindness. "I remember your mama, girl. She was just a child as old as you when I brought her Harleston way. Years ago now." He shook his head and then said, even softer, "It is good you have left this all behind." Then he tipped his hat to me and walked away to the stables, consulting his watch and sighing.

"Watch out," said Mrs Thurlow sharply, pulling me to one side. Above, a man laughed as the dregs of his ale splashed past us onto the cobblestones. "See there – some throw beer down on those who have just arrived. Stay away from the gallery." But she smiled then and had brought out a plate of food, a pie and a hot, sweet drink that she said was winter cider. I drank it as it steamed in the air, crammed in the pie, as did she. Then we were off again, for we had miles to go before we were at Hackney. I must have slept again because I woke as the coach door opened and the two of us limped out into a wide empty yard. A door opened and a girl stood there waiting.

She beckoned us in, saying nothing as we trotted down the stairs to the kitchen. I must have fallen asleep again, for I woke to find Mrs Thurlow tapping me, my head near to my empty bowl. The same girl was standing, patiently, by the door. Cook said, gently, "Maria, can you take Mrs Thurlow and Hannah up to the room we prepared for them?" The girl nodded, and bobbed a curtsey.

More stairs, a full three flights, and we came out on a bare swept landing; we were ushered into a clean room, lit by a small fire that flickered, and shown two beds, heavy blankets heaped on each. We sat down and Mrs Thurlow unlaced her boots and sighed with relief. "Did you mark that the child who brought us up here could hardly speak, poor soul?"

I nodded, but I could scarcely stay awake. "Let me help you get undressed," she said, and then, with a quick wash of our faces, we both slid under the covers and warmed each other and I remember nothing more until I woke. I crept out and stepped on my tippy toes to look out on the Hackney Road, which was teeming with people and horses. Where the road bent round, beyond the turnpike I could see fields, covered in a clean blanket of frost and, yet further, an open flat countryside.

At the front of the refuge, I saw a long, low building built of soft stone, and outside it, sitting comfortably, were three old men, smoking pipes, rugs over their knees. Young oak trees shaded them and as I peered out, I saw one of them strike a light and light his pipe, his hands shaking. The other two started to play a game on a board, while he watched, puffing away, the smoke rising in the cold air. I leaned out as far as I could and then heard Mrs Thurlow stir.

"Child, come away from there."

I stepped away and she swung her legs out of bed, brisk and ready for the day. "We must tidy you up, you still look unkempt. I'll wash you." She soaped the water from the ewer and cleaned my face, arms and hands with a rag, then patted me dry, and combed and plaited my hair, talking all the while.

"You will be taken to the committee at one p.m. prompt, and there you will be examined. I will go in with you, and I may be called on to give testimony about your conduct in the town."

She stood back, studying me from my head to my shoes and then nodded, satisfied. "Sit next to me, child. We will dress in an instant."

"The Refuge for the Destitute, as it is called, is just three years old and you, girl, are right lucky to have an audience here, for many clamour to enter, Mr Fox told me, but few are admitted. Child, you must show that you have erred, not from your own fault, but because you are unfortunate."

Such a word, it could not cover everything that had happened.

"You and others who have lost their parents, and have nowhere to go, are favoured here."

This was where bad luck could turn, then.

"You need to be admitted here."

She had taken a breath and looked straight ahead, swallowing.

"I have been instructed to tell you this, my child. It comes from Mr Fox himself. From the town, if you like. It will go better for you if you condemn your mama in your interview. You must say that you are alone in the world through no fault of your own. You must condemn her iniquity, speak it out right loudly, for you have no other choice."

I shook my head at that, without even thinking. How could I do that to my mama? None of it was her fault. If anything, the fault lay with me. For what I had done to my sister. But Mrs Thurlow turned me to her.

"I know this is hard for you, but many in the town do not want you there any more. You need to be honest about the pilfering as well. It will count in your favour. I will tell them that you are no longer welcome in the town. Child, I am not doing this out of spite, but for your own good, for Harleston is not right for you and you could prosper here. Your mama would have wished it." Then she put her arms around me tight, and embraced me, and I knew that I would do what she told me to do, for the town had turned its back on me. I must pack the past away. All thoughts of justice for my mama must be folded tight and small and stored, for I must move forward now.

Or I could stand up straight and tell them the truth, as their virtuous faces turned black when I told them what had happened to my mama, and how I would never blame her for what she had done to protect me. But I had given her my word, after all, and so I betrayed her when they asked me, true to my word.

At the end of that Saturday, I was sent for again and Maria walked in front of me again and then waited outside the door for me with Mrs Thurlow – this time I went in alone. The clerk showed me the minute he had written about me and to check it was right. He read it out loud as I followed each word with my finger. "A person attended from Mr Fox, attending Hannah Tyrell, who stated that the mother had destroyed herself, that the Girl had then given herself to all kinds of pilfering. The Mother had murdered one of her children and in the face of apprehension destroyed herself. The Girl stated to the Committee that she was now sensible that her mother had committed a great iniquity, and that she begged to be admitted."

I nodded, and blinked back my tears for not a word of it was true. Then the clerk took up his pen once again, and he wrote five more words in his finest script, to round off the minute.

The Girl is illegitimate. Admitted.

Later, picking her way through words, clicking and stumbling, Maria told me that the committee had conferred for many hours.

"It took far longer than most meetings," she said. "They disagreed about you. I heard two of them say that they felt you might taint the great reputation of this place."

She paused then.

What could I say, for I could tell her nothing. At last she went on.

"But Mr Haskin spoke up for you, and said that you were just a child, that he would take you under particular care and that he had faith that one day you would give great credit to the refuge."

She looked at me then and I wondered how much she knew.

Maria told me that he wrote two further minutes that day. Another girl of fourteen was found to be of good standing and she was deemed not in need of reform. She was refused and sent with a letter to the workhouse in Bethnal Green. A boy of eleven was admitted to the male refuge.

When it was all done, and the ink dried, Mrs Thurlow kissed me and she told me to say my prayers and to be diligent, and that one day I could become a servant like herself, all being well, and even rise to the state of housekeeper. As if I wanted to do such a thing, I thought. Then I said goodbye to her, and the gate closed behind her and Maria tapped me on the shoulder and gestured for me to follow her. I was a brand new object, ready for forging.

Chapter Twelve

I must be instructed on how to become an object, and so we arrived at Mr Haskin's room, off the great hall of the refuge, opposite the Committee Room. A fine room, smelling of beeswax, the wood panels gleaming with it, a fire flickering in a grate. Neat it was, and I thought that must be Maria's work, to dust and sweep and put all to rights.

Mr Haskin sat behind his desk, pen in hand, entering words in a large black leather book. Maria bobbed in front of him and after a moment, as she looked at me, I did the same and then straightened to stand in front of him. "Maria, fetch Miss Clements and Mrs Clark." He cleared his throat. "You are now a new object here and as such, will receive the charity and protection of the refuge. You may wonder what an object is. You may rest assured that it means that you receive charity from our Institution and that is all. There are others here in Hackney, including one for orphans where others on the committee argued that you should have rightfully gone, but I argued that you should be admitted here, as I felt that I could reform you."

My attention drifted. From Mr Haskin's window, which looked over the courtyard, I could see the old men. They were playing chequers now, slow and steady. "Those men live in the almshouse below," he said. It was small and grey and low, not like the refuge, where all the windows upstairs were barred, and with a high wall around it. "You will see that the windows are barred here. We had an escape from the male refuge, and I barred the windows myself." He looked right proud with his own conduct, puffed up with it. "I barred some forty windows in just one day. Nobody here in the refuge is above manual labour such as that. I was in such a place myself as a boy, and I know that I can steer you onto the right course." In a lower voice, as if he was talking to himself, "I was like you once." I looked at him, his black hair combed and neat, his perfect whiskers, his brushed coat, and I could not understand what he meant at all.

There was an excited knock at the door. A tall young woman burst in, brown hair falling out of her cap, pushing past Maria, followed by a woman of middle height, unsmiling and resplendent in a white cap that covered all her hair with a gleaming white apron over a wide girth. Mr Haskin paused, frowned. "Miss Clements, Mrs Clark, our new object." Miss Rachel Clements spoke up to welcome me, fluttering her hands and pulling at her lace collar, her brooch. Mrs Clark stood, quite quiet, by her side.

"I will take the child around, Mr Haskin, and issue her with the requisites."

He raised a hand and she quieted, flushed. "You may show her around the different areas and then Maria will take care of the object afterwards, until she is fully accustomed to how matters are conducted here. Maria, wait outside and the new object will join you." He waited until the door was closed behind her. I wondered, was she listening, as I used to?

"We must keep the object's story to ourselves," he said.

"The other objects should be protected from such horrors." Then he looked at me. "You will not tell your story to other objects. It is forbidden to do so. Neither will we. You will commence here on your path to reform. I hope that is clear to you?"

I stared back at him fleetingly, full in the face. I knew that look on his, when people thought they knew me, what had happened to me. Pity next to fear, fear next to contempt. He hadn't heard the half of it, for I had smoothed it out for the committee so the clerk could write down the version they would accept. My story taken from me and locked away, as if I should be ashamed. Was it for me or for them, I wonder. They never knew the whole of it at any rate, put away for safe keeping. It is only now that I take my fragments out, mend them so they are one. I have to, so I can be whole, past and present fixed together so I can go on.

Mr Haskin cleared his throat. "It must never be forgotten that we have several purposes here: to relieve the destitute, such as yourself, to reform and restore the criminal violator of the laws of God and man, and to promote the best interests of society." I wondered how a boy like him had learned to speak like that.

And to this end, he continued, he would measure my progress every week. He held up the book he had written in when I had entered. In gold lettering on the front, The Regulator. "I note your conduct in my book. Look, here is your name." He turned the page, and I saw that by my name there were two ruled lines, above them the words Virtues on one side and Vices on the other. In black ink, by the weeks of the year in lined rows were several other columns, for industry and idleness, piety and impiety, obedience and disobedience, gratitude and ingratitude. "I will note your faults and merits here, and then when I feel it is necessary, I will summon you again. That is all." He closed the great book with a clap, and I saw how scattered motes of dust flew upwards as he placed it on a shelf. Miss Clements beamed at me, quite suddenly, then threw open the door so that Maria could come back in. He spoke again, in her hearing, as sternly as before, looking at me all the while. Then he rose and beckoned to me and we all left his room together; he locked it behind him with a key on his belt. Mrs Clark went on down to the laundry and I followed Mr Haskin on, Miss Clements behind him, and Maria behind her.

He paused at a door on the corridor, near the hall. Turned round to me.

"If you misbehave, you will be locked up in here." He took another key and opened the wooden door and we peered into darkness. There was no window at all and I had to screw my eyes up to see a wooden platform in one corner. A thin straw mattress on top, a folded blanket, a bucket with a lid. Like the lock-up. Then I saw something more. Two loops of iron, fastened to opposite walls. I shivered.

"One girl stayed a week in here, so do not make the same mistake. I sent her to the temporary refuge next, and her case was discussed again at the committee." With a nod he locked it, then took his leave. I was left with Miss Clements, who led Maria and me up the stairs, all the way up two flights to a whitewashed room, quite clean and bare, with hammocks strung up all along on each side, a row of beams in the middle and metal hooks to fasten them in place.

Miss Clements told me the rules. She was new herself, she said, coming from Lincolnshire. The words poured from her like drawn clear water from a clean jug: how her mother had died and her dear father lived in Lincolnshire with her sister, and how she sent her wages home to keep them snug. Then she checked herself, and the words came slower. "There are fifty of you girls, twenty-five hammocks on each side of the room. There are some forty boys in a separate establishment. You will stay here for a while, and then Mr Haskin will find you a situation. When you are ready." Her face softened when she spoke of him, and then she blushed, jangled her keys. Miss Clements, as if she could not help herself, reached out and patted my head. "If you misbehave you will go to the temporary refuge, but I am convinced that you will be a credit to us. Child, put out your arms."

She then bestowed on me a whole quantity of goods. These were the items that would complete my transformation: two smart new dresses of crisp, dove-grey cotton, with a crisp white cap and apron with a pocket at the front, just like Maria. "They can be washed twice a week," she said. They were neat, I thought, looking down. She added, in a rush of words, that the clothing was plain but serviceable, and I caught an echo of Mr Haskin as she spoke. "And so you will avoid the love of dress that can be so destructive of the virtue and happiness of so many of your sex at your age. We will instruct you to clean, cook, and you will continue your lessons. Can you sew, child?" I nodded. She was off again.

"The chaplain, the Reverend Zachary, who was one of the gentlemen who admitted you, reads prayers morning and evening, and we will go there now at a gallop, for we are nearly late and that would never do." Then she took me, almost trotting, down the stairs again to the refuge chapel, with Maria by my side. We sat down next to each other and Miss Clements took the seat in front where she sat in a smart row with Mrs Clark, Mr Haskin and the other adults. I looked up and saw how the Reverend Zachary had alighted onto a small pulpit, as if he had floated down from a cloud. As he started to pray, as the objects knelt on the wooden floor, I noticed that he rubbed his limp black hair, as if something was irritating him beneath. "We welcome a new object into our sanctuary," he intoned, smiling at me and baring his teeth although few were left. "We give thanks to the Lord for his great mercy, and for offering the object a place in the refuge. For you have been retrieved from misery and sin, and you will be allowed, God willing, to lead an honest and industrious life." I noticed that Miss Clements was never still, stealing looks at Mr Haskin, or pushing a strand of loose hair back into its bun before it escaped again.

Maria nudged me sharply, and I looked up to see that something was moving in her apron pocket, running to and fro. Maria moved her fingers nimbly inside the stiff cloth, as if a mouse was running, and grinned, swiftly, before composing her face so that she looked quite pious, gazing up at the priest as he concluded prayers.

Maria walked next to me and talked so quietly that I could hardly hear her. Halfway between a whisper and chant, she recited: "Beef on Sundays, greens and potatoes. Broth on Mondays, broth on Tuesdays, suet pudding on Wednesdays. Thursdays it's pease soup, Friday fish, and milk puddings and cheese on Saturdays." I noticed that if she sang her words, they came more easily. She took me around the refuge one more time until we were back in the ward. Sitting down on our hammocks, set opposite to each other, Maria swung hers from side to side, then whispered again, slowly pushing the words out. "I will look out for you."

My first laundry day. The coppers had been filled already, and were steaming with warm water. Mrs Clark presided over the objects and their work. She told me that I would work here every day except Saturday, when there was a half-day, and Sunday, our rest day. "We take the soiled washing in on the Monday. It comes from our patrons and other well-wishers, who pay their subscription to keep you all here, so you must wash with great care. They take an interest in you all, destitute as you are. You enter the items into the account book, here. If you damage or lose anything, I will reprove you.

"Maria, you will work with Hannah. Separate the materials one from another, and then wash the coloureds," she said. We set to work, sorting out white linen from muslin, coloured cottons from white cottons and linens from woollens, greasy clothes straight into a tub of lime and water. "Careful now, it can sting," Mrs Clark said hurriedly, as she was called away.

As soon as she was gone, Maria grabbed a long wooden paddle, climbed up to the copper and banged on it so that the whole room was ringing with sound. Another girl joined in. Then came footsteps outside.

Maria jumped down, and the girls composed their faces. Maria lifted the heavy wooden paddle, pounded it suddenly with a thud into the water, the sodden clothes. The sound went through me, pointed and sharp. Took me back to the great silence, the screaming.

I woke up on the floor of the laundry, with Mrs Clark bathing my forehead and the girls clustered around me. "Child," Mrs Clark said briskly, "I hope you are recovered? Perhaps you are not used to the heat in the laundry." I could not talk of this. Would not.

"Yes, the heat. I was not used to it," I said. Mrs Clark helped me stand up.

"Let's get back to work," she said, and took me with her, as the girls sprang to stirring the coppers. "Miss Clements told me that you can sew and knit, child." I nodded.

"You can assist me in my room while the washing is being done, to mend any particulars that are sent over, and get up the linen."

After that I mended when the washing was done, and I got up the linen with a hot iron. When I heard the sound, it was muffled, until at last I could hear without starting, if I knew it was coming. Nobody asked me why, for Mrs Clark brooked no questions. My new life was governed by her and whatever small tasks Miss Clements dreamed up, by bells and gongs and prayers. We washed and rinsed, mangled, starched and ironed. We bathed once a week and I was clean, well fed and nobody hurt me. We objects were not slaves. If the patrons complained about the washing, well, the objects were destitute with nowhere else to go, and Mr Haskin would speak up for us and then reprove us, and make a mark in his book. We were not slapped or beaten and we knew that we were safe here, would not be cast out beyond the gates.

Harleston was a dream to me, as the endless days stretched into months and then I found I had lived there for over a year. It was only at night that everything unravelled and I woke up sweating, sometimes even screaming out loud, to see my mama and my sister rising away and passing me, quite fast and with their heads turned away from me as if they could see something that I could not, knew something that was kept secret from me. I put the sheet into my mouth as soon as I woke, saw dark figures around me groaning as the hammocks swung, then silence again. I hoped that nobody knew who screamed. I needed to put that life behind me, but it would often return. I quelled it with the dull activities, pushed away the questions that Mama had said I must not ask. Who had done this to her and to me, and what had I done to my own sister, the questions that plagued me still. I had to go on, though, and so I grew accustomed to everything, even the sound of the paddles in the coppers.

Maria stuck to me, always by my side. If we were on our own, hanging out sheets or mending, we practised talking, singing out the words together, and her words came faster, did not hang on a syllable and stick there, but instead lined up neatly and regular. By spring she was getting fluent, as long as she was not hurried in what she had to say. She asked me to tell nobody, for she wished to surprise them when she was ready. She wished to tell her aunt and uncle first, she said, as they had done their best by her. She talked of them and their only child, a girl of eight. She loved that mite like a sister, and treated her with the meagre earnings she was given as a maid.

The time before Annie arrived is blurred and smeared, each day fading into the next. I had a friend; I was liked enough. Sometimes I wondered if this was all there was now, a rhythm of work and food and a muted companionship. Then the memories came back, sharp and sore, and I pulled back. This was better. I sipped at my new life like the good wife at Godfrey's Cordial, and it kept me numb and quiet and faintly smiling, for a year or thereabouts, and my birthday came and went and then I was sixteen. Those sharp thoughts, nagging me, asking me what had happened to my mama, faded away. Then, I woke up.

It was a hot spring that year, I remember, and the stench of the river drifted up to reach the refuge, so foul that the washing stank when we brought it in dry and we had to spray it with lavender water. Committee Day came when Maria and I stood side by side, pegging out the washing on the ropes in the yard.

"An object comes from the Old Bailey today."

Maria spoke slowly still, as if the words were formed

from thick clay, but she talked well now, if she was only give time to line up her phrases with care. She knew everything that went on. The committee had determined some months earlier that the refuge would admit some small number of new objects from the Old Bailey, to respite their terms there and be reformed. Mr Haskin was given the task of attending trials, to decide which girls and boys the refuge might admit. The new object had pleaded guilty to thieving at a fair. A farmer's wife had seen her, turned her over to a constable. Mr Haskin had been present at the first day of the assizes, seen how she had begged for forgiveness. He had thought her repentant and must have written to the judge that evening and offered the refuge to the girl, who was just seventeen years of age, saying that her sentence should be respited and that the refuge could reform her and give her an honest trade, put her to service when she was ready. Maria had seen the letter when she was dusting his room.

"I heard Miss Clements say to Mrs Clark that the new object reminded him of his sister Clara, who died of a fever, and then she wondered out loud why he would want such as her, a light-fingered girl, to remind him of his sister, and then Mrs Clark had shushed her, and told her not to be bitter." Mr Haskin had told the Old Bailey that she should come to the refuge after the verdict was handed down. "The committee will admit her, though Miss Clements thinks that she should be interviewed all the same. But he stood surety for her." We looked at each other as we pegged the last of the washing, for the story was odd and Mr Haskin's behaviour was different from normal. As if he was looking forward to a change.

Mr Haskin sent for me as the committee dispersed, the men shaking hands in the hall with fervour. I wondered what I had done, but his voice was gentle and the Regulator was up on its shelf, not open on his desk. "You will assist a new object who has been admitted. She will arrive tonight."

I asked, for I was confused, "But Maria is the house servant and so is it not her position to do so, sir?"

He thought for a moment, then said, "I feel that the object may need to talk. You may assist her with that." I did not tell him how Maria had fought for every word, every sentence. She could talk now, although I had promised her to tell nobody. That was not quite it, though, if I am truly truthful. I was curious.

I rose to go, but he held up his hand.

"She has suffered, as you did," and his face softened, as if the mask he wore melted away. "Her whole family died of a fever and she was left with an uncle and it did not suit." I wondered at that, for his voice was gentle. "Be kind to her, Tyrell."

Maria was waiting for me in the hall. I found it hard to meet her gaze, mumbled that I had been ordered to take the new object around. I saw how Maria drew back from me though she tried to hide it. I did not want to hurt her, to step over my duties onto hers, but this is how it happened and I am sorry for it, but not for what happened next.

Chapter Thirteen

Annie. The first time I saw her was from above, a girl who was cloaked and bonneted, her face in shadow. Maria walked behind me and I found I was annoyed that she hovered so. Annie Simpkins stood in the hallway and as we reached the bottom tread, as we stepped onto the swept wooden expanse, she lifted her hands, untied her bonnet. I caught my breath as the dying light net in her golden hair, tangled from its covering. I felt Maria's breath on my neck.

Mr Haskin swallowed. His voice strangled as he commanded us, "Hannah, take the new object to your room. She can meet Miss Clements and Mrs Clark tomorrow." He turned on his heel. "Maria," he called, and beckoned her to him.

Annie turned to me and I stumbled a little, as I told her my name and led her upstairs. She followed on silently and I felt her gaze on me, all the way to our dormitory. We stood for a moment by my hammock and I set it swinging, and looked to see if she would laugh. I gestured to the empty one next to me.

"You can sleep here, next to me," I said, my voice catching on the words, and passed her new clothes, for she had scarcely a thing with her. The chatter rose again, and she sat down and turned her back to undress. Her garments came loose, one by one, and I saw how she glanced at me, removing a small black book from her clothing. "My mama's Bible," she whispered, as she folded her clothes neatly in a pile on the floor, patting each garment as she did so. At length she came to her shift, and she lifted her arms and pulled it over her head. Again, she spent time folding it, stroking it flat, sitting quite naked on her hammock.

A memory came back to me, of the young man at the fair, putting his fiddle to his shoulder and how the fiddle sang out as the light fell on a great body of people dancing, and how they stopped when his bow stroked the string for the last time. The farmer, holding his wife so tight that I could not see a gap between them. Annie's back, in the candlelight, curved like his fiddle, catching the light of the darkening room.

She reached up then, unpinned her hair. It fell down and swayed as she brushed it, the tangles subdued, and as the candlelight found her hair it moved like a wave of wheat. Then she reached up behind her back and caught her hair between her hands, and started to plait it, fingers gleaming white in the dimness as she fixed it with two ribbons.

I must not stare. I dragged my gaze away, dressed myself hastily in my night shift and got into my own hammock. Before we blew the candles out, I looked at her once more. Annie had knelt by her hammock. Then she climbed into it, Bible in hand, and lay completely still on her back before she placed the book on the floor. Her eyes were still open and shimmered with tears. As the lights went out, I reached across to her, and in the moonlight, she reached out until at last, our hands touched. Hers felt soft against mine and I held it until it loosened, and fell away.

I woke in the morning before she did, and looked at her as she lay sleeping. Her hair had come out of its plaits and was spread out all over the hammock, and her hand dangled down. I reached for it, to shake her awake, but then I checked myself. Maria was watching me from her own hammock and her mouth had turned down at its corners. I opened my mouth to talk. She turned away from me, dressed and left the room.

Annie stirred and my gaze moved back. Mr Haskin had commanded me to look out for her. She needed me and I would be present for her. It was not my fault that I had been chosen for this task, to show Annie around, to demonstrate the tasks to her, as Maria had done for me.

Annie was docile, quiet even for those first few days. At night I heard how she stifled her tears, and so I held out my hand to her, gripped on tight. The feel of her hand, as she folded it around mine, stays with me still.

Mothering Sunday dropped on my mama's death day that year. Some objects walked out to spend it with their relatives. Miss Clements took them into the small garden she tended, near the temporary refuge. She took her snips in her hand, and cut and tied small nosegays for them, tied a ribbon around them, gave each one out with a blessing. Maria took hers and I wished her a good day with her family, but she edged past me, as if her words were lost again. I watched her go through the gate that was open for this day and then Miss Clements tapped me, offered me one of the white and yellow flowers, the daffadowndillies scented. I held it to my face and thought of how I had gathered flowers in the meadow for my mama, and how the goodwife had helped me tie a ribbon around them. I would beg Mrs Clark for a cup of water, keep them by me.

"Annie, one for you too," Miss Clements said, and I turned around.

Annie held out her hand, as if to take the nosegay. Then she slapped it down to the ground and ran away.

"Well, I never," Miss Clements said, staring after her. I picked the nosegay up, but it was broken.

"I will go after her," I said. "Thank you for mine, Miss Clements," and then holding it tight, I hurried after Annie.

The refuge was empty that day, with the objects scattered around London. I found Annie in her hammock, her face down. I sat down next to her, reached out and rubbed her back.

"What happened, Annie?"

She turned towards me then. Her face was wet.

"My brother Thomas came home on Mothering Sunday and when I ran to welcome him, I saw that his face was shining, and his hand was hot. I saw that he was carrying a posy of flowers and they were all wilted from the heat of him but he wanted to give them to Mama all the same. By night-time he was shivering and groaning in the bed.

"First the fever swept Papa away, and Mama cried that what should they do, for the cottage was tied, but by the end of that day my brothers were dead and Mama five days later. I was the only one to live on."

This is the moment to tell her what happened to my mama, but I hold back. She needs to speak more than I do, the desolation of her. And anyway, I am forbidden from sharing my story. Since she has come, anyhow, the dreams have stopped.

Her voice trembles.

"I should not have slapped the nosegay away. I will tell Miss Clements I am sorry. But this day, it hits me. All my family were gone, a week after this day." I think of my mama. My sister. My poor family.

"It went from bad to worse. I had to go to my uncle, a single man."

She had never understood why her papa had made black looks at his brother when he asked her to sit on his knee and jiggled her up and down. Her mama would laugh and take his gifts but Annie would jump down as soon as he loosened her, for something was not right about him.

There was a housekeeper there, who lived in a room at the back of his shop.

Annie woke one night to hear sounds that she dimly remembered from her childhood, when she was lifted, half asleep in her papa's arms, and placed in bed with her brothers so that the parents were alone in one bed. A woman groaning, then a thump, thump, thump, as if wood was hitting a wall. A door, ajar, showed her uncle, back to her, britches down, and the housekeeper, on her knees, eyes closed. She was afraid. She feared that it would be her turn before long and no one to protect her.

"I didn't know where to go, so I went back to the farm, but the wife there blamed my brother for bringing the fever to the town. The farmer said I could stay till fair day, and then he would find me another position."

Fair day came and Annie wanted money so she could leave if she needed to. She slipped away from them at the fair, stole a quantity of ribbons to sell. But the farmer's wife saw her, and got the constable to take her in hand, and then she was alone again, and to stand trial for thievery at the assizes. She would have been sent to the house of correction after the Old Bailey, but Mr Haskin spoke up for her and so her sentence was respited and she came to the refuge, after just a few nights in the parish lock-up.

"Then I came here. I met you." She sat up, took my hand in hers. I felt the thrill of it, how she trusted me. "Take my nosegay and pin it to your dress," I said, and pressed it on her. "Say you are sorry to Miss Clements."

I could not tell her my story, how could I, for she had

given me hers to hold, to give her strength. I could not weigh her down like this.

Annie took the nosegay and kissed it, and as she pinned it, she said, "Thank you," and all of a sudden, she stood and took my hand, and whirled me round, just once. We stopped then, and I felt how our bodies warmed each other, and then she whirled me again, until we were flying and everything left us except our hands held together, until at last, we collapsed on the floor and still everything spun as we lay together in a heap.

The days caught colour, laughter. One day, when we were sorting the laundry, for I had found I could tolerate the thuds again, now Annie was there, she grew tired and threw a great pile of dirty handkerchiefs in the air so they came down like wilted flowers and all the girls put their hands to their mouths and laughed out loud. So it went on.

One day I even grew bold myself, threw trousers at Annie and told her to put them on, for she was as tall as a young man and full grown in every way. Annie strutted the length of the laundry, dressed in britches, as the girls laughed till they cried. I could not take my eyes from her, this fine young man from the back, and from the front something else, for her shift clung to her in the warm laundry and outlined how she curved.

We sometimes took the fine handkerchiefs, if they were not monogrammed and might not be missed, and could forget to enter them in the laundry inventory, and we hid them in the capacious pockets of our aprons for why should we not have pretty things to enjoy ourselves. I loosened three floorboards below my hammock, and put together what I remembered Mama had called her trousseau. Stored against a future. With Annie. I hid the thought underneath, next to Mama's dress, folded in paper, so that each time I added an item there was a crackle.

Maria seemed to disappear, the spring that Annie came. She was busy with her duties, or so it appeared, as she rarely came to the laundry, and only came to bed when the lights were about to be snuffed out, and then she turned away and pulled the blanket over her head. I wondered, when I could catch breath, why she was so quiet, but then I was drawn back to Annie, and the stories she told after the candles were out for the night, for I was swallowed up whole by my new friendship, and had no time for anyone else.

She was a teller of yarns, smuggling stories from the West Country and tales of ghosts that lay in wait down country lanes. The girls would draw in breath sharply, in unison, at her spiels of horror, and fall to sleep with trepidation. Except for me, who smiled at her as she talked, and Maria, who turned away from Annie when she spoke. I stopped repeating her words with her, although that was not for want of trying, for every time I looked for her I could never find her. She slipped away from me and to my shame I did not seek her out and ask her what I had done to offend her so. I was busy, all the same, for each night Annie and I whispered of how we would collect things and set up house together, and in my dreams each piece of laundry was another stone we slotted into a house that we were building together out of nothing.

At the end of April Mr Haskin gathered us all together in the great Committee Room, Miss Clements stood to his right and Mrs Clark to his left. We were lined up in neat rows before him.

"Tomorrow is May Day, and I have a fancy to celebrate it this year, with some country dances in the yard outside.

I have agreed with the committee that this will be an annual event, to thank the objects for their hard work." I saw how his eyes moved along on our line, focused for a moment on Annie. The day was a furious whirl of activity, as we practised our steps where we worked, up and down the laundry, in our ward around the hammocks, in and out, until at last Mrs Clark came and told us all to go to bed, although even her eyes twinkled at the absolute scene we made.

One by one the girls got into bed and the hammocks swung to and fro as the lights were blown out. I watched from my hammock as Annie knelt, a dark figure, as she did every evening, and prayed, her hand on her mama's Bible. At the end of her prayers she looked up and saw me watching. She smoothed down her Bible, placed it on the floor. She straightened up for a moment, then moved towards me without hesitation, and stepped into my hammock, one arm on the rope so that it hardly swung.

We lie face to face, and I smell the whole of her, lavender water and a scent of sage from her mouth as it finds mine. I feel the folds of her gown, stiff and clean from the laundry, and nothing is said but our hands find each other and I feel their softness again, for she begs Mrs Clark for goose fat after every washday. Then her breath laps against me and she is asleep and I dare not touch her but I feel the shape of her as I am rocked to sleep, as if on water.

Dawn broke, and I heard the sparrows as they started yelling, flying in and out of the ivy that had crept up the wall. In the dim light I saw that our hair had blended together, the brown and the gold, and hung mixed through the ropes of the hammock. On an impulse I plaited some of our hair together, and then I fell asleep. When I awoke, she was smiling at me and working to take the strands of our hair apart. Then she swung her legs around and tiptoed back to her own hammock and I must have slept again.

I wake to hear voices. Annie is shaking my hammock. The girls are taking them all down so we can practise dancing along the full length of the room, and before we are even dressed, we gallop through a strip the willow and a Scottish reel. Miss Clements runs in, hair falling out of her bun and giggles like a girl at the tumult. We do not care; we do not stop for her until Mrs Clark arrives and restores us all to calm. We wash and dress for we are to dance at noon, so that we may eat a late meal afterwards. I plait Annie's hair for her, she mine. Then she hands me a paper package, tied with string. I pull the string loose and inside is a linen square, and when I unfold it, it is a clean white handkerchief, and she has embroidered our initials together, linked with running stitch.

Her voice is shaky. "Do you like it? It is my way of thanking you, for everything." I hold it to my nose for a moment, inhale her scent of lavender that comes off it, and then I hold her hand and I thank her and I see how her eyes do not want to leave mine, nor mine hers. I slip it into my apron before we rise together and go down.

The yard is swept and ready. Mr Haskin refused the maypole, even though Miss Clements begged at first, remembering how she had danced as a girl in Lincoln. He said it was improper, even pagan, and he struck out another dance that the committee frowned on, but we could dance six dances and that would be enough. Mrs Clark takes out her fiddle, puts it to her shoulder. I never knew that she could play. Miss Clements has procured a large saucepan and a wooden spoon to keep the rhythm.

Then we are off, girls matched against taller girls, moving in and out, round and in figures of eight, up and down, and some of us breaking into missteps but it doesn't matter, for we all laugh as Mr Haskin calls the turns, and even he is smiling. Miss Clements keeps banging out the rhythm and each time she strikes the saucepan another strand of hair comes loose.

Strip the willow comes last and we all know it, and the girls laugh and beckon Mr Haskin to the dance. He takes off his coat and seems younger, shirtsleeves rolled up and his hair rumpled. He stands opposite Annie, and Miss Clements beats the saucepan and we are off. We turn and turn about, and at one point I take Annie's arm to dance across her and round and we look back at each other even as we dance away and onto our next partner. Mr Haskin arrives opposite me now and his face has changed and he is scowling at me. I do not understand and I dance past him to the next person and forget. I forget how he looked because I remember how I danced with my mama until my feet burned and then the dance comes to an end, and Mr Haskin claps his hands and the thing is over.

When she beckons to me in the darkened room I go to her, a hand on the rope so it is almost still as I step in. I feel the heat come from her but still I draw her close. As she lays her hands on me and mine on her I feel that I do not know where I end and she begins for we are mirrors to each other. That is the start of it, and spring turns to summer and every morning that I wake a part of me is quite absent from the long day and waiting for the moment when we put out the lights.

I could have told her everything, I should have, for however much I squashed the memories down, the thought came back. What had happened to my mama, who had done this terrible thing to her?

Sometimes Annie cried, remembering her family. I dared not. I had promised the refuge, but they would never find out, so my mind went back and forth, for surely she would not betray me. No, that was not it, not really. What if I told her everything and she looked at me differently and a great wall went up between us. Then we would be cut in two, separate again, and never lie together so close that I could not feel the join. Instead I would be alone and she might tell others and rend our handkerchief in two ragged parts. I would be naked like Mama, in front of the great concourse of girls, and then be staked out by sharp laughter and pointing of jagged fingers. I had left it too late – by the time I was ready to tell her I had too much to lose.

I do not know who went to Mr Haskin, and if that girl had known about us as well but chose to spare us. There were other girls who took some comfort, sleeping together in their hammocks. More than a few who, at dawn, woke as the sparrows sang out, and separated. But we never spoke of what happened at night amongst us.

One day, towards the end of summer, Maria came down to the laundry, spoke quietly to Mrs Clark. Mrs Clark rapped hard, cleared her throat.

"Leave everything," she said. "You will all go to the Committee Room."

The tubs were steaming and I saw how the whites and the coloureds were ready for stirring and thumping but she pushed us before her and we walked behind Maria, up the stairs.

Mr Haskin is by the dark cell door and turns the key. He has a lantern with him, I see, and he goes in and I hear the sound of chains. I understand now what those loops of metal are for, on opposite sides of the cell. But there is no time to think, for then Harriet and Phillipa stumble out. I hardly know them, except that they came in together, sleep at the other end of the room and are never separated from each other.

He pushes them before him, as they grope their way forward out of the darkness. I see that both of them rub their wrists. He must have chained them up, facing each other. In the darkness, so they could not touch for comfort.

Now, at last, he throws the chains back in, turns the lock again and they stumble on into the room and we follow on behind.

I smell the stench of the river before we are in the room, even though each window is closed and the room is sweltering from the heat outside. We file in and stand in damp lines, our hair clumping under our caps. I feel how the sweat runs from my arms down my body.

There he is, Mr Haskin, again, as he was before the dance, with Miss Clements on one side, Mrs Clark on the other. He has the great Bible in one hand, which he gives to Miss Clements, the Regulator in the other. He lifts it up, opens it on a page. We hardly dare breathe.

Harriet and Phillipa stand before him, backs to us. I see how flecks of spit gather at each side of his mouth as he shows us two pages from the Regulator, with the names of the two objects written there and a great black mark by each.

Then he takes up the Bible and makes the sign of the cross. He calls the girls unnatural, vicious, un-Christian, and then he exhorts them and all of us to go down on our knees and pray for their repentance. We fall to our knees in a wave and I see how drops of sweat land on the floor from my forehead. I cannot breathe. I close my eyes and wish for this to be over. Annie is next to me.

"No."

I open an eye and see Phillipa, still standing, and how she has turned around so we can see her, and how she bends down and lifts Harriet to her, off her knees and how their hands twist together. How Harriet nestles her head into Phillipa's neck and straightens up and stares back, defiant.

"I am not sorry. What should I be sorry for?"

Mr Haskin opens his mouth and I know he will roar but before he does the two of them walk out into the hall and then we hear them running to the front door and it closes with a heavy thunk. We never see them again although we ask everyone we know where they might have gone. They disappeared and it is as if they were never here, except for the fear they leave behind them, and something else, a glimpse of something real between them.

That night the ward is completely silent and we dare not go to each other, for nobody knows who told Mr Haskin, who might next be at risk. We wait instead until all is quiet and then I creep to her, and her breath wafts against my ear and I creep back later, sleepless, before dawn breaks. His eye is on us all and I am brought to the committee on the sixteenth day of September. I am quaking with fear.

I stood there, before them, the great and the good, sitting behind the oak table that Maria had polished so that it gleamed even in the dim light of an autumn day. Mr Haskin told them that I had been admitted when I was fourteen. Now that I had been there for coming up to two years, as was the habit at the refuge, I should be re-examined for admittance. He added, "Tyrell is altogether destitute and conduct very good." I watched as the clerk read over the minute, and told me that I was well praised by the staff. I sighed then, for surely that meant that we were safe.

Mr Haskin cleared his throat. "I have not yet finished. I received visitors here this Saturday, our patrons Mr and

Mrs Harding. They require a maidservant. I thought of you, Tyrell."

That was it then. The punishment for dancing with Annie, for not being able to break that gaze between us. I could hardly breathe for sorrow, or look at him.

There was a rustling of papers, and then he spoke again. "We have restored you to the society of the virtuous. You have been rescued from misery, and now you can pass to the next stage of your life, for you are sixteen now and more than ready for service. You may live it well, in honesty and comfort, in the house of Mr and Mrs Harding." Mr Haskin approved the minute, then opened his Regulator. My life as an object was concluded, he wanted me gone. I was to become a maid.

Chapter Fourteen

We will be parted. The last days and hours before I leave come closer. I count them down, from the moment I wake and I remember again, with a dull pain, that I am to leave.

Forty-seven hours before I am to be collected, we are in the laundry's side room, set to folding laundry, sprinkling it with the scent of lavender and putting it ready for Mrs Clark to check before it is tied in a bundle for each patron. Mrs Clark is busy elsewhere and I whisper to Annie, "Let's go upstairs." She shakes her head but I persist. "We will take the brush with us, then we have a reason to be there."

She agrees, then we take the great brush and the pan and tiptoe upstairs to the ward. I have taken a knife from the hall and now I take it out of my apron pocket, crouch down and lever up the floorboards underneath my hammock. We squat down together and I pass her out our trousseau. So few things we have to call our own. A few smart items that we washed, then took away to make our collection. One thin muslin blouse, a small quantity of handkerchiefs; they were never missed. That pair of britches that Annie wore, to strut up and down the laundry, we had marked them down as rotten, hidden them away. Underneath everything is my mama's dress. Annie feels the thin fabric of the handkerchiefs between her fingers as I cradle Mama's dress. I feel how the paper is dry, how it splinters as I unwrap it. I just wish, long to see it. I unfold it, run my finger over the flowers she had sewn, hold the fine fabric to my face. Her scent has drifted away but for a moment I close my eyes and she feels nearby. I wish I could summon up her voice but it is faint now, as if she is somewhere in the sea and calling to me, as the wind whips away her words.

I am dragged back to the present, to Annie. I feel how Mama leaves me then, slipping away as I put my arm around Annie, hold her close. She wails, sharply. "Don't leave me here." As if I have any choice. I take a handkerchief from the pile and wipe the tears from her face.

"Somehow, I promise, I will come back. Look, the trousseau stays. I will visit you, I promise." But I take the scrap of linen she embroidered for me. I need something from her with me, so that I do not feel what is underneath everything: that I have already left her, as if my body has shrunk back into itself, for we have not lain together for so long. I hear the sound of footsteps, light and unsteady, and we bundle our items back below the board, spring up and Annie takes the broom and starts to sweep as I lay the pan down to receive the dust.

Miss Clements rushes in. "But what are you doing here? You know Mr Haskin has strictly forbidden it during the day." She looks earnest, concerned.

I think back to the girls, the chains, and stammer, "We had seen dust on the floor this morning, Miss Clements, and wanted to sweep the room clean, for our task downstairs was nearly done." I tread on the board as I speak, press it down as flush as I can without a sound.

She sighs, then says, "Well, come along, girls," and we go down together, down the back stairs, and I hope that she will not think to tell anyone, as we go back to our folding, place the brush and pan back in the kitchen. Before she turns and leaves, she puts a hand on my arm. "Come and find me tomorrow, Hannah, for it is your last full day." She does not say why but I do not think we have anything to fear from her.

Mrs Clark has returned and so we work in silence as she moves between rooms, checking every folded bundle and then calling out for the girls to hurry with the mangle, for all the washing must go out today or tomorrow.

I go to her when the lights are out that night, my heart full of so much that I have not had the chance to say. One more night after this, I think, as I wake before Annie to the sparrows' chatter. and look at her for a moment, as the weights on my heart are added back by an unseen hand, one by one. I touch her face, lay my heavy head on her chest to feel how she beats against me. Then I turn away and rise to dress as the tears fall down and I go down early to see Miss Clements.

With a great flutter she presses a gift wrapped in paper into my hands and tells me it is a Bible and that I should read it day and night. Then she says, "You must not worry about your friend, for another girl is to be seen by the committee today, and Mr Haskin says he is quite sure that she will be admitted. I have asked him to permit Annie to have charge of her."

Just as I had charge of Annie. So that we had time to grow close, safely. I speak up, before I can check myself, sharp.

"But that is Maria's task, Miss Clements."

Miss Clements snaps back, "This is not for you to decide." More gently, "Maria has more than enough work. The new object is called Phoebe Potter."

I linger in the hallway after committee and I see the girl

as she comes out of the room. Then I note that Maria has fetched Annie, and they are hastening down the stairs towards Mr Haskin. I see how Mr Haskin welcomes them with his solemn nod, then calls Maria to him and presents the girl to Annie. Annie glances at me, and then she walks away with the girl and I watch them as they go. I feel how Maria looks at me and wonder, for a moment, whether it was her, my friend once, who had gone to Mr Haskin and betrayed the girls.

I am to leave at six the next morning. Phoebe Potter has a hammock opposite us and she has a cheerful look for everybody and Annie must smile back for Potter is her charge. I remember how I did the same to Maria, and I regret it, how I became so distracted by Annie that I forgot my first friend. But this hurts when it is done to me.

The room is full of noise. Phoebe brings the room together and Annie shakes off her sadness that I am leaving and joins in. I dare not go to her that evening. The last touch I have of her is when I reach out, scarcely daring to, and take her hand and she hardly responds, though whether that is fear or anger that I am leaving, I do not know. My last night is spent alone and without sleep and at dawn I rise and dress and take my items with me. At the ward door I look back and see that Phoebe regards me with her bright eyes. I turn away and feel how the flush rises in me, and I go down to the hall, where the Hardings are waiting for me.

Chapter Fifteen

I kept my eyes down as I stepped into the carriage. It jerked, and then we set off, in a stately kind of silence, along the Hackney Road. Then I peered out. An autumn sun shone out and daylight streamed into the carriage. The streets were busy and some people, dressed soberly in black and white, were on their way to church. Water-carriers, milkmaids and finer folk jostled for a place on the narrow pavements. The roads were heaving with carriages and carts. For a moment I was distracted from the ache, that I had lost my dearest friend, and I craned forward to see more of the city. The blind came down, all of a sudden, with a crash. Mrs Harding looked at me, as her husband looked down at his hands. "No looking out. We are not a spectacle. Sit back and be upright in your seat."

We halted and stepped outside a terrace, small and coated with soot so that it was as grey as the door itself. This was Gracechurch Street then, just a straight long line away from the Hackney Road – and Annie. Mrs Harding led me straight down to the kitchen, where the cook welcomed me with a cautious nod. "You will sleep in the attic. Cook will show you later. First, come with me to the parlour." Mr Harding was already there, with a small child of about nine or ten, holding a doll nearly as large as herself. She looked away when I smiled at her and clutched her father's hand and nestled into him. The three of them stood in a row and I noticed how Mrs Harding was a little taller than her husband and how her bosom went out in front of her like a well-built shelf. Mr Harding was stringy and his coat had a sheen to it that matched his shining hair. They were like three steps, I thought. Every time his wife spoke, he nodded, and then the child did too and so did her doll. Mrs Harding cleared her throat, straightened her back and the great shelf of her bosom rose stiffly up.

"My daughter is called Hannah and therefore I have determined," then a pause, "that you will be known as Susan in this household."

I stammered, looking at the child, as she and the doll stared back at me. "That is not my name. Please, let me be known by my surname. Or perhaps by the name Annie." Mrs Harding shook her head. "No, Susan will be your name here. It is easier for my child, as our previous servant was a Susan." Then she hurried on, although I hardly heard her, for my mind was in a tumult from the thieving of my name. "We expect you, Susan, to be correct, sober and industrious. You will rise at six and clean the grates, and prepare the fires but quietly, so you do not wake us. Then you may carry hot water to all of us and clean yourself before family prayers." The list of duties stretched out in front of me, for I was also expected to help Cook with breakfast, change beds and do extra cleaning.

Then Mrs Harding swept out, with me in tow, and showed me first to an enormous cupboard below the stairs that was shelved and neat with items for my work. "I will teach you which cloth or broom to use where, the feather, the pocket handkerchief." I drifted off, snapped back as Mrs Harding shrilled in my ear. "Listen, Susan, when I am speaking to you. Here is your uniform." She pulled out a dull brown twill dress, two white caps and two aprons. I could smell the grease rising from the dress, for surely it had not been cleaned when the last Susan left. Sure enough, she said, "You will spot clean your dress; there is no need for you to have two or to wash it. There is enough laundry to send out already." Then she took me to Cook.

I saw even as I stood in the kitchen that Cook would have little time to talk to me. Her days passed in a blur of meals to prepare and cook and wash up and I must help her, for there was too much for one cook to do. She told me, as she made a pie, that the last Susan had gone one morning six weeks earlier and that nobody knew what had happened to her. She rolled out the pastry with a thump. "A nice girl, and helpful. I hope that you will be as industrious as she. She never stopped, morning till night, and even helped Mr Harding in his study when he had copying out that needed doing. He says he is publishing a pamphlet on fallen women." A sharp look at me as she fitted the pastry in a dish, cut off the edges, but there was no time to wonder at what she had said and what she meant by it.

The day passed, and it was well after seven before Cook and I sat down to eat, both of us too tired to talk. But all the same she squeezed my hand and thanked me, and passed me a sweet currant pie she had made from the leavings of pastry, and then we washed the last few dishes together and went to bed.

At six the next morning, as I took in the milk with my eyes still blurry from the day before, I saw a girl, pretty and freckled, standing on the steps next door. I noticed that a strand of bright red hair had worked itself loose from below her cap. I followed her gaze. She was looking over at the inn opposite and I saw then that it was the Spread

Eagle, where I had arrived in London with Mrs Thurlow, when I was sent away. I was just a child then. How much had happened since. As we looked on, two men staggered out of the courtyard and weaved over the road. A coach clattered in, and one man stepped aside to avoid it and fell onto the cobbles. The girl laughed out loud as he sat there, cursing.

She looked at me, curiously. "You are the new Susan?"

I nodded. "Yes, but my name is Hannah." She frowned. "I liked the old Susan; she was called Louisa and she left overnight, without notice. They forced her to lose her name, just like you." We both looked outward again. The man had taken his companion's arm, and they were lurching away from us. "Look, Hannah, old Tom's out on his walk." A venerable goose, with six others following on behind, swaggered towards the steps of the Spread Eagle. The landlady stood there, holding out her hand, and we watched as the geese, one by one, pecked grain from her, then moved on quite stately as their heads bobbed in a neat line.

Cook shouted up at me to get a move on, to come inside for the trays needed carrying. "I'm Jane," she said, as I left, and bobbed a curtsey at me, with a swift grin. "Wednesday afternoon, we are both off. Let's go out together, for my young man Richard will be working."

I asked Cook if I could leave with Jane on Wednesday afternoon. She nodded, but then said, "Mrs Harding will be out visiting, but you must ask her permission and whether you are needed for Hannah."

So I might not be able to leave. I swallowed my disappointment, asked instead,

"She has no governess?"

Cook hesitated, shook her head. "No need for that, poor mite, for she finds it difficult to learn. She should not be part of your duties but Louisa often took her on all the same."

I asked Mrs Harding, timidly, just after lunch, whether I might go, for Cook had no need of me. She stared back at me, looked me up and down.

"You have no need to return to the refuge or to venture into London. I see no reason why you should leave."

I stammered, "I understood that it was permitted, usually, if you had no need of me?"

She was impatient all of a sudden, and relented. "You may go, Susan, but do not think that I will always permit it. Hannah will need a sleep today, in any case."

It was a grudging permission, but all the same I thanked her and ran upstairs to put on my own clothes. As I walked downstairs, I saw how Mrs Harding was dressed in her best clothes for visiting, a forest-green velvet that strained over the great shelf, so much that I questioned if the stitches would hold all afternoon. I might have mending to do that night, and I wondered fleetingly if she had thread that matched.

As I walked towards Jane, who was waiting outside, I looked back, as if a gaze had pinned me. There was Hannah's small face pressed against the window, and her doll was waving at me. I waved back, then joined Jane and we walked away, arm in arm, from the soot-covered houses. "Poor child," said Jane. "Louisa played with her when she could, for the Hardings do not seem to know what to do with her."

Then she pulled me into the market. I had only glimpsed it, shuttered and empty. On a weekday afternoon there were the boys running into our path, men begging, holding up dirtied stumps where arms had been – and food everywhere: periwinkles, mackerel, crab and lobsters, live poultry in the shops, in coops, and hot pies for sale. I remembered the taste of the one I had shared with Mrs Thurlow, bringing back that evening when I first came here, the warm cider. But there was no time for that, and besides we had no money. We arrived at the back of the stalls, where the rubbish piled up and naked children played in puddles, then laughed out loud as they splashed.

Jane threw open her arms and beamed. "Look at it all. We'll visit theatreland this Sunday, or I'll take you up Mayfair, you choose. Richard, my young man, works there on the buildings; the great houses are still being thrown up but he's shown me the ones that are sold and lived in that he had a hand in building. They have stone pots outside with flowers in them and high hedges, and if you wait outside in the afternoon, you may see how the ladies come out for visiting in their finest."

I wanted to see everything, but I had promised Annie. "I must go back to the refuge this week, to see friends there."

Jane was not deterred. "One day, let me show you. You cannot walk all that way every Sunday. One day we should even go to Vauxhall."

She laughed again because I must have looked blank. "The pleasure gardens, you must see them. Richard took me – we crawled in at a place he knew, for it is costly. There are hot air balloons that ascend into the air and people sit in them and it is magnificent to see them passing overhead. You enter through a dark passage and then you come out, and there are flags fluttering and looking glasses and stars. I cannot even describe it; you must see it for yourself."

Chapter Sixteen

The second time I asked Mrs Harding for permission to leave, she allowed me only three hours away. It took an hour to walk to the refuge, and an hour back. It was the best I could manage, and even when I walked swiftly, I arrived after visiting hours had commenced, in a fluster, covered in sweat. I had to wait at the gate before I was allowed in and so the minutes ticked on and by the time the gate opened, I had but thirty minutes before I must go again.

I saw Annie before she saw me. She was sitting in the courtyard and the girls were clustered around her. Potter saw me first, spoke out behind her hand. I saw how the girls laughed out loud, looked at me as if they hardly knew me, huddled about her again.

Then Annie rose and came to me and I saw how Potter followed her with her eyes and all of a sudden, I felt a dread in me, for I knew what Potter wanted, and that Annie was defenceless against her, for I could not be there.

I found a place behind the laundry lines where we could stand and talk. Our eyes met fleetingly and we could not break our gaze, just as before. The first time we danced together; lay together. I forgot myself and reached out my hand, but she shook her head and her gaze moved back to

Potter as the sheet billowed and we saw how she had fixed us both with a stare. I could not bear to be with her like this, to see her look away towards the great gaggle of girls and their laughter. This was too painful, and too exposed. I should not have come; I had no idea it would be like this.

I took her hand to say goodbye and felt how she flinched, looked away as if she could not meet my eyes. There was no time to talk and worse to come, for she said, all of a sudden, "You cannot visit next weekend, for there is a luncheon for patrons after church and no guests are allowed," and withdrew her hand, hurried away. I walked back, quite forlorn, pushing my way through the streets. Was this all I could expect, was there nothing else?

I had nearly reached Gracechurch Street but I had ten minutes still. I would not return early. I walked over to the Spread Eagle, just for a moment. To look out on the market. There were two girls, baskets on each arm, tightly linked together. I looked closer and one glanced up. A flash of recognition, a nod, and then they slipped away, into the crowds. It must have been them, Phillipa and Harriet, and I plunged after them, but it was too late; I could not find them, and ask them how they were surviving. Staying together, somehow.

I dragged myself back to the house, and another day of labour. However much I worked, from day to weary day, I was always behind, and at night I found I could not sleep. When I woke up my eyes felt rough as if grit had gone in them. The dreams returned with Annie woven into them, so that I dreaded the moment when I took my candle, shut the door and prepared myself for sleep, for I was tossed about and woke with the bedclothes in a heap, as if I had been flung about in the night.

*

Jane took me aside one morning. "Tomorrow," she said, "Vauxhall. You'll meet me on the steps when your family leaves, for they are visiting relatives and staying for a grand dinner. They have no need of you; they are taking Hannah with them. Cook told me, and she will be away herself that evening. They will not even know that you are gone."

The following day we crawled into the pleasure gardens and burst out of a hedge in front of a statue that suddenly moved and yelled at us as we ran away, holding hands and laughing at our own bravado. This was how some people lived, then, who made beauty, who tumbled in the air so that others gasped, or balanced on wires so thin you could not see them.

We should have left after an hour, and I grew impatient to return, but Jane begged me to stay until the end, for Richard had told her that it was well worth the wait. Everything darkened completely and then there were bursts of light and showers of colours raining down on us. It was only then that Jane said we could go, and then we ran, for we were out well after hours.

I was still smiling, my eyes full of fireworks and dancing statues, as I groped my way into the house through the kitchen door and made for the stairs. I saw the light first, from above. The great shadow of him next, though he was a small man. The circle of light spread, moved towards me.

"Susan."

The candle came closer, until Mr Harding faced me. I must not tell him.

"I went out, sir, but only to see the maid next door."

He was silent for a moment, then said, almost gently, "Very well. Go to bed. I will not tell your mistress on this occasion. Come, take the candle and light the way. You must be silent."

I took it from him, climbed the stairs. The light flickered. I felt how close he was to me, then he clutched at me, pressed himself hard against me. His hands crept around my waist and up, cupping my breasts and kneading them. He groaned and buckled and this was my chance. I pulled away; I stumbled upstairs, and then I was in my room, pulling my chair across the handle, wedging it shut as my fingers trembled. I saw how the handle descended and there was a push. The chair held. I watched, stiff, and then heard how the footsteps went away and at last there was silence.

The child fell ill two days later. She had been quiet enough already, but now she lay in bed and shook with fever. Cook told me to go to her and change her bed linen. As I slipped the sheet off the bed, warm and damp, I heard the Hardings enter the room together.

"You should never have insisted she came to the dinner," Mrs Harding snapped at her husband. He shrank from her.

"I like to have her with us," he said. "She is alone so much."

"She is better at home. Now look at the child."

She turned to me then. "You, Susan, you will watch over her, night and day."

"My other work, Mrs Harding . . ." I trailed off.

"Cook will assume those duties and bring you food and water. You are not to leave this room."

Then she swept out, and Mr Harding followed her but looked back at his child before the door closed behind them both. I almost felt pity for him, for the child was truly sick.

I see the child now, looking up at me with her broad face all sweating and never complaining, even if I have to bathe her in bed and turn her from side to side. When she is comfortable again, she reaches out her hand and takes mine. It is a sweet thing she does, stroking my hand with her thumb, up and down until she stills and falls asleep, holding on. Her hand is still so small that I can wrap the whole of mine around it. I want her to live – I want this with a passion that comes from way back, from the baby I failed so long ago. I sit in a rocking chair by her bed and wrap myself in blankets so I can check on her. I promise her that she will recover, even if she doesn't understand. From time to time I hear footsteps and I rouse myself, sit up straight. Mr Harding comes in to see her many times a day. I wonder if he notices how I huddle away from him, as far as I can, as he bends over his sweating daughter and takes the cold cloth from me to wipe her forehead.

Mrs Harding visits twice a day after prayers but she is not grateful.

She snaps at me as soon as she enters. "Susan, you must change the pillowcase, do you not see it is wet?" And then, as I raise her daughter so I can slip the case out, she reproves me again, for hurting the child for her neck is lolling, so heavy that she cannot hold it up. It is all I can do not to weep.

Cook brings me food, even tea, but she cannot stop except to kiss the poor child, for she has no time to spare. Between the visits I nurse Hannah, poor mite, alone and at night, my head dizzy with fatigue, I fall asleep in the chair.

I wake one night and I am quite confused and do not understand where I am. I felt a warm breath on my face and for a moment I am back with Annie, holding her close, the scent of sage and lavender drifting over me. But this is not her breath. I open my eyes and peer into the darkness, for the rush light has burned out. I see a figure bending over me towards Hannah and I realise from her shape in the moonlight that it is Mrs Harding and she has something square and heavy in her hands. I must have jerked for she pulls back with a start. She raises Hannah's head. It is a pillow then, I think, as she slips it underneath. Hannah does not stir. Mrs Harding says nothing, but straightens and leaves.

Hannah's fever broke at last, a day before I was due to visit the refuge. They summoned me to the parlour and I held fast to the bannisters on the way down, for I swayed with fatigue. I saw how they sat together on their dark green sofa and I wondered if they might thank me at last for nursing Hannah and restoring her to health. Perhaps I would even be rewarded with more time to recover, for I was exhausted from the night nursing.

Instead Mr Harding rustled his newspaper, turned it down and folded it into squares that got smaller and smaller until at last he stopped and spoke.

"Tomorrow is your day out, Susan?"

I nodded, cautiously.

He said: "I hope you won't be disappointed, but we cannot permit you to go."

I paused. Breathed in. I could wait. I needed sleep after all, as well as to see my friend.

"I'm sorry, sir, but if it can't be helped, I suppose I can wait till the week after," I said. I could send word to Mr Haskin, to Annie, if Jane might take them notes, or pay a boy to deliver word. Perhaps if I did not go, she would miss me.

He shook his head. "No, Susan, you must forgo your days off altogether. It is for the health of the family and in particular for Hannah."

He rose up and came towards me then, held out the square of newspaper and told me to read the article. I shrank back as much as I could. A health officer had said that servants carried germs into the houses, when they got out on Sundays, so the visits should cease. "I must be firm, Susan, no more visits out, for I must think of our family."

So they have imprisoned me now, I thought, bitterly. After all the nights sitting up with Hannah. And on Sundays Mr Harding stayed in his room, working, as he called it, and Mrs Harding and Hannah attended Sunday school and church. I would be on my own in the house with him before the family joined together for a late meal and evening prayers. I did not know what to say and so I nodded, and left the room, and went to the kitchen and cried. Cook was sorry for me, and gave me tea and a brisk hug but said that I must bear it all the same, till the master relented. But they let her go out to Sunday service with her sister, so why not me?

It was perhaps two or three days later. I was back in my room, for the child was recovering well and even Mrs Harding accepted that I must sleep in a bed. I lay awake shivering and saw how the ice had crept across the window and drawn patterns on it. I dressed underneath the bedclothes and crept down to the kitchen, shivering as I went. At last the water was boiling and I could make tea and warm by the fire. I must get the milk in. I could not see out for the windows here were also covered in crystals and as I opened the door, I saw how each one was different from the next. I pulled at the door and stepped out into the frost, looked up and saw Jane, milk jug in hand, just like me. Then I saw how her face changed and her hand clapped over her mouth so quick I heard the sound echo in the crisp air.

I follow her gaze and how it twists away from me to the area by the steps. There is a bundle there, clothes wrapped in ice. Jane's footsteps crunch on the frost and come down to join me. We crouch down on our haunches. I pinch my fingers together and lift up the rags.

There is a crackle below my fingers. Underneath is a girl and she is our age. Then Jane breathes in and sighs out one word and it is a misty cloud around us. "Louisa," she says.

We are still for one moment more and then I lift the rags away to see if she is, if she could be breathing for any chance and yet she is all shades of ice and white and blue and she must be dead. We both gasp and stand up then and cry out for help and the men in the street come running and then Mrs Harding comes to the kitchen door with Cook. Her face is black with anger that I am in the street, shouting. Then she sees the mound of rags. She steps out as the men peer down and she speaks.

"Susan," she says, and her face is quite blank and then Mr Harding comes too and she looks at him and then bustles him inside. Men come with a stretcher and the girl is carried away with tender care and Jane and I fall towards each other. "She had an aunt in Richmond, I thought she must have gone there. She hated the work here."

I do not say anything. Should I tell her what Cook had told me, of how Louisa had helped Mr Harding, of how Mr Harding had touched me? Of Mrs Harding and the pillow? She is as powerless as me, and so there is no point except to hold her hand and comfort her.

I waited until lunch time. Then, as the family ate and Cook was busy downstairs, I packed my belongings up and took some money from Mr Harding's desk, and then I walked out and left the front door wide open and did not look behind me as I crunched my way back to the refuge, and knocked on the great door. I would never wash up for them or carry their trays again. I would miss Jane, and little Hannah, but I dared not stay. I should have written a note for Jane, but there was no time.

Chapter Seventeen

Miss Clements permitted me in, but she would not allow me up to the ward until I had been interviewed by Mr Haskin. She took me instead to the room I had first stayed in, locked it from the outside. Later she brought me broth and water, then locked me in again, hardly spoke to me. Here I could sleep again, and I lay down fully clothed and I piled the blankets on me and slept soundly till the morning, when the door opened.

Maria stood there, quite silent. I opened my mouth to speak. She looked away and so I smoothed myself down, and splashed my face and followed her down to Mr Haskin. I looked at her back and wondered how I had let her slip, wished that I could say I was sorry. She opened the door and let me in, stepped outside. Still she did not meet my eyes. She had not said a word to me for months.

"I should charge you for this," he said, without looking up. "You have disgraced us." He took the Regulator down and opened it, and entered a great red mark in it next to my name, in the column for Vices.

I wanted to tell him about Mr Harding, about Susan. Louisa. It was so complicated, I didn't know where to start.

But he stopped me from speaking. "Mrs Harding is outside, and you must apologise to her."

She rustled in, in her fine green silk, and let forth even before she was settled.

"She was idle, impertinent, and," she spat out, "dishonest."

Mr Haskin started at that, his pen hovering again over the black column. "Tyrell, what do you say?"

"The situation did not suit me, Mr Haskin, for they withdrew my time off and asked me to work without any proper rest. I had to nurse the child, work as the servant; I could not have worked harder. I only took my earnings; I was not dishonest."

Should I tell them that Mr Harding had crept his small, greasy hands around me, so close that I could feel his whiskers brush my neck; pawed my breasts so I could feel his hands still, his body pressed against me, moving. How I had woken to find Mrs Harding hovering with a pillow. How Louisa had come back to the house and died there. They would never believe me, but I would not be called dishonest.

Mr Haskin held up his hand. He considered silently, then said, "If you are not to go back then perhaps Simpkins could serve." He would give up anything as long as we were separated. I fell to my knees then.

"I beg pardon, I will go back. I am sorry for my impertinence. Please, take my wages."

But Mrs Harding shook her head at that. "No, I do not want Tyrell back or another maid from here." Relief burst through me and I begged her forgiveness again.

She rose and swept out, still rustling and angry. I breathed out. We were both safe.

"I have not finished with you, Tyrell. You are the first object for over a year that has run away. You have disappointed me."

He sighed. "You may return, but be warned, Tyrell, there are black marks against you now in the Regulator. You may go down to work here. For the present at least." He dismissed me and I opened the door, sketched a curtsey to him and went out and closed the door. Then I whooped, silently, and ran to the laundry to find Annie, for I had made my way back to her at last.

I heard the sounds of laughter and talking before I went in and for a moment I stood, hesitant, in the doorway. I felt like a stranger, as though I was beginning all over again. Annie was at one of the coppers, face flushed, stirring the coloureds with a paddle. She looked up and the paddle slid out of her hand into the hot water. Kept staring and then, at last, she looked around to see who was there and finding that Potter was absent, beamed at me.

Mrs Clark snapped at her to continue stirring. She dipped her hand in, brought the paddle back to the surface. I murmured, "I told you that I would come back." This time we both smiled, and it touched her eyes for the first time since I left.

At last it was evening and the lights were put out in the ward, and I swung my legs out quietly to come to her hammock. She put out her hand, shook her head.

"We must be more careful," she whispered. "Potter watches me all the time, I am afraid that she will inform on us." After that we snatched our moments together, but it was not the same. All the time one of us looked over our shoulder, for Potter seemed to be in every darkened doorway, around every corner, behind each hanging sheet.

December Committee Day came and Maria arrived in the laundry and told Annie that she had been summoned. Her gaze flitted over me. Annie came back just fifteen minutes later. Her face was pale and she said nothing at first but pounded at the laundry as if she could destroy the day, but she would not talk then, as Potter looked on at us as if her gaze was stuck.

Later, when lights were dimmed, I crept over and put my face by her so she could tell me. At first, she said nothing, but I felt how the tears ran down her face. Then she told me, "They came back. The Hardings changed their mind. Mr Haskin has decided that I must go there." For the first time in front of her I cried too and then I crept into the hammock so close that we could whisper. "I must leave in two days. Please, Hannah, I cannot go."

Then, her breath on my ear, "Let's run away together."

I felt a spurt of joy in me. We would run and never be found like the girls who left? Potter and Mr Haskin would have no more power over us. We would set up house together and prosper. But how, in this weather?

I told her, "Last winter it was so cold that the river froze."

Annie lifted her head. Her face was wet.

"I can't leave. I can't go there."

"I saw a girl frozen, Annie."

The crackle of ice on her, carried away like a stiff board. I did not tell her who the girl was, what Mr Harding must have made her do. Still Annie wept on. She would wake everyone.

"Annie, I promise you, you won't have to go."

At last she slept and feeling her breath on me once more I slept too until dawn broke and I wondered how on earth we could escape and where to go. I wanted to leave too. But I had tried to protect Mama, all those years ago, and my best had not been good enough. I feared that the same thing might happen again, and everything that I had woven together would unravel, leaving me with nothing but frayed thread, my life in rags and tatters. Yet I knew we would go, for both Annie and me.

Chapter Eighteen

I knew, even then, that this could be the downward slope for us, but if I had known how far we would fall, I wonder now, would I have looked for another way? But still I am not sure what else I could have done. I left her sleeping and slipped on my clothes in the half-light, wrapping a shawl around me to belt it underneath my cloak. Potter seemed to be sleeping as I edged out.

I reached the top of the stairs and peered out until I saw Mr Haskin walk over as the clock struck six; he unbolted the great door, opened it and breathed in, then clapped it to. Sometimes, when he walked to his study in the morning he came back, bundled up in his coat, to walk down to the temporary refuge and give orders, but he walked away and I heard his door close. I crept down and across the hall and out as fast as I could, to walk to Gracechurch Street.

I breathed in as the cold hit me, tucked my hands into my shawl. The sun hit the houses as I reached the sooty houses I knew so well, frost on the ground, cold seeping into my boots. I got into the basement area, tapped quietly on the door so Jane could see me. No movement at the Hardings'. She was putting water on the range and came over to unbolt the door, smiling; her face cracked in half to see me.

"The first I heard of you going was when Mrs Harding came to my mistress to complain and ask for another maid, for the refuge had none that were ready yet for service," she burst out, as we hugged. A rap at the door, a tradesman with meat. Another, too, then we sat down. "I don't have long, Hannah."

I asked her how the child was.

"I see her sometimes at the window, looking down on the street. I wish that they would take her with them more, poor soul."

Then, as I asked her straight for help and how we wanted to leave, her face clouded.

"It's still freezing, Hannah. You remember how we found Louisa. How she crackled." She swallowed. I had seen her carried away and nothing more had happened; life had gone on as if she had not existed. "Her aunt buried her. Richard and I were the only ones there. Her aunt has nobody now."

"I wish I could have been there too," I said. She did not speak. "She trusts me, Jane, and she goes into service in just a week. The weather will only worsen if we do not go now."

I saw Jane's eyes travel over my face. At last, reluctantly, she said, "There's a woman my papa knew back in the days before he married, before my mama made him straight or else. Old Ma, she knew his family. She lives down in St George's Fields, sells on laundry and other items. You know her by her limp, Papa told me. I could ask Papa to send her a message, if my mama is out of the room."

But she added, frowning, "She's a Hedger."

It should have meant something to me, I could tell. She slammed her cup down on the table.

"You'll be cheated or worse. A life in service, it can be endured; not every situation is as bad as the Hardings.

There are ways out after. You could have hope beyond this. Annie too."

She put the tea tray together, her hands shaking. "She should stay close to the child and she will not be the only maid jamming her door shut at night. You saw Louisa. Girls like us cannot survive. We need people." I knew what she meant, for only men could protect us from other men.

She knew then, or guessed at least what Mr Harding was capable of, but she was still right. Annie and I were swimming together, into the weeds, where the witches slept, and if we continued, we would be pulled underneath, deep into the water and would never rise again. Yet we could not turn back.

"She cannot come here, I have to help her." It was not just that. Images swam up, of Annie and how she bent people to her, most of all me. How she might at last submit for the ease of it, let him buy her the pretty things that made her eyes sparkle, each time that she copied a page well for him. Or she might beg to come back to the refuge, on bended knee before Mr Haskin, be paired once again with Potter. The thought of her made me fire up. They could not have her – we had built something together, we had come so far.

I wonder now, did Jane see the desperation in me, for she relented at last.

"If you are set on it, you need to take everything you can carry, all the laundry, for Old Ma will cheat you and you have nobody to defend you and so you need a huge quantity. You will need every penny. I will get a message to her, at least get her to take you in for my papa's sake." Her voice changed. "But I have news too. I am marrying, leaving this place, and we will settle out west, where Richard's mother lives, stay with her until we can find a place for the two of us, set up house. I leave in a matter of weeks."

I stood up and went to hug her. She stepped back, looked at me and said, "Tell me you know what you're doing. No friendship, however loving, should mean this much."

My hands dropped and my face burned up and my eyes spurted, hot and wet. She came towards me then, and took my hand and embraced me after all.

"Thank you, Jane. I cannot ever repay you."

Then I crept out and when I looked back, I saw how she was dressing the tea tray, with her precise hands, and shaking her head, and then she ascended the stairs and was gone from sight. I ran down Gracechurch Street and I saw the old goose trotting along until he stopped as the landlady of the Spread Eagle came out and held out her hand, full of corn. He pecked her hand clean and empty and walked off, as if he were leading a procession, and his courtiers waddled along behind him, free and defiant. I turned my face to the refuge and the long walk back.

The streets are thronging, all of a sudden. People are streaming towards where I stand on Gracechurch Street and I cannot move north, it is too crowded. I am carried along west and I see how the throng is looking forward and it is all I can do to stay upright. It is as if they are running for something that they do not want to miss. I am too small to look up or fight my way through as I look for a turning that I can take. I am borne on in this great concourse and then I realise – this must be December's hanging day. It is seven thirty and I see nothing but I hear a roar moving through the crowd until it reaches us, and then like a wave moves on.

There is a high platform, even I can see it now; there is a woman there with a white nightcap on her head. A shout goes up which I cannot make out but all around me men remove their hats. I can see clearly now. A man is struggling with her, so he can bind her wrists. Another rope to bind her nightshirt with. He loses balance for a moment as she kicks out. She laughs and there is a great silence and then she takes her nightshirt and peels it upward so she is fully naked. Then she throws it into the crowd. "He'll not sell it when I am gone," she cries, with a frightful laugh, as the crowd roars and the fabric is quite rent into pieces. I put my hand out, the one that can move for the crush, and I cover my eyes with it, for I cannot see this. I can still hear though. There is a sudden rushing of guards onto the platform then, and a short prayer and a crash and then I hear no more.

I find that someone is pulling me loose and then I fall into an alleyway, the man almost on top of me, my rescuer. But he laughs, short and harsh, and I freeze. He is above me, fiddling with his garments. He drops his trousers. I want to cry out but nothing works; I cannot make a sound.

He bends over me, starts to pull at my clothes.

My head. I lift it, somehow, and then from somewhere comes the sickness. The splash of it hits his naked legs.

"Bitch," he says. He kicks me once.

My face is covered in vomit.

There is noise outside the alleyway. He kicks me again, hard, in the ribs and pulls up his trousers. Then he is gone.

I am alone, and the stench is overpowering. The crowd is cheering outside the alleyway. Two women walk past me, step aside. Disgust on their faces.

The cold has seeped into me. I am shaking. At least he is gone. I prop myself against the wall. I need to get back. I might have been missed already.

I stagger up. My ribs hurt from where he kicked me. I lean on the wall and step by step ease myself out of the alleyway. The streets are emptying fast of people.

By the time I return to the refuge it is already darkening,

for daylight was at its shortest then and I had fair staggered back, jumping at every jostle. The kitchen gate is still open, and I hear the sound of the girls finishing off in the laundry for the day, and I ease myself in, hide my shawl and cloak which I will need to wash. My ribs are fair burning now, from the kicking. I must return to folding the laundry, but first I wash my face, and then stagger in.

We must withdraw from this scheme; it is foolhardy. But I do not know how to tell Annie. She should go into service instead. She could be safe there.

She is folding the laundry as I walk over, but I cannot speak. My head swims and I sit down before I fall.

There is a breath and then I am soused in cold water and Mr Haskin looms over me, empty wash-tub in hand. "You must show good conduct, Tyrell," he warns, before he turns on his heel and walks away. He has never lost control like this before. Somebody laughs and then others, until the laundry is ringing, but then Annie comes up with a towel and I dry myself as Potter leans against a wall, smiling at me.

I cover my face with my towel so I can cry into it. I feel that cruel gaze on me, and turn away. That night I tell Annie that if her mind is set on it, we must go soon. I do not tell her the rest of it, and my sleep is broken by pain. And by terror.

Chapter Nineteen

I held the thoughts I had in my hand as we whispered together the night before we left, cutting the refuge buttons from our garments so that nobody can identify us as objects, packing together what we owned.

The night we escaped, it was dark and chill. We had first unroped our hammocks, knot by knot as the rope stung our hands, holding the line so that the swing did not betray us. Then we went down to the laundry late when the washing was done and wrung out, and bundled it into two heavy bags, as many items as we could sling on our shoulders, damp and heavy. I knew Mrs Clark's room, and so I had taken her keys and unlocked the door to the back yard and then put them back. The air hit us as we left. The temperature had lifted and I could see no stars. Snow threatened.

We passed outside unnoticed, hammocks and bundles knocking together. There was a ladder there in an outhouse, used to whitewash the laundry room. I held the ladder as Annie climbed, reached down at the halfway point so I could hand her the bundles. They thudded as they reached the ground. The back yard was still and quiet. I climbed up carefully, kicked the ladder away. One more wall and a hook to hit in the dark. My hands trembled as I knotted the hammocks together. Annie aimed, twice. At last the hammocks caught, held firm as we tugged on them. A harder climb, as they swung with our weight, each with a bundle, reached the top and sat there together. Below us was a yard that led onto Gorsuch Place and freedom. But we could still turn back. The hook stayed strong.

Annie whimpered, held out her hands. "They're burning," she said. Mine were too.

"Should we go on?" I asked her, rubbing her hands. She said nothing, but took her bundle and threw it into the yard below. I did the same. It was decided, then.

I unhooked the hammocks, threw them back down, for we could not sell them, filthy from the climb, and we slid down the brick wall together, picked up our bundles and squeezed through the yard gate. There was no way back now. We pulled up our hoods and set off, for we had the whole of the Hackney Road to walk down first. Our cloaks flapped loose and cold without buttons.

We followed the road due south, as it merged into Shoreditch High Street, then became Bishopsgate until we passed Leadenhall Market, shuttered and still, then Gracechurch Street itself and then out into fields before we crossed over the river. I looked right as I passed Jane's house.

"My friend Jane lives there," I said, pointing. Annie hardly glanced. Was Jane working by candlelight, or in bed at last? The Hardings' house was dark, for Mrs Harding instructed everyone to extinguish the candles early, to save on wax. I thought back fleetingly to how I felt, shivering in the attic, my chair pushed against the door, the handle slowly moving up and down, and so I picked up our pace and we went forward.

Lights blazed out all along the bridge as we reached it, but underneath the water slid, cold and silent, as the snow came down. Annie stopped for a moment, looked round at me.

"We are mad to do this. We should go back. We should never have done this."

My shoes were soaked through. I had done this for her, and so I could not help it, I snapped back at her, "There is no way back now," my mind circling back to my attic room, the breath of Mr Harding on my neck, his hands cupping my breasts. Darker still, the feel of Mrs Harding, solid and powerful, bending past me towards her child as she lay sleeping. It is a dark and dangerous house, that one. Yet at the front of my mind is a white nightcap, a woman facing the noose with a defiant bravery, and behind that still the naked body of my mama. Women facing an unequal justice. Every choice we have just sets a new trap, teeth ready to snap shut.

She had thrown her bundle down first. She had decided we should go.

She said nothing but I could see how she cried again and I turned away and trudged on until at last I heard her footsteps behind me, like a reluctant child. I knew she would blame me; I knew that she was right. I also knew I had no choice.

Jane had told me that we must not offend Old Ma, that if we had committed to bring her the laundry we could not turn back. Once the family had owned an inn there, but then it was pulled down and instead they had built houses, huddled and crowded together, on land that had not been drained, extorting rent from families that lived each in one small room in the houses on the Fields.

Once we were over the bridge, the lights ran out and the dim lights that glimmered, from house to house, illuminated houses without roofs, narrow courts and winding alleys. I knew that smell, of a kind of closeness, as if the old things had fallen together and left to perish. We were looking for a lane known locally as Dirty Lane. In this street lived the last barber who let blood and drew teeth in London. Old Ma lived there in a large brick house, next to a house that had no roof.

She had ordered us to meet at the obelisk, in the middle of the Fields themselves. She ran a laundry nearby and if the clothes were good, she would buy them and she would offer lodging and a fair price. I thought over the clothes in the bundles, writing my inventory, handsome clothes that would surely sell well, and the lawn handkerchiefs we had put by. But I had hesitated, then folded Mama's dress over and slid it deep underneath the floorboards, for I would never sell it.

We reached St George's Fields as the buildings around it blazed with light, places like the refuge itself. I recalled what Jane had told me. Bethlem, for the lunatics, was on one side, and it was white and wide with great high pillars, and it put me in mind of the asylum, and the clacking needles in Great Yarmouth. Then, on the north side of the Fields there was another large building, the Magdalen. Over the doorway it proclaimed that it welcomed 'Penitent Prostitutes'. Around it loitered women and men, entwined and sighing or groaning from time to time, before each pair dislodged themselves and went their separate ways. The area smelt of marshland, and the ditches all around the fields smelt foul. Dotted in between the smarter houses and institutions were tumbledown houses, with broken windows patched with rags and paper. Jane told me that each room was rented out to two families, so each had it only for day or for night.

I couldn't see Old Ma anywhere. We found an alley, worked our way inside. I felt Annie breathing fast, as she did when panicked. My anger left me, and I set the bundle down, put my arm around her, and peered out in front as the snow came down. If she did not come, I wondered where we would sleep that night, and even if we could somehow return to the refuge, if that, after all, was better than this. I felt Annie shaking against me, and reached a hand outside my own shawl so that I could envelop her hands inside mine. I rubbed them till warmth flickered in them. There was movement at last, as the snow came down. A woman, cloaked and hooded, limped towards the obelisk. She had a small child with her. This must be her.

I nudged Annie and we reached down for our bundles. The woman had come to a standstill near the obelisk and was peering into the darkness. We swung the bundles on our shoulders, and started to walk towards her. The snow leaked into my shoes as we half slid, half walked. I raised a hand in greeting and started to speak. She turned, then, wordlessly, pulled the child sharply so that it yelped before being dragged away.

I stared after them, for I did not understand. But as the figures disappeared into the night, I heard the sound of a carriage, wheels pushing through snow. Then I felt a hand, heavy, on my right shoulder. I looked around and Charles Haskin was there, his hand on Annie's shoulder too, and for a moment the three of us stood there quite still, as if we were companions, out for the evening. The snow ceased and the stars came out in a sky that was suddenly clear and dark.

He had found us, then.

He spoke, all of a sudden. "Come," he said, and we made no resistance, and walked back to the carriage; he pushed us in and shut the door behind us. There was a glimmer in the carriage, a lantern held by a girl. It was Maria. So this was her doing then. It must have been.

I grabbed her by the arm, shook her. "What did you say?" I pulled the words from her, between sobs. There were hardly any stammers, I thought, bitterly. All the easier for her to speak up and betray me. Us.

The door opened, as she came to a close. Mr Haskin snatched the bundles from each of us and put them by him as he sat himself down. Maria huddled away from me, as if she was afraid of my anger. I put it away and wondered, could this be enough for him, could this be an end to it?

He had recovered the property of the refuge; he could forgive us, or even just Annie. He could send us to the temporary refuge and watch as we ground shells until our hands ran red. Nobody had ever stolen so much from the institution. It would go before the committee and the men would ask him for his advice, and there would be silence until he had pronounced. He could do what he wanted. He could keep Annie under his eye and find her another position if the Hardings now drew back, for her character was now tainted. I could be sent away, but at least Annie could be saved.

"Newgate," he said in the crisp air, as the snow fell.

Annie started to cry. He spoke at last and I remembered that tone from when the girls had stumbled out of the locked room.

Ordinarily, he said, errant objects would be returned to the temporary refuge. He paused. I could live with that if only we were together.

"But you have brought shame on us, with this theft. From us, who have taken you in." He took a breath, and then continued. How men loved to talk when they condemned us, in words and lines and black ink. "You have offended against charity. The refuge took you in when none other would, and we put our faith in you. Now you have thrown it back in our face, and I will have to justify your conduct to the committee, which showed you both so much mercy." His voice had risen so that the very carriage shook with his anger. Annie shrank away from him, clutched at me.

He pulled her away from me, pushed Maria into the middle of us. Then he pointed to me. "You ran away from your mistress. I took you back in although she called you idle, impertinent and dishonest. Mr Fox warned me, and I should have heeded him. What is bred in the bone is there for good, he said. That seems to be true of you."

He looked at us both. "So I must make an example of both of you, for the sake of the other objects. Like Maria, who has never transgressed like you."

Then he fell silent, and the carriage moved slowly through the snow.

Chapter Twenty

"They belong in the parish lock-up, you should know that."

The gatekeeper shook his head, started to close the door. I could hear Haskin's voice, the irritation spurting out of him. A chink of coin, then, "Keep them until Friday at least. Committee Day."

We could slip from the carriage and run for it. I could feel Maria's eyes on me as Annie grabbed me and whispered, "But we will not be hanged?" as if I could work some magic.

"We were not violent," I said. My voice shook. We had only stolen clothes. But this was personal for Mr Haskin. All those fine words from the refuge – compassion, forgiveness, reform – counted for nothing now.

He came across the snow towards us, but he was not alone. Next to him was a wardress, cloaked. There was a dull clank to her walk, keys around her middle. He would not look at us but instead just opened the carriage door and gestured for us to descend. I looked at Maria as I stood up. "Traitor," I said, and I saw how she shrank away from my bitterness. Then Annie stood up, too, and we left the carriage, and went out into the snow. The wardress walked us towards the prison, Mr Haskin ascended, and then I heard Maria close the door of the carriage behind us. I would not look as the carriage moved off. We walked through the gate and it thudded shut behind us. We were prisoners of Newgate.

If I could refuse to breathe I would, I thought, as the wardress hustled us through the corridors. We stumbled down the glistening stone flags. Door after door was unlocked, then dragged open, clanking shut. The lamps hissed gently. The reek of the place took me back to the lock-up in Harleston except here it was stronger, and then grew stronger still as we entered the Female Quarter. It rushed out to meet us as we hovered on the threshold, so strong that I felt that I could touch it, that familiar mixture of blood, vomit, urine and night-soil, of unwashed bodies sweating despair.

She opened a cell door. Two women looked up, then resumed their talk, a dialect so strong that I could only pick out a few words. There were girls younger than me there, two mothers with babes in arms. They should not be in such a place. They clustered on the wooden beds and there was no space between them.

There was screaming from the next cell, then a sudden silence, as if it had been cut off, mid-shriek, a sound of utter desperation. I felt the wardress at our back, a sharp shove. I looked around, found a space. Straw had been scattered on the bare planks, but as I drew nearer, I realised that it stank, for the pot in the corner was full, and there was nowhere to go. I took the edge of my cloak and brushed the filthy stuff off, onto the floor. I would rather rest on bare wood than that reeking mess.

The wardress thrust some bread and meat towards us, spoke for the first time. "Mr Haskin paid for this," she said, hissing through a gap in her front teeth.

"You can buy more food," she added. She turned to leave, then spun back abruptly and thrust a blanket at us. Annie looked at the blanket. It was crawling with lice. She tossed the foul thing into a corner. She lay down on the plank and I next to her, and we held on to each other for warmth and wept on each other's faces for all our house was crumbled to dust.

The key turned heavily in the lock, then back again: another woman, the scent of rum rising from her, cheerful enough and stumbling around looking for room on a bench. I gave in, offered her as much space as we could bear. She spat on the floor at that. "Thanking you," she said, slurred and merry. "I came here tonight," and of a sudden she spat again, "in the hopes of seeing Mrs Fry." Then she bowed and told me that her name was Lily and would not stop talking, although I could make no sense of her. At last another woman shouted at her to stop, and she fell asleep next to me, snoring all night. I pulled my cloak tight around me, found that I could not stop shaking, whether from shock or the cold. From time to time I heard a bottle chink, other women curse. Sobbing and then a baby, wailing weakly, and at last there was nothing except Annie's hand in mine.

Chapter Twenty-One

I woke on that first morning in Newgate to a tugging, then air on my cold skin. A woman was ripping at my shawl and when I jerked it back, she bared her teeth. They had been filed to points. I saw the rat before she felt it run over her foot. Once I had seen the farmer's terrier bring one down, then eat it whole as the tail swished desperately, dangling outside the dog's mouth, till it was still. That image rose to me and I felt sick to my stomach. Annie roused herself, saw the rat in front of her and shrieked. It snarled, then ran into a hole in the floor. Annie started to weep.

The cell door opened, and the women lined up. The warders jostled us as we walked out into a yard, narrow and lit faintly by the winter light, where we were lined up again. I counted. There were twelve of us and then other women staggered out, till the yard was full. I looked down and realised that the snow was yellow and brown underneath our feet. As if a bell had rung out, the women lifted their skirts, squatted in a line. Annie looked at me. I squatted down and watched the snow beneath me run yellow and steam, briefly. I caught the eye of the woman who had grabbed at my shawl. She bared her teeth again and I looked away. The women stood up, mingling. I saw a woman lean against the wall, take her thin breast out, let her baby latch on. The baby cried, weakly, and the woman squeezed her breast until it turned white and at last the baby suckled and was silent as its mouth moved in and out.

Before we had ended up in this place Annie had laughed with me during prayers, although she had always kept to her evening ritual, said it comforted her and took her back to her family. But then she found true religion. How could I follow her, after all that men of God had done to me, even if the only good thing about Newgate wore a white bonnet and a grey dress and her name was Elizabeth Fry. She and the other ladies, who called themselves Friends, visited poor sinners like us in Newgate. Mrs Fry had even persuaded the governor to whitewash a room, put a fire in it so we could work in there.

We were taken there that first morning and allowed to wash first. I had not expected this, a warm clean room. As I looked around the ladies came in, led by one who was holding a babe in arms. The women around me sighed as if they were one, and fell onto the flags in a wave until all of us were kneeling. The baby woke and cried, weakly, then another lady took the baby and sat with him, as Mrs Fry began to pray. Annie did so too, and then a silence fell and the women stood up again and I found Mrs Fry in front of me, holding out her baby.

I felt her open my arms and place the baby inside them. He lay there squirming and I looked at his whorl of silken hair, his blue eyes, long lashes closed, and I felt the weight of him. He was kicking, he was warm. I could not help myself: I stroked his head, felt how a vessel beat strongly underneath my fingers. Mrs Fry addressed me, smiling. "You stroke Harry's hair as if you were used to it," she said, and then she took him from me, and my arms were light again. She sat down and held her child, whilst another one of the ladies addressed us and told us what they did and how they visited every day except Saturday. Mrs Fry spoke on Fridays and visitors were admitted then and we must show good conduct. I must have slept as she talked because I jolted upright when a scream broke the hum of her voice.

It came from outside, and then grew clearer, until it filled the room. The same as the night before, I recognised that awful desperation in her voice. Harry roused and cried too, and as the scream faded again all we could hear, in our ringing ears, was his weak echo of that sound. The ladies crowded around Mrs Fry and the child, and then Mrs Fry, her face soaking with tears, gave her child to another Friend, pulled up her skirts and nearly ran from the room.

She was called Dinah Belshawe, the other jailed women said, and she had been told that there was no pardon for her, and she was to be executed. She had uttered false bank notes with five men, and the judge had put on the black cap and sentenced them all to death. She had children, and Mrs Fry had begged everyone on her bent knees, from the governor to the king, for her sentence to be commuted, but that morning the message had come that there was to be no mercy. She would be removed to the condemned cell the next day.

There was no more screaming that day, but a heavy waiting instead. When the keys turned in the lock the women took out what liquor there was and everybody drank. I saw how Annie prayed with a fever, as if it might save her. For if Dinah could be executed, with children at home, what would happen to the rest of us? Midnight came and we heard the bellman in the tunnels ringing his handbell, singing out for the soul that was to depart.

We must cover up this awful ringing that echoed down every corridor so there was nothing else but the dreadful warning of what would happen next. Lily started to sing, quietly at first, and then we all joined in the old tune, about the boy that was sent to Botany Bay, and we sang so loudly that nobody could hear the bellman. We sang ourselves hoarse and then there was silence, and a sobbing in the darkness, for all of us could imagine the fear of being the condemned woman, locked alone in the cell in the middle ward, with the bellman outside.

The day after the long drop was visiting day. We washed early and were given clean white caps to wear and then marched to a room that the warders called the lecture room. I peeked out and saw that there were almost two hundred visitors there, clutching their tickets and seated on benches; the male prisoners were seated opposite the visitors. A bell rang and we filed in, listless, still stupefied. The warder hissed, "No speaking. No talking to Mrs Fry. Get in line."

A chill breeze wafted in. The glass in the windows had fallen out; in its place was oiled paper. One corner was flapping, as the wind crept in. I pushed my hands inside my sleeves, tried to stop shivering. Mrs Fry rose to speak and all turned towards her as she preached, eyes brimming, as she said that even the fallen were extended God's mercy.

When she had sat down and closed her eyes, a sheriff stood up. He spoke out loudly, said he had a message of repentance from Dinah, an exhortation even, that we must find God, reform. I looked at Annie, but she would not meet my eyes. I saw that she was looking at the great ladies and gentlemen who had come to hear Mrs Fry speak, holding their tickets, and the men on guard, looking stern. Lily overflowed, then Annie, and then the whole row of us swayed together and wept. Annie's hand came reaching for me, and I held on tight. We were all lamenting together, and it was both for Dinah and for ourselves, and for the end of everything that had come to her, on the night when she bade farewell to her children and felt their bodies against her that last time, and knew that she would never see or hold them again in this world.

Then I saw them in the third row up, opposite us. Mrs Harding looking resplendent in her green velvet, Mr Harding quite tiny beside her, twitching slightly. I knew what she was thinking, as she looked down on us. She had come to see us condemned, to see the impertinent object punished more than she had managed. So I dried my eyes and looked back, looked her straight in the eye and smirked at her. Mr Harding could not meet my gaze, I noticed, as he shrank into his wife's side and looked everywhere but at me.

On the way back to our cells, I was clapped on the shoulder, pulled to one side. "You too," the warder said, pointing to Annie. The women snaked past us, raggedly. "Your trial date is in January. The first day of the sessions." Then he pushed us back into line and we filed on.

We had begged pen and paper just before Christmas came and written to the refuge together. We offered penitence and we asked for forgiveness, a second chance, and also for a little money, a few coins to buy hot food. We were sent money, told that the committee would gather before our trial, to consider what should be done with us. But our trial would go on regardless. When Annie read the letter, her face crumpled before me and when I reached for her hand to comfort her, she pulled away, looked at me with brimming eyes. "I should have gone into service, we should never have run."

I had no answer except the thought that I had done this for her and Jane was right, there were fates worse than service after all.

Chapter Twenty-Two

Trial day. They shake us awake at dawn, command us to hurry, to dress and tidy ourselves. There are twenty of us on trial at the sessions and we line up, file through the corridors. I count seven gates to be locked, unlocked, locked again, until we arrive at last at a great wooden door and stop. Behind it, as it opens, I see a long brick passage, and we pass through it and into the fortress. The Old Bailey. Eight times a year they hold the sessions there, and the death sentences are handed down after the king has considered and confirmed them.

This is the Middlesex Sessions, and the jurymen file in as we stand up straight in the dock and then the judge comes in, Judge Newman Knowlys, and then the clerk intones the date, 10 January 1822, and our trial starts. The staff from the refuge are there and so is Potter. I look for Maria.

Just for a moment I look sideways at Annie. She holds the edge of the dock, her fingers white, and is trembling. I had forgotten that she had been here before, and that last time Mr Haskin had seen her and looked kindly on her and so her sentence had been respited. I see how she gazes on the jury and the judge, perhaps hoping that again she can dodge punishment, but I refuse to do so. I see how the jurymen are crammed in a stall to our right, and how below us are clerks, lawyers and writers. I look up and see a mirror above our heads. I remember talk in our cell of why this is, that the jury can examine our faces, tell whether or not we are telling the truth. I look up at the chandeliers and see that they are shining bright and for some reason wonder that they are shined to such a buff and how a servant must be put on a high ladder to go up there and balance as they polish. The clerk glares at us, tells us to look forward. He reads out the charges. The minute hand on the large clock ticks round twice before he is finished, for the list of items that we stole is long and carefully detailed. He intones at first, then speeds up and gallops through the list.

"They are accused of stealing three gowns, value nine shillings; eight aprons, value four shillings; three remnants of printed calico, value four shillings; six petticoats, value six shillings; three pair of stockings, value one shilling.; three caps, value sixpence; four shifts, value four shillings; one dresser-cloth, value sixpence; two slips of muslin, value one penny; two combs, value three pennies; two handker-chiefs, value two pennies; one shawl, value ninepence; two pair of stays, value one shilling, and two bonnets, value two shillings, the goods of Edward Forster, Stephen Lushington and Peter Martineaux, trustees of the Refuge for the Des-titute; and one gown, value two shillings; one bag, value one pence; two gown bodies, value two shillings; two yards of muslin, value one shilling.; one pocket-book, value one pence, and two yards of lace, value one shilling, the goods of Rachel Clements, spinster."

How far would all that soiled and dirty washing really have got us, I wonder, as he nods, sits down. Where would we be now if Old Ma had come earlier, and we had gone with her?

Charles Haskin is called first, and he gives his name and his title. I see a writer setting down his account in squiggles I do not understand. He does not look at us once, although I steal a glance sideways, see how Annie gazes at him with those great soft eyes, framed by glistening lashes. She must have done this last time to win him over, reminding him of his poor sister. "I am superintendent of the Refuge for the Destitute, in the Hackney Road. I live in the house, and have the charge of it; Tyrell was admitted first, and Simpkins came to the refuge from this place the following April. I commanded Tyrell to have care of Simpkins, but she abused my trust, as did Simpkins. I sent Tyrell away to service, but her mistress returned her. On the tenth of December, between seven and eight o'clock in the evening, they both left the house without notice, and this property was missed. Between eight and nine o'clock the same night, I found them in St George's Fields, walking in the road. I took a bundle from Tyrell and Simpkins, containing the property belonging to the institution." There are no cross-questions, and he leaves the stand. I wonder where Maria is, for she had been there, she should be a witness. I realise that I have missed her, that quiet companionship we shared, our small jokes; that I should have tried so much harder, that I didn't need to choose between loving Annie and liking my first friend.

Miss Clements comes next. She has been taken in hand and neatened by someone, I can see it, for her hair is tied back in a neat bun and greased down and not one strand falls out as she speaks. "I am bookkeeper and housekeeper to the institution. The prisoners left the house on the tenth of December. Here is a pocket-book and a gown body in the bag. They are mine, among other items; they were kept in the counting house." She brings them out, shows them to the jurymen and I wonder, why do they need to see them? Then she bursts out, "Please have mercy on them, the girls, the poor girls," and the judge hammers down and she leaves the witness box in tears and I find I am crying too. Poor Miss Clements.

Mrs Clark is next; she climbs up to give evidence with a heavy sigh I recognise. She looks at us both and shakes her head.

"I am the matron. The prisoners left unknown to me; part of the property was under my care. I know it to belong to the Society."

I am called to defend myself. I cannot, will not hurt Maria or Annie. But there is one person I can lay the blame on. I stare at her. She will never have her now, and nor will the Hardings, and so it was worth it. I stand up and I fix the jury with my gaze. I will not beg. I will blame.

"A young woman named Potter persuaded me to leave. She encouraged us to steal and to escape, and said if we did not then she would tell vile tales about us. I was kindly protected there, and if I was permitted to return, I would behave with great propriety."

I pause and look at the staff. They sit together and Miss Clements has a handkerchief to her eyes. The others do not look back at me. But Miss Clements does, just for a moment, and her eyes are bright red, as if she had cried for hours.

Annie stands up. The judge asks her if what I said was true. The silence stretches out and then at last she speaks. Surely, I hope, she would never betray me. But I am not sure.

"I am very sorry for what I have done," she says, and gives the judge an imploring look. "I have found God in here and truly repent for everything that I did."

She does not back me. Her silence pours down my throat.

When the jurymen come back, they do not look at us, but instead at the judge. We stand to be found guilty, and the judge's face is grey stone.

The judge tells the court that the Old Bailey had asked the committee if we could be respited and readmitted, and that the two of us had written and repented. But then comes the shock. He says that Simpkins had written again later, alone, and begged for forgiveness for both of us. She had never told me this, she had never asked my permission to do so. I felt my body shake as he read out the committee's reply.

"The committee is of the opinion that no good is likely to come of readmitting the two girls to the refuge, one of them having been in the care of the institution for some years and the other having been received on the recommendation of the Old Bailey in April last, and that it would be injurious to the other objects of the refuge."

The judge folds the letter, looks straight at us both. "You have betrayed the Refuge of the Destitute, which took you in. You have stolen from those who sheltered you. Those good people tried to reclaim you, yet to no avail. This is the best punishment for you, as it ejects you, you two delinquent girls, from the bosom of the society that you have so grievously offended. Take them down. You will be transported for seven years."

Seven years, seven whole years, and how would we ever return from it? And yet the words numb me for I cannot take them in, even as Annie bursts out into weeping and then clings to me. I look down at her arms and mine fall away from her.

I look out at the courtroom as she sobs and I see, as if through a smeared and dirty pane of glass, that Miss Clements is still imploring the judge, weakly, for mercy, and Mrs Clark wipes her eyes too, angry and fast. I see how

Potter smirks at me as if to say that she has won at last, though what do her winnings amount to, for Annie is forever beyond her grasp.

On that day Judge Newman Knowlys, the second highest judge in the whole of the land, transports four children altogether, including the two of us, and the oldest is Annie, who is eighteen. He sentences two others to be whipped, and six to be jailed. The other judges pass twelve verdicts on the same day. There were three boys on the male side, who were prosecuted for stealing apples and pears. They were set onto the treadmill for three months, with the youngest of them only twelve. Others who were convicted that day were to be whipped. Two walked free. One woman was sentenced to death. There will be bells, there will be singing on the female side but we will not be there.

We are taken out but not back to our cell. A warder tells us that we will be jailed and then transported on the first ship of the spring, when the tides turn, and we would then leave our country for evermore, for nigh on nobody came back, once they had sailed for the other side of the world, to Botany Bay.

Chapter Twenty-Three

For evermore. But there is no time to take this awful sentence in, this utter banishment, because we are hustled and bustled down corridors until we halt and are chained together. The great door opens then and the air rushes in. So the other women spoke right. We would be sent to the Millbank Penitentiary first, and then transported four months on, or more, whenever the first ship was ready and the tides and wind judged right.

"Tide's up," a voice shouts, urgent. It is the captain of the longboat, and the warders pull us out and down the river steps. I count them, one to nine, and slide on one, and then we are in the barge, and the captain cries again, and we are off, the men pulling hard as we go upriver, reach the deeper channel. All around me, the sound of sobbing, the slop of water off the oars.

I feel the chain pull tight on my wrists as Annie shrugs her shawl over her head. I tug back. I think, suddenly, savagely, that I hope it rubs her skin. Maria first, then her, traitors both.

The men row fast, past barges heaped with coal on one side of the river, on the other timber yards down to the water's edge, stacks of wood piled up.

"Heads!" the sailors sing out, in unison, and we duck as they do, and slide under Westminster Bridge and there is the Abbey, the Houses of Parliament, catching the last of the winter light.

We are near the potteries now, the bone-crushing factories, the gasworks and the kilns that lie upriver. The stench of it suffocates, as the fog comes down in drifts and the odours are trapped around us.

"Heads!" again and we duck, slide under Vauxhall. We must be nearly there then.

A shout across the water. The fog clears. A boat shoots out from the river steps. The men rowing wear handkerchiefs across their mouths. The boat comes nearer. There is white sacking in the boat; bodies underneath, I see now, with a shiver. In one where the sacking has shifted, I see an arm, motionless. My mama looked like that once. Then the boat is past us and we arrive at the steps and I try to look back but we are dragged up them.

This is the place where the bodies must have come from. I look up into the sky but it is blocked out by the building, its casements and turrets and a long wall that stretches all around. This is Millbank then, and the great door opens. We are halted outside.

There is a screaming now from inside and I see two women in the light. They are struggling over a stretcher, pulling it to and fro. "This is not God's work," one shouts, pulling the stretcher towards her. But the other woman steps in front of her, squares up to her, and in the end she nods reluctantly, and permits two men to take the stretcher from them. They are wearing scarves around their mouths and as they walk past us a stench rises so bad that I hear Annie gagging. They dump the stretcher by the steps. The sailors cross themselves.

The woman who shouted has composed herself; the

other woman has disappeared. She walks towards the captain, holding a long stick by her side. He hands her papers – they must be ours – and I watch as he walks away, and see how the stretcher is loaded on the boat as the men hunch their jackets around their mouths. She looks at us then, and yells out so that it echoes. "You will address me as Wardress Brimley. Welcome to Millbank." Bitterly, then, "A place forsaken by God."

I look back now, along the winding passage of my past, and I see the doors that locked me into all the places that I lived, as a child and as a woman and this one turned out to be the worst. It was a kind of hell; we feared for our lives, from the moment we arrived. And I faced the place alone, at least at first, for the thread that had bound me to Annie, and she to me, had frayed in Newgate, and here we took an end each and snapped it off.

Other wardresses came, then, and led us inside. I saw a bare yard lit by flaring lamps, and then an inner gate, which was barred shut. We were pulled across to it, pushed into another room, bare and cold, and lined up.

Brimley studied our papers, called out our names in turn, then read again.

I saw the contempt in her light blue eyes, and how one corner of her thin upper lip rose and curled as she looked at us. She took her stick up then, pointed with it to a long paper on the wall.

"These are the rules. If you are idle or negligent, or if you mismanage your work, or behave irreverently, or curse or swear or fight, you will be punished. And you will not damage the articles you are given, or deface the walls, or damage anything."

The list was endless. Each word read out clearly, and "punished" said with satisfaction. We were all shaking with cold before she was done.

"If you misbehave, you will be put away in a dark cell, for an allotted number of days. You will be fed bread and water."

Then she pointed outwards and we shuffled on, down more corridors, to the reception ward. "You will strip here, so that you can be examined by the surgeon. But first, you will bathe."

The chains were removed and, shaking our stiff hands until the blood flowed back, we started to remove our clothes. One prisoner could not bear the shame of it, covered her breasts with her hands when she was naked. She was so thin that every rib showed on her. Another dropped her clothes straight away. And then we all stared, for she was painted in the most beautiful of hues; she had been inked in blue and green, in the shape of a mermaid, up one leg, a naked woman winding around the other. She winked at us all as we stared, and then lifted one leg up so elegantly, and then the other, to step into the bath that I laughed out loud, then coughed from the shock of the cold water and was silent. A shout from the same wardress and we were hauled out, still naked, and allowed to rub ourselves dry with towels.

"Come straight this way." She led us, dripping, to the surgeon's room, holding our towels around us.

He looked up. "Thank you, Brimley."

She nodded, then turned back to us.

"You," pointing to the first one of us in the row, "drop your towel so that Dr Latham can examine you."

It was the woman who had covered herself, who now cowered back. Brimley walked over to her, wrenched the towel off her, pushed her towards the surgeon as she yelped. He looked her up and down as if she was a cow at a show, muttered and made his notes.

When it was my turn, I tried to look up straight,

like the woman with the mermaid, not to be ashamed. The cold from the flagstones was shooting through my legs now.

He noted down my eye colour, height and hue.

"Do you have any insanity in your family," he asked, adding, as he looked at his notes, "Tyrell?"

I thought of my grandmama. Those clacking needles. My mama, and those spills of powder. They had been driven to what they had done. I shook my head.

"No, sir."

When we were all covered again in our towels, the wardress pulled us out impatiently to another room. A row of chairs had been put out, ready for us.

"Hawkins," she cried, and the two wardresses nodded at each other, grimly. Hawkins was as tall as a man, and so thin that her clothes seemed to hang from her frame. She was holding a pair of blunt scissors in one hand, in the other a large grey bag.

Brimley pushed each one of us down on a chair. Hawkins held the bag, handed the scissors to Brimley. I was the first in the row and she took the scissors up and started to cut my hair. She had to saw it off, for the blade was blunted. Hawkins swept it into the bag, and then they moved on to Annie. Her golden hair fell on the floor, was swept up in an instant.

At least, this time, she was not crying. She had her eyes closed and seemed to be praying, as the wardresses moved on until all of us were shorn.

Then we were lined up again, and given drab grey gowns and other items, damp to the touch. We carried them before us as we were escorted out and Hawkins vanished into another corridor, scissors and bag aloft. Brimley walked on at the front of us. All the time she held her hand to a red line, chalked on the wall, as she ushered us through corridors that made no sense, that twisted and turned until I had lost my bearings completely.

Annie walked ahead, head bowed. Then we stopped, and a cell door was opened. Annie was pushed in and the door thudded shut and was bolted behind her. Good riddance, I thought, as I realised that now we were truly separated. A pang then, at my own spite.

I felt Brimley's hand land heavy on my shoulder and then propel me towards a cell door. I noticed that it was curved, almost circular. Everything here was queer, bent out of its natural shape. She stopped, lit a candle, and gave me a thin stick.

"This is the signal wand. Push it through this hole if you require anything. The black end is for a special need, and the red for anything general. You will make your bed up as you find it, for Mrs Martin, the Matron, will inspect. In the morning you will dress yourself in the belongings on the bed."

With those last instructions she gave me one final push between my shoulder blades so that I stumbled into the room, and slammed the door shut behind me. The key turned, heavy in the door.

The candle showed me that there was a table, and on it a pile of books and other things. I set the candle down and picked them up. There was a Bible, a prayer book, a hymn book, an arithmetic book, a book called *Home and Common Things* and a slate and pencil. Also a wooden platter, two tin pints for cocoa and gruel, a salt cellar and a wooden spoon. Underneath the table was a broom for sweeping out the cell, two combs, a hairbrush, a piece of soap, and a utensil like a pudding basin. There was a washtub and wooden stool. Two buckets, uncovered, one for washing. A bell rang faintly outside, then a sharp knock at the door. "No lights after dark. Blow your candle out." I looked behind me and saw a bed with a thin pile of garments on top. I climbed in, fully clothed, pushed the items to the floor, dragged the bedclothes over me, then blew out the candle and shivered until I finally found sleep.

Chapter Twenty-Four

A rap at the door woke me. "Fold your belongings and dress. Neatly, mind you." A blear, blue winter light struggled in from outside. I pulled on thick, scratchy woollen socks first, as the stone flags chilled my feet. Then I dressed in the same rough grey clothes from the night before and put on a white cap and apron from the pile. I put the bed to rights, in five folds as it had been, with my nightcap on the centre of the middle fold. I stood back and was satisfied with my work, and then I sat on the bed and at last the tears came. But there was no time for this, for I heard the key turn, and I dabbed my eyes and stood up.

I heard the hall before I entered it, a hum of voices, and then I saw it, a great dark wooden hall, with long tables and slippery stone flags underneath.

"You go there, and take a portion of food," the wardress said, pointing to a table where most of the women I had seen at trial were sitting, Annie among them. A pan of thin gruel was at the end, and I took a bowl, a wooden spoon and helped myself to a portion. The only space was next to Annie. I sat down and took up my spoon. I felt her eyes on me, as if she wanted to speak.

I tried the gruel, salty with a rotten taste, and pushed it away. She broke the silence between us then. "You know it wasn't Potter. Why should I lie for you?" I banged my spoon down at that, saw how Brimley turned and stared at me with cold blue eyes.

"You will eat silently!" she yelled suddenly.

I turned my head away from her, snapped back to Annie.

"You only had to nod. It would have cost you nothing."

She shook her head. "You swore on the Bible, Hannah. Then you lied."

Annie had always come back to this, to her God.

"It was our fault, not Potter's," she said flatly.

I stood up then and cleared away my bowl. Just for a moment I bent over her. She looked up. "I ran away to save you. You begged me. And now you blame me. Don't come near me here." I left her behind me, tears in her eyes no doubt, looking for another fool to comfort her.

Brimley caught my arm as I walked past to the kitchen.

"You, Tyrell. No talking at mealtimes, hear me." Her grasp hurt, fingers digging in to where my skin was bruised from yesterday's chaining. "Simpkins," she shouted then. She came towards us, head down.

"Governor wants to see you now. Matron, too." She released me then, and we were marched to his room.

Governor Chapman sat behind a wooden desk, like Mr Haskin, a tall and fully imposing man, dressed in black with a pure white collar. Behind him stood a woman of middle age, who looked steadily at the two of us.

This was the woman we had seen yesterday, struggling with Brimley.

She was broad and of middle height; her grey hair was

neat and her grey dress quite smooth, yet her face was rumpled, as if it had left creases where she had smiled.

Brimley hovered on the threshold.

"You may go, Brimley," said the matron. Brimley stood stock still. The governor looked up. "Brimley, you are dismissed. Mrs Martin will take Simpkins and Tyrell around." Then she went, but not before she had glared at the matron and she back at her.

The governor cleared his throat and began. He had a deep voice and I noticed how it boomed around the room, and through the door that was open to the corridor. He enjoyed speaking, that was for sure.

"The object of imprisonment is to awaken reflection, and a due sense of your situation. You are young both of you, and I wish to become acquainted with your characters, which I will note down in my character books. Simpkins, you are first."

He took up his pen then, dipped it and asked her for her history. I heard it first, I thought. You be taken in by her now, you feel sorry for her. She kept it short and soft, and turned her eyes to him from time to time. I knew that beseeching look, up through those long dark lashes, from how she used to look at Mr Haskin. And me, I was taken in first.

"Tyrell, you now," he said.

Which story should I tell now, for what was left to lose? My pride won out. I clattered through the story I had told Annie before. The truth, but not the whole truth. The governor noted it down, then closed our books with a clap, cleared his throat.

"I have determined that as you are young, and were under the care of Mrs Fry, I will enter you into first class. Matron, you may address the girls for I have meetings." He sighed, then left at a brisk pace. Matron stepped forward.

"I will watch you both closely, for life is hard in here."

I thought of how she had nearly fought Brimley. Is that what she meant?

"You may come to me if you feel uncomfortable."

She was choosing her words carefully.

"You are young, as the governor said, and your punishment is to be here, nothing else." I wondered again what she meant.

A knock on the door and then, without ceremony, Brimley threw it open.

"I have not finished with them yet, Brimley," the matron said, rising. A bite to her voice.

Then she ushered us out with her and led us through the corridors. I felt Brimley following on behind, and how the matron bridled, but said nothing.

There was the laundry, with its cold wet floor and the prisoners stirring the coppers in silence; the kitchen, which reeked of damp; and the hospital ward upstairs, where small still figures lay, covered in sheets. "All of those who live here come to the ward if they are sick."

She backed out and opened a door next to the ward.

"This is for persons subject to fits," she said. It was about six foot high, with mattresses ranged around the walls, enough to cover the room if laid out. I noticed hooks on the wall, fixed opposite to each other. "We try not to use it, and few suffer, thankfully. I hope not you." We gazed inside, staring, and I thought of the girls who had been locked in by Mr Haskin, and how they had escaped. Then she locked it behind her.

"You may go with Brimley now," she said. She started down a flight of stairs but looked behind her first. Later, I understood why.

Brimley watched her go, then gestured with her head to the matron, now at the bottom of the stairs. "Don't go running to her, hear me?"

She stared at both of us with her strange light eyes until I nodded, and so did Annie. Then she took us to the laundry and set us to work, and the silence suited me.

The girl with the mermaid was called Bridget Sefton and was from Lancashire, or so she said. She slammed her broth down opposite me when at last it was time for lunch. "Eat it," she said, pushing my soup back to me. "You won't get anything else here, for sure."

I took up my spoon again, saw how Annie did the same, swallowed the cold soup down, mouthful by mouthful. Then Bridget gestured with hers towards Brimley and whispered, "I was in here before. Last winter. You need to watch out for those two. Her and Hawkins. They believe that they should run the penitentiary, not the matron."

The two women struggling together, with the matron only just in control.

I found my voice. "I saw them fighting when we arrived. There was a stretcher . . ."

I trailed off then.

"People are dying here." She frowned. "They call it marsh fever, and it spread through Pentagon One. Where the men are."

A pause, then, "A woman died yesterday. Perkins, she was called."

I stopped eating, lowered my spoon. The whole of the table was listening to her, fearful.

"Be careful," she said, then stopped talking. Brimley was walking towards us.

The next skirmish was just a day later. I was in the laundry, folding damp clothes to be handed out to new inmates. Brimley walked in, looked around. Walked over to an older woman, Mrs Lacey, who was stirring a copper, her grey hair clinging to the edges of her cap. She grasped her by the ear, and we all gasped. Lacey struggled for a moment.

"You stole tea," she spat at her as Lacey slipped on the flagstones, put a hand down to steady herself. She looked up and spoke back, gently, as she struggled up.

"I would not do such a thing," she said.

Brimley stood over her. The slap resounded through the kitchen and Lacey fell back. Her face was scarlet.

"You're nothing better than a whore," she said. "You will work on half rations until I say otherwise."

Bridget walked over to Brimley then, stood in front of her. "Leave her be. Lacey is a grandmother. She is no whore."

We waited in silence to see what Brimley would do next. Lacey struggled to her feet.

She laughed, and the sound echoed in the room. "Not like you, then," she said, and she called out, "Hawkins!"

Together the wardresses took Lacey by one arm each and yelled out for the dark cell to be opened.

We found our voices then, and yelled back, until other wardresses came running, but I noticed that Annie did not join in. One by one we were dragged out but Bridget called out to us, "Kick your feet against your cell door. For Lacey."

Once I was thrown in, I kept my boots on and lay down on the cold floor and thumped them against the door. I heard how other women did the same until the corridors were ringing with the sound.

The next morning, thirsty and hungry, we were led out and down to the hall, lined up in ragged rows. Bridget stood next to me, a bruise on her face. But all the same she looked down at me and winked. Annie stood, head down, saying nothing. Mrs Martin walked in and stood before us. Brimley and Hawkins stood to her side.

173

"I have freed Lacey. Back to work."

She turned then and walked out as Brimley and Hawkins stared at her back, and then at each other.

The next incident unfolded before me. I saw how Brimley followed Mrs Martin closely on the stairs as we walked behind them, and how the matron seemed to slip on a flag and then fall with a thump, down the stairs, until she lay at the bottom, quite still. Brimley walked down, slowly, and crouched down next to her. We crowded around her, and at last Brimley grabbed me and Bridget. "Carry her to her parlour," she rasped, and I shot back at her, for Mrs Martin was struggling to move, "She should go to the infirmary."

Brimley kicked out at me then and Mrs Martin spoke up. "My parlour," she managed, so we took her up and carried her, as gently as we could, to the sofa in her room, and laid her out and covered her over.

Brimley came to the door of the parlour.

"Sefton, you go back to work. Tyrell, you may stay with her." Bridget stared at Brimley, then rose and closed the door behind her.

I stayed by Mrs Martin's side and looked around her parlour. I saw how there were piles of paper on the desk and that dust had settled on her bookshelf. She was breathing quietly now, so I took the edge of my apron in my hand and gently dusted her shelves, stacked the papers in piles.

"Tyrell," I heard, a note of anger in her voice. I turned to see that she was struggling to sit upright. "You must not touch my papers, or look at them, for they are private," she said.

"I am sorry, Matron. I was dusting a little." I looked over at her. "May I fetch water for you, or anything?"

She shook her head, then gestured for me to sit down

next to her. I saw that her face was a strange colour, almost yellow.

"What happened?" Mrs Martin sounded fearful.

I was silent for a moment. Bridget had told me not to take sides, to stay out of it, but Brimley had her eye on me, and I was afraid.

She pointed to her leg then. "The bruises will heal." But she added, "What did you see? Was I pushed?"

I thought back to what I had seen, how Brimley had followed her so closely there was no gap between them. "I am not sure, Matron."

I dared not take her side.

"You were there, at the gate, when the first woman was carried out."

It was a statement. I nodded, then, reluctantly.

"My father used to shoot on the marshlands hereabouts and wore thigh-length boots; it was deep in water. First thing I did as Matron was to recommend that the prison be moved to higher ground. The governor said it was too late, for the foundations had been laid. I should never have come here."

"Are we in danger?" My voice quivered as the thoughts came fast. She had a choice, she could leave. Not us. Would we survive this place?

Things begin to make sense now. The atmosphere here, the feeling of chaos. There is fear underneath, fear of death, and what person can control what happens when that takes hold? She talks on now, as if it is a relief to share the news.

"I told the committee not to reduce the rations. The governor said there was nothing to be done. I have seen how bad the broth is, the porridge."

She struggled to her feet, rummaged on her desk and thrust paper after paper at me, reading out scraps. There were pamphlets from Members of Parliament, fulminating that our food was an insult to honest industry.

"They called it the fattening house. I tried to hide the wastage, for I sent it to friends nearby, who keep pigs, but the committee cut your rations in half. They did not want to hear me, when I explained that I only threw away what was rotting and not fit for you to eat."

She gulps then.

"The men sickened first. I pleaded with the governor, but he had no power to help."

A vision of the governor, almost running to a meeting. Leaving the matron to face Brimley alone.

"You could help, Tyrell. If you were my maid."

I would single myself out. Bridget had warned me not to take sides.

"May I consider, Matron, just for a while?"

She dismissed me then and I left her alone in her parlour and went back to the laundry. I did not tell Bridget what Matron had asked me, but I saw how Annie leaped up whenever Brimley needed anything. I dared not trust her now.

It was a few days later. Matron was limping still, and kept to the ground floor, and looked around herself fearfully as she hobbled from parlour to the governor's office and back again. Brimley had taken her place. She had sent out for more laundry for us to do and we worked now on Sunday afternoons, mending clothes for patrons.

It had been quiet there, as we mended clothes and sewed others, and Lacey had been telling us about her grandchild, and how she hoped to live with her daughter once she was released.

"Lacey," Brimley said, jerking her out of the circle, scissors and needle still in her hands. "Your grandson is gone. Gone, dead of a fever. Buried already. You can give that sampler away. God rest him."

She started to walk away then. Except that Lacey took her scissors and stabbed Brimley in the arm, then, before any of us could do anything, had sliced at herself, her hands, her face. Brimley grabbed the scissors and called for help, as the blood ran and the rest of us screamed out loud. Hawkins came at a run then, and the two of them subdued Lacey as she sobbed, and we shouted at them. Mrs Martin arrived in the doorway but Brimley pushed past her, half carrying Lacey, blood running. I saw how Mrs Martin stepped back at last and let them go.

She was taken to the padded cell and screamed all the way so that the sound was heard throughout the building and we set up a scream to keep time with her, until we were all locked in our cells. Then we drubbed on our cell doors until at last we fell silent and all that could be heard was Lacey's lament for her Robbie, who she would never see again.

Chapter Twenty-Five

I saw how Annie crumpled, then fell onto the laundry floor, and then how Bridget bent at the knees and did the same. I ran and knelt between them. The damp floor oozed into me but their foreheads burned to the touch. The wardresses came running, shirts pulled over their mouths, carrying two canvas stretchers. That stench again.

Mrs Martin arrived and we watched as they were carried up the stairs, heads nodding. She spoke low. "Hannah, you should go with them."

There were seven in the ward already, I knew. Hawkins was there, another wardress had only just come back on duty, her face yellow. Two of us had died.

"I might sicken."

Only weeks ago, I would have done anything for Annie. For Bridget, too. Now, I was afraid.

"There is nobody left to nurse them."

I hesitated again and she said, in a low voice, "You should come before it is too late." She handed me a scarf; we tied them close to our mouths and walked up in silence.

They had been lain down on two iron beds, a small chair between them. Both of them had thrown off their blankets. A warmth coming off them, the stench of covered buckets. The windows were open. I could not die here. They could not die.

I heard a bell ring out in the early morning and Annie's eyes flickered open. I tied my scarf tight again over my nose and mouth, and walked towards her.

Her eyes fixed on me at last, focused.

"Don't leave me, Annie. We had such plans."

This was a pain so sudden that I gasped from the weight of it, the love buried under so much hurt. The trousseau underneath the floorboards. The hammock where we had lain together, come together until I hardly knew myself. It had worn down to almost nothing, but I could not let her go.

But she closed her eyes again, and turned away from me.

I stood up, eyes starting with tears, and stumbled to the window. I had not seen the outside for so long. The Thames still rolled past the prison, the boats still sailed, and on the other side of the river I could see boys playing by the water, blurred shapes that tumbled and jumped. There was a world beyond this, beyond the bars.

Brimley had come in, face hidden behind a scarf. She trod over to a bed. Then came a most anguished scream. She had torn the scarf off her face, and cried out, "Hawkins!" and laid her head down on the sheet.

I dashed to my friends and felt their wrists. Each had a pulse. Weak, but pulsing still.

Two men come in then, a stretcher between them, the surgeon behind them, and Mrs Martin at the rear. Brimley stands in front of them. "No, absolutely not. She is no criminal; you cannot cut her up." Then she wails, desperate, and puts her hands up as if to bar their way.

But the surgeon passes her and the body is loaded onto the stretcher, gently enough, and covered in the sacking. Hawkins will be dissected then, the second of us to be probed, to find the reason why we are dying here. Brimley shouts after the matron then, as they disappear. "You will pay for this. This is against God's will."

Mrs Martin begged the committee to close the prison that day, but again they refused. But they allowed the sick women to leave. Annie and Bridget were brought out on canvas stretchers and put on a cart. I stood at the great door with the matron, and watched them go.

"The hospital was only built a few years ago, for blind soldiers returning from the war in Africa. It was closed down just last year and has lain empty; it is clean there, away from this miasma. They can recover there, Tyrell."

"But I might never see them again," I said quietly, my voice catching. Mrs Martin reached out a hand and held mine, against all the rules, till the cart turned a corner to head north and it rumbled out of sight. I wiped my eyes and asked her then what would happen to the rest of us.

She did not answer me, and instead stepped away from me and spoke out loud, told the turnkeys to gather the rest of us in the hall. We were so few now, gathered together, that her voice echoed as she spoke.

"The committee has decided to send you to two hulks, moored off Woolwich. You will be sent to either the *Heroine* or the *Narcissus*. The prison will close."

It was midsummer when the great gates were opened and we were led out in batches of six to walk down to the river. Names were called out in alphabetical order. I stood, shaking, inside the gate. Those first called went to the *Narcissus*. The others were bound for the *Heroine*. And so I watched and waited, as other inmates shuffled forwards, and then I was called, to be sent to the *Heroine*. The longboats to take us were moored at the steps, sitting heavy in the water and chained to stone bollards.

The prison guards walked out too, and lined up by the steps. All the disposable taskmasters, turnkeys and patrols were armed and stationed from the outer lodge to the River Stairs quay. The governor had decreed that we were to be placed on the launches without being in irons. Then the master came on board each launch. Chapman was on our launch himself, a last act of his governorship.

Mrs Martin looked down at me, as I settled into the boat. "They live," she said softly, and blessed me with a breaking voice. As the longboats cast off, onto the stinking river, I looked behind me and raised my hand to her and she waved back, as she stood alone. Annie lived, then. But I might never see her again.

Chapter Twenty-Six

The time on the hulks, those long sad months, passed by in a dreary muddled stupor, for we had tobacco and drink on the *Heroine* and there was nothing to do but play cards and wait. The first warning of what it would be like to be imprisoned there was the smell of the ships when we arrived, of rotting wood and filthy flesh and the hulks rearing out from the Woolwich flats in two long lines. They were moored close together and I can still recall the awful reek, as the men leaned over the sides and cheered to see us before the shouting started and they were set to work again.

There was another muster and another counting and another uniform. It felt damp to the touch, as if everything on board oozed a kind of despair. I feared that the women would remember how close I had become to Mrs Martin, but nobody cared; the quarrels of the last days of the penitentiary were quickly forgotten here. On the first night aboard the *Heroine* I recall how there was the sound of steel on flint, a flare of char cloth and flame, and then I saw that Lacey was passing out candles, until there was light.

She struck up a ballad then, and another, faster; then

another woman brought out tobacco, and the cards came out. We played until dawn, by which time our throats were sore with smoke and singing.

But Lacey must have been carrying the illness even then. Two days later she said that her throat hurt, that she was burning up, and then the convulsions came. She was dead by dawn and we covered our faces and took her up on deck.

The captain said first, "I may as well take more to bury. That will save on rowing upriver twice." At that we set up at him and spat until he shrunk from us and ordered that she be covered in a sheet and her body rowed away. We cleaned up as much as we could and we all survived. But we could not bring ourselves to sing again once Lacey had left us.

Until Bonfire Night came and the fires were lit along the Thames and all the hulks were singing, and at last, as the men's voices rang out across the water, I struck up first, and then my friends joined me.

"Pray remember the fifth of November,

Gunpowder, treason and plot.

I know no reason, why gunpowder treason, should ever be forgot.

A stick and a stake, for King George's sake.

A stick and a stump for old Oliver's rump."

Where was Jane, who had shown me the delights of Vauxhall, and where was Annie, who had whirled me round? Bridget, who had winked at me, even when her face was black and blue? I sang for them, for every bit of joy I could grab from the misery. Even though I knew there would be more to come.

The scurvy spread amongst us before Christmas, for there were no oranges to be had any more for the price that the prison governor would pay. The stomach pains returned to us all, and we feared that we would die on this hulk and be forgotten.

The surgeon gathered us on deck on a freezing morning before Christmas. "You have complained to the captain that you have stomach pain, that your motions are liquid." We stared at him as he spoke. "I believe that you are breaking down your motions with your fingers and mixing them with urine. That is reprehensible of you, to repay the kindness of your most considerate captain in this way."

There was a silence, and then I held up my hands, palms turned towards Surgeon Pratt. One by one the other women followed my lead, until all had our hands up, facing him, scrubbed as clean as we could manage. He snapped at us to put our hands down, but the captain walked along the line and then stopped, squared up to him. "Their hands may not be as clean as you would like, Surgeon, but there is no evidence for what you have said." Dr Latham came from the penitentiary and argued that we should be given oranges again, whatever the cost. As he left, I broke out of our line.

"Dr Latham, please," I said, and he held up a hand to the guard and let me speak. "Do you have news of the women at the Ophthalmic, where my friends were sent to with the other sick women? Simpkins and Sefton were with them."

Would he tell me? I had a vision, suddenly, of a knife and a slab and a tattoo sliced open on a leg. I would have heard if they were dead, surely.

He looked back at me, kindly enough. "Most are recovering. But I do not know their names."

They were bodies to him in beds, after all. Prisoners. I turned away, desolate, and watched as he was rowed away.

He went straight back to the prison governor and the

committee and argued for mercy, went over their heads when they were reluctant to act.

On a fine wintry day our surgeon and our captain called us to muster on deck. Dr Latham stepped forward, unfolded a letter. "This is from the Prime Minister. He writes that there are grounds for clemency for all of you, and that you are granted a free pardon."

The silence was complete. The surgeon folded the letter, put it back in his pocket.

"You will be leaving the ships this week. Your friends and families will receive you."

Then, at last, we understood. We held each other and sobbed, and the other women cried out the names of their children and grandchildren, and where they would go. I wept for Lacey, who would never see her daughter, and for myself, for I had nowhere to go.

What crimes had I committed that I should be forgiven them? I had stolen clothes to escape from the cruellest place. That had been pardoned, with the flourish of a pen. A nothing, a chance of a survival, that could have cost me seven years of my life. But the other guilt, the one I had carried since I was just eleven, that could never be pardoned like this.

"Tyrell," he said.

I looked up.

"Mrs Martin has sent word to Mrs Fletcher of the Ship, and you will work there. Mrs Martin has written to tell me that she will visit you when she returns to London."

I stammered then, for there was so much to take in. "And my friends at the hospital?"

But he was shaking his head already and making ready to leave.

"I know nothing of your friends."

I watched him go, and looked at my shipmates as they cried out thanks to him, and felt a desolation fall on me like a heavy blanket.

Ten months after I left the Millbank, a longboat brought me back close by, to Millbank Steps and pulled off straight away, into the deeper channel. I held on to the stones as I climbed to the Row. My head swayed as I sat down on dry land, my legs unsteady. My friends were waving at me as they were rowed further downriver, the men bending to their oars. I heard how one struck up a song until they were all singing, even the sailors, and I watched and waved until they were joined by other boats in the channel and I could see them no longer.

Chapter Twenty-Seven

I was here. Free. Alone in the great wide world, again.

The Ship Inn was right by the penitentiary. I remembered how Mrs Martin had drunk there, heard first about marsh fever from the male warders. How she had told me that she would walk to the inn through a tunnel that ran from the laundry straight to the Ship and how I had wondered, could I escape with Bridget, or even Annie. But then the fever had taken my friends from me.

I looked out on the river. The timber merchants were busy, sawing wood into logs to be floated down the river and sold. Barrels bobbed around and men rowed skiffs across to Lambeth, while others leaned against the river wall, smoking their pipes. It was half-tide, and three boys were rowing across to the other side. The tide was running hard and the boys were dragged off their course, so that they veered diagonally, all the way from the steps of the penitentiary to a mill on the other side. Perhaps it would not be so bad to be here and wait for Mrs Martin to return, as she had told Dr Latham she would, to seek me out there. She might have news. I pushed myself upwards, walked the few steps to the Ship, and went in.

A woman stood behind the bar, with thick meaty arms and a face that seemed entirely blank. She looked up at me and then away, as if I had disappointed her. "Tyrell," she said. "Mrs Martin recommended you." Then she tossed her head and gestured upwards. "Your friend has made herself comfortable already. You may fetch her down when you have taken your items up, for there is work to do."

I did not know what she meant but my heart beat faster. She grew impatient. "Upstairs, room at the top, and then come down again with your friend – and hurry." I walked up the stairs and saw a room at the top. A straw mattress had been flung in one corner with two thin woollen blankets on top; the window had a tattered cloth over it. A girl was looking out of the window, so thin that her clothes fell off her. She turned around, her face in shadow, hair hanging loose. Annie, alive, after everything.

I put my bundle down and walk towards her. Before I can think we are in each other's arms and we crumple together, thin and weak as we are, to land on the mattress. She is here, restored to me, and I do not hate, I cannot hate Annie, why did I ever think that I could? I stroke her hair, even though it is lank and I seek her out, with hands and lips.

A heavy tread outside, an impatient knocking.

"I expect you downstairs, for you are here to work." The gruffness in Mrs Fletcher's voice cuts through. She descends, step by step until she is gone. I look at Annie again, but the moment has passed. She pushes me away now and then she is on her knees by the bed. So close I could still touch her.

"This is unnatural; it is vicious what we did together and we must be forgiven." The prayers pour from her and do not stop. I am transfixed by her hands and how the veins stand out on them, for all the flesh has fallen away as they come together and find each other, the fingers pointing upwards. I leave her alone there and as I descend to work. I look back and she is still kneeling on the wooden floor as the sun finds her hair and lights it up. We are together and free, and I feel sadder than ever.

There was one long bar downstairs, and then upstairs another room, lighted by gas, where there was often music and dancing. By early evening the inn was already full of men, and even a scratchy orchestra, with fiddle player and a trumpeter. There were men from Thorn's brewery, who came in smelling of hops and who worked long hours. There were men off the coaches, from Vidlers down Millbank, who smelled of horses and the long roads out of London. There was a gas light company, right by Westminster Bridge, which was illuminated every night. Some of the stokers drank at the Ship, faces blackened. They were strong in the arm but moved like weak men, coughing and then spitting on the floor as they ordered drinks. Then there was a whiting factory close by, and those men, who came in with whitened faces, were more cheerful. And there were Irish paviours, with arms like trunks of wood.

That first night a man called Skillem, a local tailor, joined in, singing out, and leering as we filled glasses. I tried not to listen, for it reminded me of Harleston, and the company that had come to the farm.

"And for which I'm sure she'll go to Hell, for she makes me fuck her in church time."

"One night as I came from the play/I met a fair maid by the way/She had rosy cheeks and a dimpled chin/And a hole to put poor Robin in."

Then, with a grin and a bow towards us, he sang out, with a great roar and a laugh:

"First he niggled her
Then he tiggled her
Then with his two balls

189

He began for to batter her
At every thrust I thought she'd have burst
With the terrible size of his Morgan Rattler."

The songs ended with a shout and a crashing of tank-ards. I saw how Mrs Fletcher cast glances at us both, and in particular at Annie.

"You could earn more, you know," she said. "You could double your wages. It's easy work and you're full grown," nodding at Annie, then gesturing at two sailors sitting in a corner. A woman sat between them and then all together the three of them rose and Mrs Fletcher nodded, and they stumbled upstairs. Annie looked uncertainly at Mrs Fletcher and then as I walked to the door to look out at Millbank Row, Mrs Fletcher beckoned her over and they started to talk, fast and low.

In the distance I could see Vauxhall Bridge, glittering, as people walked across, carrying lanterns. Jane had told me that if the lights ever went out in the gardens the people on the bridge would fall silent and listen, then walk towards the music.

At midnight when the door was closed, as I cleared the last few glasses, smeared and filthy, I saw them whispering again to each other. They were both smiling and Mrs Fletcher had a hand on Annie's hair and was stroking it. Annie, looking back at her, hesitant, then a nod at last.

I remembered how she had looked when I first knew her. That golden hair glinting as she strode down the laun-dry in britches, laughing and unafraid. What did it all mean to her – who was she, the girl I was still tied to? I could make no sense of her and how she acted, how she had pulled me towards her then pushed me away.

I climbed upstairs behind Annie, and we washed in silence, turned away from each other to put on our night-gowns. I looked away as she prayed, then I got into bed first, moved towards the wall. I felt the draught as she lifted the bedclothes, but no warmth from her body, stiff and distant. The candle guttered and in the light her hair framed her head as it had done the first time I saw her. Then she blew out the light and all was silent.

It was dawn before I lapsed into sleep and when I woke, I was quite alone.

The first sounds I heard when I awoke were the river slopping and splashing, and the watermen crying out for custom. The bed was empty and the room was cleared of Annie's belongings. I remembered, and my stomach turned.

Unnatural. Vicious.

As I walked down the stairs I saw her, bending over a chest and putting her items away carefully. The room she had moved to was bigger, and light streamed into it from the open window. The bed was covered with a pink bedspread, and there were drapes over the windows, tied back with red ribbons. I watched as she walked over to a looking glass, sat down. She took up the rouge and outlined the bones of her face with a shaking hand. She saw me then, in the mirror, and might have spoken to me but I walked away.

How was I vicious, how was she virtuous? I worked feverishly, turning it over in my head, polishing the bar, shining the glasses, sweeping the floor, anything except look as she gathered her regulars and led them upstairs, one by one, with a swing of her bony hips. I learned their names. There was Skillem, the singing tailor; Robinson, a glazier and Wood, a carpenter. Mrs Fletcher had dressed Annie up in her finest. She offered them to me as well, though she said that I was undersized and too young, but I shook my head. She pushed one pink dress on me and would not take no, for I must dance on the weekends when the music struck up and if I was paid, give her half of everything.

191

That Saturday she took me to her room and dressed me herself, and put rouge on my cheeks and curled my hair in ringlets. I saw how Annie hovered at the door for her turn. She pushed me out then, and Annie went in and I heard how Mrs Fletcher laughed. I went away and polished the glasses.

When the dancing came, when the men led me around, I looked over at Annie. I saw her brushing a stray hand off her, then turn away to the tailor, who led her upstairs. She looked quite blank, her hair tumbled out of shape by the end of the day, loose and lank and still her clothes hung from her. I could not reconcile this, how she prayed and then laid herself out for these wretches. I could not stay here. There must be someone to help me – Bridget, or Jane. There must be a way to live that was not like this. I must put away the thoughts, that we could have faced the future together, like Phillipa and Harriet.

The laugh cut through. The glass in my hand fell, shattered on the flags. All those years ago, he had gripped me and his laugh had turned into a belch so I could smell the ale on him, as his hands held me so tight that I was forced to see what no child should ever see.

I crouched down as my head swam and picked up the glass as Mrs Fletcher shouted at me to get a move on, to clear up the shards. I pulled myself up and focused. It was him, in the corner with two paviours. I had noticed their accent before. They must be from Norfolk too. He rose and came towards the bar. The tankards slammed in front of me as he shouted for more beer. He had never spoken. I remembered that, how he shouted wherever he was. The smell of him, of beer and meat as he belched. He opened his mouth again to shout for service and then I slid down onto the floor.

The landlady called for help and Summers himself,

always ready to handle a female body, hoisted me, his hands on me as they had been so many years ago. He carried me upstairs, as I tried to struggle against him. Annie came out of her room, smoothing down her hair. Then he started at me and roared out, "Tyrell."

He climbed up further, and Annie must have followed on behind, and then Mrs Fletcher, with her heavy step. I found myself on the mattress. I could not move. The three of them in a line, looking down at me.

"Her mother was a murderer. Like mother like daughter, peas from the same pod they are."

He slurred his words but he spoke clearly enough to take a spade to my past and dig up the story I had buried.

"She had fallen pregnant from whoring in the town, she was infamous for it. And she concealed it, wicked woman as she was, and she gave birth alone, although some whispered that her daughter might have attended.

"The parish overseer's brother was pulling water out of the pond, hard by the windmill and the workhouse, and then he felt a tug on his bucket and a weight, and he pulled it in and it was a bundle. He laid it on the side, by the pond, and unwrapped it and there was a baby, a newborn, God rest her soul."

His story unfolded, his story that he had heard from others in the town: how the rector had ridden there, right fast, and then Mary Tyrell had been taken up for questioning, with two other women.

"On the third time they went to unlock the parish lock-up, the beadle found her dead."

The voice of the man faltered as he held onto the door jamb, as he slurred a version of my life, my mama's suffering.

Mrs Fletcher came towards me when he had finished, pulled me off the bed. I struggled to my feet. She threw open the drawers, flung my belongings up into the air and they came down like ragged rain.

"Get out."

But Annie spoke up at last.

"She's no murderer, she has done nothing."

Now she chose to defend me. Why now, after everything she had put me through?

"I'll not have her here. Get her out of here, or you will both leave, I swear."

She left the room and Summers stumbled after.

I heard her heavy foot on the treads, then the sound of the door to the bar opening, then closing again. Annie put her arm around me and held me, as if a feeling had come back to her. How could she change like this, like lightning?

"He accused you and your mother. I knew nothing, Hannah. I told you everything. I thought we were friends."

"Friends, after everything that you have subjected me to. I don't want your pity or your prayers. I looked after you, Annie, I did my best."

I pushed away from her, weak.

Annie spun round at that, a flash of something.

"You wanted too much from me, you worshipped me and I was fair smothered by it. You covered me over in love and protection. I never said I wanted that. I wanted us to look out for each other."

She sobbed, said no more. She was lying. She had told me that she needed me, never pushed me away.

I tore my hand free.

"You said I was unnatural. Vicious. But you were the one who wept, the one who asked me to come to you, the one that took comfort from me and never asked how I was. Enough now. This, whatever this is, it's finished. You stay here and do whatever it is that you are doing."

I could not help it; as I gathered up my belongings and

put my shawl on, I looked at her: "You're a whore, nothing else." I walked away and she sobbed as if I had stabbed her with my words.

I walked along the river for over an hour, all the way to Blackfriars Bridge. I could turn north here, walk up to the refuge, be there in an hour. I was not too proud to beg them for admittance, just one last time, until I could find a new situation.

All light had left the sky by the time I reached the bridge. The water flowed fast and black away from me, and I could not drag my gaze from it; it pulled me in. I hoisted my skirts, climbed up onto the arch and then finally curled into one, put my arms around it as if it was a branch.

I had nothing left and so I let it all go and howled. I threw it all away into the cold wind, and then I looked down. The water would take me if I let go.

A gull swept past, screeching. *"You go on now."* I had promised Mama one thing only. But now our secret was gone. I had to discover what had happened to my mother. To fight for the memory of her, so that I had the courage to go on. So I clung on until light came, and then I clambered down, took my bundle, and walked north.

Chapter Twenty-Eight

I saw her coming down the path that led to the temporary refuge. She was so very different now. Previously, Miss Clements had galloped everywhere, with hair streaming and escaping so often that I had spoken up one day and offered to plait it for her so that she looked more decent. The new Miss Clements was immaculate in a black dress, with a snowy-white tucker, stiff and starched. I saw, though, that halfway down the path as she processed, quite slowly, she stopped completely still, and smoothed her dress down, threw a speck of something pale onto the path and looked down at herself, as if satisfied. I stood up as she entered.

"Tyrell," she said, looking at me, and for a moment her eyes softened. "I preside now over the temporary refuge." She stretched quite upright, as if she had practised her triumph in front of a looking glass. In spite of everything that had passed between us, I knelt in front of her and I was not too proud to beg. I knew, in the end, that her soft heart was still there, underneath the black dress, the bib and tucker. She touched my hair, gently.

"I will have to examine you," she said, with a pause. "We will go into a private room together, and you will undress."

I took off the few clothes I had and wrapped my arms

around me as Miss Clements brushed me with her warm hands, up and down, across my stomach and breasts, pressing in carefully. She concluded her examination, took a blanket from a cupboard, gestured for me to sit down and wrapped me warm.

"You are free from pregnancy and disease, and I have the authority to admit you."

Then, as if she came back to how she had been, how she was really, "Your feet are bleeding, child – I will dress them for you."

But as she knelt by my feet and cleaned them, wrapped them in clean rags then warm socks, she looked up at me, a shadow passing over her face.

"I must warn you that not all will agree with my decision. I have fifteen girls here under my care, and my calling is to reform them. If I admit you, you must own yourself willing to repent, my child."

"I will do anything, Miss Clements."

It made me giddy, how she put on a coat over her kindness, then threw it off again.

Her face took on the look it had held in the Old Bailey, and she spoke sternly.

"Mr Haskin was devastated by what you did. You have no idea how shameful your conduct was. He felt that you had corrupted Simpkins, brought shame on the refuge. And I reasoned with him, and reminded him how weighed down you had been by your mama's great iniquity. So I will admit you here, but you must obey all my rules and keep out of sight of Mr Haskin until I have informed him of my decision, your presence here."

She recited her rules.

"You will be instructed in the Christian religion, taught how to work in the various branches of household employment, and then, if all goes well, at the right moment, after the committee and I have determined that you have reformed your behaviour, you will be placed in domestic service. You will grind up oyster shells, and you will pick oakum. A virtuous woman should be pure in body and in mind. The aim here is to check depravity and to give succour to forlorn objects." Religion had taken Annie away from me, but I had to bend myself to it.

And then, as if she could no longer restrain herself, she put her arms around me, just for a moment, and she kissed the top of my head though I must have stunk. She called for warm water, and helped me bathe and put on a clean uniform, which was dark brown from top to toe, and admitted me to the temporary refuge.

I wanted nothing except to be left alone, to remember Mama and her stories, and forget everything else; just work and eat and sleep and stay there forever. I dragged myself from bed, to labour, to food, to bed. I put Annie, the life we had lived, away. I wanted to dream myself back in time, to Mama's stories, when the gulls cried above the jetty and Mama ran down the rows, shouting, with her brother, until she scooped him up and ran down with him into the sunlight, to the harbour, to wait till their papa was back.

Mr Haskin arrived two days later. I had been put to work in the kitchen, as my feet were still bandaged from the glass. Miss Clements had told me to sit down and make bread, and so when the knock came on the door my hands were floury as I kneaded the dough, and Miss Clements rose without thinking and went to open the door.

My eyes followed her and so I saw the scene before it changed: Mr Haskin, smiling at Miss Clements, with a bunch of flowers in his hand. Then I understood how she had become orderly and immaculate, for she had always been determined to win him and now, with Annie gone, her heart's desire was within her grasp. I couldn't blame her for it.

Then, as he took in the scene, and Miss Clements gasped, her hand to her mouth, his face changed as if the weather had turned. She wailed, "I was going to tell you!" A strand of hair sprang loose. He held his hand up. She fell silent.

"She cannot stay here." He broke the silence, laid the flowers on the kitchen table. My hands froze in the moment of kneading.

"She has nowhere to go, Mr Haskin, and she is truly repentant. I have examined her and she is free of pregnancy and disease. I implore you, please," and then Miss Clements broke off, for ultimately it was his decision. But more than that, for he had, unbidden, brought her winter flowers, catkins and rosehip berries, gathered from the grounds of the refuge and I could tell she was right pleased yet torn, and I had put her in this position.

The silence grew between the three of us. Mr Haskin pulled a chair back, sat down. After a pause Miss Clements sat down next to me. I could not meet his eyes. I looked instead at his bouquet. I had gathered red berries like that once, that cold spring day that I had slipped out of the doctor's house, picking what I could find to lay at the willow tree where Mama lay.

"Tyrell, the parish from whence you came should take you back and find you employment. I will write to Mr Fox. It is their duty."

Miss Clements babbled, asking Mr Haskin for patience, forbearance, to allow the child to stay. But her voice faded and soon I heard nothing. I stretched out my hand, touched the red berries. When I was just a child, I had bitten into them, spat out the soft seeds and the hairs and sucked on the tart flesh that was left, such as it was. I had not seen them since. Such a small thing, but it had woken me. Mama had told me to leave the past alone, but it had come after me.

If I could have nothing else, Mr Haskin was offering me the chance to seek out justice for my mama. I could go back; I could discover what was hidden from me when I was a child. I could lay the thought to rest that had haunted me for years, for somebody must know the truth about my mama. Someone must pay at last for all the pain I had endured.

Miss Clements was still talking, begging Mr Haskin to have mercy. I stood up and looked at him.

"You may write to the attorney; I will deliver it when I arrive. May I have sufficient funds for the stagecoach, and food for the journey?"

Chapter Twenty-Nine

The Accommodation set me down at the Magpie, on a late afternoon but I did not know the coachman and had no heart to ask after Mr Salter. I wrapped my shawl tightly around me, put up my hood. I climbed down and nearly missed a step. No Mrs Thurlow to hand me down, I thought, as I looked out on my old town. The market stalls were all shut up, but the shops blazed out and I saw cloaked figures enter them, the bells overhead tinkling and the doors closing behind them. I could imagine the warmth inside, but not for me this time. I had shopped here on market day, run along the high street, the fleetest of all the children. Seen my mama in the lock-up. Nobody noted me. I passed down the street. I was a ghost here now, except that Mrs Thurlow would admit me, even give me a bed for the night if she could. I clutched the letter to me, my small purse.

I remembered the knocker, shaped like a fox, and the box trees on either side of the great door. I stood there, hesitantly, and then at last I rapped it. It opened almost immediately to a young girl in a bright white cap. A mourning band on her arm, I noticed.

"I am here to see Mrs Thurlow. I have a letter for Mr Fox

as well." I realised then that I should have gone to the back to see her. The letter gave me an excuse for my impertinence.

The young girl snuffled.

"Dead, miss. A sennight ago."

I could not speak. I had always thought that if I returned, she would be there.

The maid asked timidly, sniffing, "Miss, can I be of service to you?"

I gave her the letter, thanked her. Then I put my hood up again and walked away. I saw how the constable stood in front of the lock-up door, turning the key, and wondered how cold it would be for the unlucky one who had ended up there. I walked past Cage Walk, and into the Swan Inn. I had enough coins for some warm port, and sat down by the fire. I had no idea where I would stay that night now. But I must put that aside, for I had work to do if I was to get the morning coach.

I warmed a little, found that I was shaking. I must have closed my eyes for a moment and seemed to hear that the fire had hissed, perhaps spat out embers. I opened my eyes. A woman had come close to a man sitting by the fire, opposite me. I saw how he seemed almost unconscious, slumped there, breathing heavily. She walked away, looked back. "Disgrace," then walked up to the bar and asked the landlady, loud and angry, why such a man had been permitted in. The two women argued on and on.

I had not recognised him. The big man of the parish, shrunken into the chair. His legs looked like long twigs. I could snap them off. His stomach was swollen and his breath wheezed in and out. He stared into the fire. His nose seemed to have bloated. He looked over at me. It was Wypond, right enough.

His tankard clattered to the floor.

"You . . . you . . ."

He pushed himself upward and stumbled towards the door, as if he was frightened.

The landlady called over to him, "You're not to come back here."

I followed him out. He had not gone far. He staggered along the high street, one hand on the wall, with a curious, bow-legged gait, like a sailor home from the sea. I put a hand on his shoulder and peered into his face. He shrank away, hissing slightly. His breath, laden with liquor, floated away like a cloud in the night air.

"Mary?"

He pushed me off, stumbled into Cage Walk, then steadied himself against the wall. In the cold air his breathing came and went in fits and starts.

"No, not Mary. Hannah."

"Hannah. Hannah." He did not recognise my name. Slowly his body crumpled, so that he slid down the wall.

"The girl who was sent away. Whose life you ruined. You were cruel to us."

He was calmer now.

"I remember you now. You were just a child when your mother took poison. You could be her now, like peas in a pod."

He coughed again, and then started to laugh. I could not help myself; to stop the laughing I crouched down and slapped him, right across the face.

"What did you do to her? She died; my mother died."

His words came out between the fitting, the laughing and the coughing. "What did your bitch of a mother do to me, you mean? She led me on, and then she put your bastard sister in my pond. My daughter even. The whore that she was. Dragged me down with her. I lost my situation in the end. My reputation."

It was my turn now to collapse, to cough. The feel of my sister in my arms, her dark hair, her clear blue eyes. Her dark eyelashes, closed against the cold.

I understood now the sounds I had half heard when I was just a child; nothing was missing any more. At last I knew what had been done to my mama when she had sent me to bed, faced six men alone in the kitchen after Harvest Supper.

"She led us on, all of us. Danced with all of us." He spat again.

She had put me behind her and joined the dance. First with Summers, then with Wypond. A year before, and then they had come back. The tale she never told me.

"Summers started it," he said. A coarse laugh. "She was bending over the table, wiping it clean."

I could imagine the rest. How he had pawed her, and there was nobody there to protect her.

I must have spoken out loud.

"The farmer."

"He wouldn't. Not him, my dear brother." A laugh again, steaming in the air. "He watched, but he never said a thing. Not till he wrote to me."

Cook's voice came back then: how the farmer had taken a rope and slung it over the rafter a year later, and hanged himself whilst the cows lowed, restless to be milked.

All of a sudden Wypond was weeping, and calling out his brother's name. I wanted to slap him, to bring a spade down on his head, this man who had taken turns at my mama.

"I was the fifth," he said, "then we pushed her away upstairs and told her to look after her daughter. My brother had gone by then, he wasn't man enough to stay."

I found my voice then, pushed out my words.

"You should have left her alone. And he should have

defended her." A coarse laugh, then his words slid out again.

"We did leave her alone, we went back to Harleston on the cart. I looked back and saw how the kitchen was lit; my brother had brought rags and a bucket to your mother, and she slapped him away."

She had dragged herself up the stairs to me and done her best to put the violation behind her. But the harm was done. And I had tried to protect her then, but failed her. She had put herself between me and those men, one final time, when she stopped up her mouth with poison. So that I could go on.

Matthew Wypond, the overseer, he had done this. They would not have violated her if he had not permitted them to do so, arranged for them to come to the farm when his brother was still beside himself with grief. He had tried to help, the farmer, and had done himself harm as a penitence. I knew that now. But there was more.

"Answer me. Did the archdeacon know what you did?" And I could not help myself; I grabbed him by the hair for a moment.

He coughed again, and this time blood trickled out of his mouth.

"Later. Not then. He told me to resign from my position. But it was too late for your bitch of a mother."

He laughed. I imagined the spade coming down on his head. The blood spilling out of him, into the snow.

"You are the spit of your mother. I'd do the same to you now as I did to her. And the others did too." He spat on the ground and groaned, holding his belly. "But now I am always limp, like a soft worm." He touched himself then, and sighed, as if I should pity him.

I loathed him, the ruin of him who had destroyed my mother and left me a shell. He had taken my life from me and I could not recover. I ached to hurt him, this awful man who had bonded me to him, destroyed my life, such as it was. I could not see him any more and so I turned and I walked away and left him sitting there on the ground and I left his wheezing behind me.

I walked the length of the Low Road, two or even three miles, and my breath steamed in the air as I walked. I had walked here before with my mama, and then carrying my sister, for the first and last time. She had scarcely drawn breath but she had shaped my life, every step of it, even up till now. I had never got free of her, or of my mama, and I could not see how I ever would. At least she was spared the shame of being the daughter of one of those men. I was not forced to be her sister, or Mama her mother. I was glad, then, that she was dead.

I had knowledge now. And one more call to make. One more step to justice.

The rectory was a dark presence, except for a lantern, flickering, over the great wooden door. I stood on the doorstep, looking up.

I stepped up and rapped sharply.

He came to the door himself, in his shirtsleeves, as if he was a common man. I could smell, somewhere behind him, a warm steam and a sizzle. Somebody was ironing.

I stood there, my breath floating like fog in the air. Archdeacon Tom Olderhall held a candle to my face and I thought I saw that he drew back, astonished.

He peered at me, held his candlestick higher, wonderingly. "Not Mary. Hannah Tyrell." And then, as if to himself, he said, "You are the child."

"I am grown now. I am not a child, to be put off, to be shamed in church by you. You of all people. You say you are a man of God."

The bitterness in me. I had no idea how deep it had soaked the whole of me until I spoke out loud.

"Did you know what had happened to my mother?"

He stuttered, and then was silent. This was not the man who had preached at me, who had sat on Black Bessie, quite silent, as I screamed. He was smaller now. A winter apple, shrunk and wizened in its spill of paper, came to mind.

"She was violated. Did you know?"

He remained silent, and I saw how his countenance changed. So he knew; he was guilty as well.

At last he spoke, uncertain, clutching at his open collar.

"You shouldn't be here. You were sent away. You should never have returned."

He shrunk back from me. I remembered that I had looked up at him and wondered if his countenance had been carved from stone. Now it was soft, falling in on itself, creased like a sheet before it was put through the mangles I had seen at the refuge, just before I left. He had become an old man.

I would not let him off this hook, though, after all he had let happen to my mama. To me. When he had the power, he used it.

"Wypond violated my mother. With other men. You judged my mother. You had her staked. You let them walk free. Shame on you."

The candle shook in his hand.

Finally, after what seemed like an age, he said: "No. I did not know." Then he added, as if the words had been torn out of him by sheer force. "Not till later."

"You judged my mother. You sent me away. You gave a sermon about her, with me sitting there, so that the town would judge us. Her only crime, my only crime, was to be poor and friendless. You sicken me."

I waited for him to judge me, preach at me, but instead

he leaned against the door jamb, quite still, heaved a dry sob, and then slumped to the floor.

"The child," he said, as if that justified what he had done. I looked down at him. "The baby died in her sleep. My mother did nothing. Except protect me."

The candlestick blazed for a moment, guttered and died. I pulled my cloak to, in the bitter cold, turned around to go.

I looked back and saw him, in the flickering light of the lantern, his hands clasped together, then at last he heaved himself onto his hands and knees, and the door closed to.

My feet took me all the way along the Low Road, all the way to where one life had ended, at Lush Bush. My fingers were so cold that they could hardly move, but I tore the last flowers and grasses I could see, standing proud and frosted on the verges, and then when I arrived where the willow grew, I stopped and knelt and laid them by the tree. I felt how my blood was running out of my hands, warm where I had torn it against the harsh grasses, and I wondered that I was alive at all.

I tucked myself into the lee of the hedge there, shivering, but as near to Mama as I could be. It snowed during the night and I curled myself as close to her as I could get, buried six feet under, and I looked up at the flakes falling on us, onto my face, my arms, my legs. I could nestle here and not be found, and when I woke up, I would be walking hand in hand with Mama, along the lane where the flowers bloomed, and all of this would be gone. But Mama wanted something else, she told me, as I lay there. I heard her quite clear, and she told me that one day the sun would rise over me and I would laugh again, somewhere else; that we would meet again, but not now, not yet.

Chapter Thirty

I woke to find myself in a small room, warm, wrapped in a blanket. Flames flickered as I opened my eyes. Two people, one on either side of me, crouched down. I tried to struggle up. The woman looked uncertain.

"John, my husband, he found you outside. By our woodshed."

John took up the tale. "I was fetching wood for the morning."

I heard my mama in their voices, a softness. Saw curiosity as their faces swam into focus. The woman took my hands, rubbed them.

"You're warming up now. I thought you might be dead when John brought you in." Then added, "My name is Elsie. John works up at the hall."

"Gawdy Hall," I said, as if in a dream, and the two of them exchanged a glance.

"My name is Hannah Tyrell," I say at last.

I saw how they exchanged a glance, but said nothing. Surely nobody knew of me any more. Elsie slipped her hand under my neck, and gave me hot sweet tea to drink.

I could feel my body coming back, thawing, and I shivered. The room came into focus, a thick-walled cottage with small windows. Elsie watched me look round, then burst out proudly, "It's well-built, with a privy outside."

Their words tumbled out and over each other in turn as they told how in the spring and summer they dug and planted the triangular garden belonging to the cottage, which divided it from the road. They kept chickens, but no pig. They didn't have enough space, and besides, they were both busy. I saw them look at each other as she talked; John followed Elsie with his eyes and then she would catch him, and look back at him, lovingly. John tucked the blanket around me; Elsie banked up the fire. John brought me a mug of warm milk, sweetened with honey.

"How did you arrive here? We are right at the end of the town; how did you wander so far?"

I said, each word chosen, "I came off the coach today. I went to see Archdeacon Olderhall."

They were very still, both of them. Elsie said, carefully: "And what happened?"

"I went to ask him something. I was not happy with what he said. Then I went away."

They had saved my life. I owed them this. A fragment of the truth at the least.

Elsie burst out, as if she could not prevent herself from talking. "None of us attend Redenhall, not any more. Nobody visits him, not even his father."

Elsie looked at her husband, a long look. He nodded and she rose, went over to a table, and pulled a crumpled piece of paper out of a box that sat on top. She started to read, slowly. "To the church wardens and overseers of the poor of the parish of Pulham, from the church wardens and overseers of the poor of Redenhall with Harleston, upon our complaint, that this woman, a single woman, Margaret Nicoll, came to inhabit in the said parish without legal settlement. And on December 13, she was delivered of a bastard child."

It was a bastardy order. I remembered that Mama had one too, on which my name was inscribed, and beside it, in clear writing, it said "base born".

"Enough, Elsie, she can hardly speak."

But Elsie brought the paper over, and showed it to me.

"She was examined, and then Olderhall proclaimed an order." I read it, and saw his signature, written proudly in black ink at the bottom and sealed with his signet ring. A justification for sending a woman and her child to their death, ordained by the church, by the archdeacon himself.

We do adjudge Samuel Flowering of the parish of Pulham to be the putative father of the said female bastard child and that the same is let living and is likely to become chargeable to the said parish as doth appear us. By the complaint of the church wardens and for the relief of the parish of Redenhall with Harleston, as also for the provision and maintenance of the said bastard childhood, it is determined that the putative father must pay the sum of one shilling and his successors to the overseers of the poor and further order that the sum shall be paid to the churchwardens for the maintenance of the bastard child.

John spoke then. "The child was chargeable on the parish of Pulham, so he said that they should go there without delay. It was snowing that day, but he would not listen."

Elsie had tears in her eyes now.

"Olderhall and Wypond held a town meeting, and they agreed that notwithstanding the lack of response, the single woman should leave the workhouse before Christmas, and strike out for her own parish, where the man who had fathered her child should either take her on or pay for its upkeep. They refused her a carriage, although she should have been conveyed out, as she was still breastfeeding, for Wypond said it was a matter of just six miles, and she could walk it."

Elsie turned away. Her shoulders heaved, and then John put an arm around her as she wept, and took up the story. "She got to somewhere just beyond Pulham St Mary. She had to walk just two miles further, to the workhouse on the Norwich Road. We surmise that the baby cried and she stopped to feed her. She called the baby Martha." A memory, of the good wife Martha sitting at Harvest Supper, before everything was lost.

The silence spread out in the room, and it was white and cold. "She was found, like you, outside in a ditch, with the snow covering them like a blanket. Martha was at her breast."

There was silence in the small, dark room. The fire flickered, spat out embers that glowed for a moment on the hearthstone, then were extinguished.

Elsie let out one sob. But she was not finished.

"She was like a sister to me, and we had begged to house them here but the house is tied, so we were not allowed to. We could have saved them."

We spoke in whispers then. I could feel their breath on me as we talked.

I spoke. "You said Wypond, the overseer?"

"Olderhall excommunicated him one Sunday. Women made complaints against him, and at last, he was forced out."

My head was swimming now. But I must keep my secret.

"We knew about your mama. Everybody knows here." Elsie had my hand again and said, gently, "We lay flowers for her every year. Every spring. We are not the only ones. Things are changing here."

She paused, swallowed, and looked hard at me. "Have you heard of Captain Swing?"

I shook my head.

"The workers are in revolt now," Elsie said, her voice rising. John pointed upstairs and she spoke more softly. "Olderhall tried to stop us building on our own chapel, just up from the marketplace, for which we had taken up a collection. He was sent a letter, and threatened with being swum at the witchpool. He brought in the guard. And so they hooded and cloaked themselves, the labourers, and then a great deputation went to see him in the rectory, and when he opened the door they surrounded him, and jostled him and cried shame on him for his tithe. But then his daughter came to the door, and said that she might be young but that he should mark what was being said. Then she asked to live with her grandfather in Cambridge and he was all alone."

Justice had come to them both, then. Slowly, and not at my hand, but they had been broken for their cruelty.

We had been talking all night. The fire had burnt down and was turned to ash. Now, as a winter dawn broke and silence fell, I looked toward the light and saw the frost had etched a pattern on the windows. I could hear, faintly, the sound of a wood pigeon outside, and then a magpie, defiant. I saw how John and Elsie heard it too, saluted him gently. One for sorrow. Another joined him. Two for joy.

A child cried upstairs. Elsie walked up the stairs and brought down a three-year-old with brown hair, whose eyes widened to see a stranger there and who put her head into her mother's breast. John re-laid the fire and stoked it till it caught, rubbed his tired eyes.

The London coach left at eight. I must get up. But I found I could not stand and without a word they helped me upstairs and put me on a mattress and then came the darkness.

*

213

I stayed like that for nearly thirty days, drifting in and out of sweat and cold while the snow fell outside. I found myself in a child's bed, wrapped up with a brick at my feet. Elsie sat on the bed, gave me mead to drink, helped me dress and get myself downstairs. I had shivered and shook, coughed and slept. They had given me all the nursing I needed, left me to recover once the fever had broken, brought their children into their bed and although I was weak my mind had cleared.

I watched the two of them go about their morning business. John brought the children down and they washed in a tub warming by the fire. Elsie took her brush to their hair. The feel of my hair in my mama's hands, safe and comfortable as she stroked it down, plaited it and tied it back. I wanted what they had, one day.

"I will walk into Harleston and get the coach back to London," I said. They argued with me and said that I should stay, and only agreed when I had eaten, and they had wrapped me up in a shawl, given me thick socks for the journey. I embraced them both, and held Elsie's hand, I shook it and offered them the last of my money, but they refused and pressed more on me instead.

Outside, the snow lay quite thick on the ground, and the willow where Mama was buried stood bare and proud under a clear blue sky. I walked over, kicked the snow away and laid my hand on it, and I said goodbye.

When I got to the inn, I bought myself a warm cider, and sat by the fire. Where I had met the ruin that Wypond had become. I wondered where he was now, why Olderhall had cried, admitted his faults. Bitter memories, even of the farmer who had watched. Done nothing. Olderhall had never cleared her name. Only Mama had protected me. I had not meted out justice, but at least I knew what had happened to her and how hard she had fought so I could survive.

At just before eight I drew my hood to, climbed into the coach. I had kept my promise, to go on. I did not look back at the market square, the folk who walked there, for I would never come to this town again.

Chapter Thirty-One

A garland of early spring flowers, snowdrops and daffadowndillies woven with ivy, decorated the great front door, and I understood why as I was conveyed, sodden and shivering, to Mr Haskin's room. There he was, and there was Miss Clements, and they were holding hands and smiling, and she had flowers pinned to her gleaming grey dress.

She came straight to me, but looked back at Mr Haskin. "So you are back so soon, Tyrell, we did not expect this." She is Mrs Haskin now. I am Tyrell now to her.

I fell to my knees. "I found that my friends were all dead when I arrived so I had no situation to seek out. A stranger and his wife took me in for I fell ill for weeks, and then I used the last of my money to come back and throw myself on your mercy."

Perhaps he had been gentled by marrying, for he ordained that I should stay for the time being. The next day, he would write to the committee and it would convene to consider my case. Mrs Rachel Haskin clung to him, and smiled to hear him as he spoke. He was only doing it for her, I realised.

"I will advise the committee that she should be admitted

to the temporary refuge and that then she should apply to the London Female Penitentiary, to see if they will admit her, for they take young women who have gone out on the town."

I would have spoken up then. I had never done that, at least. But Mrs Haskin burst out into a clatter of gratitude on my behalf, so I did not speak up, and then he looked down at her until she was quiet, and then he went out.

Once we were out of earshot she burst into speech, for she was brimming over with joy. "The full complement of the committee came to St Leonard's for our marriage, and the objects attended, of course."

Her words spilled out.

"The committee permitted the entire refuge a roast dinner of beef and a hot steamed pudding."

"I wish you joy," I said, then added, "Mrs Haskin."

She beamed at that. I took advantage of her happiness. "Mrs Haskin, do you have any news of my friend, by any chance?"

Her face clouded over then, and she ran a hand over her hair and a strand burst free.

"That is no longer your concern. You are here on sufferance. I will take you back to the temporary refuge until your case is settled." But she sounded uncertain, rather than angry, and as she rose and walked me down to it, I felt that she looked at me from time to time, as if there was something she wanted to say, but dared not.

I was kept apart at the temporary refuge and I remembered that when I was an object, I was not permitted to speak to those that stayed there. I saw Maria only once in the yard and ran to her, but she faded away into the shadows of the refuge, where I was not allowed to approach. She had not forgiven me then.

*

My time ended swiftly at the temporary refuge, for two men arrived and Mr Haskin brought me to them and closed the door behind us all. They told me that I was under suspicion for the murder of Mr Matthew Wypond, the former parish overseer of the town of Harleston in Norfolk. I saw how Haskin looked at me then.

"I took her in as a child," he said. "I did my best by her, to raise her to be a most virtuous object. I have failed for she is like her mother."

The two men burst out then and said that no blame was attached to the refuge but to me. They explained that Mr Wypond had been found near frozen in an alleyway, almost buried in a mound of snow.

"He murmured Tyrell, but then he lost consciousness. Mr Fox recalled that a letter had been sent from here, and the landlady of the Swan remembered seeing a young woman with him, leading him out into the cold, days earlier."

I was taken to my room and Mrs Haskin watched over me, as I picked out a few items to take with me. At last I was at this point then, I could hang – and then the thought came, that there was nobody to miss me.

But at last, as we were done, she blurted out:

"She wrote to you."

My fingers trembled and loosened. The bundle dropped onto the floor.

"I gave it to Mr Haskin and he read it." A pause, then she broke out, "I know only that she has sailed, on the first spring tide. The letter was burnt."

I snapped back at her, "*He* burnt it, that's what you won't say. Your precious husband. You should have told me."

Her hands grasped at thin air. "I have stayed awake, night after night, wondering what my duty is. She had stood trial for assault, and she was convicted to transportation. She wrote to you and I passed the letter to my husband. He told me that I must not speak of her again in front of you. I promised to obey him."

Her hands twisted as if they were knotting themselves together. "But you may never see her again, and I remember some of what she said." And then she started to talk, and I could hear Annie's voice, clear as a bell, rise in the air, as she spoke, with that burr in the voice, as if by talking she rose and walked up and down on the hills of the West Country.

"My wishes are not to leave this country, for to leave my friends behind will break my heart. If you could, get Mister Haskin to petition for me to stay here, for Botany Bay is so many miles away it fair breaks my heart. I had one friend to stop me here, but she is lost to me. And she has no friends to help her, and nor do I. Pray for me, and for her, and ask forgiveness for both of us."

A sound came from me, like a cow in long labour, and I realised that I had cried out loud. She had not deserted me after all; after everything she had suffered, without me, she had decided that she would be my friend again. She had thought of me up until the end, even when I had pushed her away. I had called her a whore.

"I did not know that he would read it, and then put it into the fire. He forbade me to tell you, and I promised to obey him, and I will in everything else, but not in this. She was your friend, and I am sorry."

She had told me everything that her conscience allowed her to say. She had taken her vows and even this tale had cost her. I wondered how much Annie had suffered, and what had happened, but no one would tell me. I must find her, somehow, I must go after her. But how?

There was a knocking then, and it was him again. I looked at her and the plea in her eyes to say nothing. I remembered how hard she had tried to help me, in so many ways, and in the end, I gave her my hand and I thanked her and I saw how he looked and understood nothing at all.

Chapter Thirty-Two

Newgate again. My fate is not in my own hands, and so I follow the warder and stand behind him as the doors lock, unlock, lock again until I am in a cell. I push the muck away, sit down on a bench, wrap my shawl around me and then my eyes adapt to the dim light.

Mrs Harding is there. For a moment I cannot understand this, nor why her hair is loose and her clothing torn. Her eyes fix on me and at last she knows me.

"I did not do it; you must believe me." I push her away. She keeps coming, sits next to me. I have never been this near to her except, I realise, when her breath woke me.

She speaks through her sobs. "Hannah died."

The feel of her body close to mine, the heavy pillow, the sleeping girl. Left behind on visits by her mother, the shame felt of having a child like Hannah. That gentle, sweet child.

I scramble up, "You killed her. You killed your own child." The women look up and all of them are listening; the silence is rapt. I shout at her now; I am beside myself for the poor child.

"You never loved her; I saw how you left her behind when you went out visiting. You were ashamed of your own daughter, who loved you. I saw you. With the pillow."

A woman steps up to her and slaps Mrs Harding. A crack through the air as she falls back on the wood. A murmur from the women, one word. *Murderer.* They might tear her apart, for some things were beyond what could be accepted.

She starts up again. "No. I loved her. I thought of doing it when she was ill. For mercy, you understand. But she recovered and I was grateful that she did. But then after you left, she sickened again. I cannot bear that she is gone, but Mr Harding thought it was my fault and they took me up and brought me here."

She falls to my feet in a frenzy of weeping. I think of that poor girl, with her doll. I see how the woman steps towards the heap on the floor. Mrs Harding could die here. I do not want her on my conscience and so I hold my hand up to the woman and pull Mrs Harding up. She sinks on my shoulder, a stinking mess from the floor. I push her away from me until she collapses on a board, weeping. The murmurs stop as I sit at the end of the bench. At last all is still.

We will stand trial on the same day of the sessions. Before that, I agree to write to Mr Harding. I say enough in my letter to allow him to think I have evidence about what happened to Louisa and to me. A threat, scarcely veiled, to save a woman who despised me. But Mrs Harding is changed indeed and tries to cling to me, but I cannot bear her. I did not do this for her, but for myself, to clear everything I can before I go to court. Mr Harding changes his evidence and so she is set free. But the child who I cared for is dead, whatever she did or did not do to her. Louisa is dead too and Mr Harding free to write his pamphlets on fallen women. I can only press things so far.

My second trial. I thought I had lost everything, until

Mrs Haskin spoke and gave me hope. The dice rolls and I have no power over it, how it lands. I die or I go. The judge and jury will decide.

There is Olderhall; there is the same judge as before. The jury stare at me, as they did before. This time it is murder, and I know that the judge has a black cap waiting. I hear how the prosecutor calls me vicious and fallen, a woman who had killed her protector so that she could steal money. They can say what they want. I will not give them my words. I stand there silent when I am asked what I have to say for myself.

I wonder what they think, those good men, and true as they look at me as though I was dirt underneath a shoe. I do not expect mercy or kindness from them or from any man. I wonder only at the power they have, to sit in judgement on me and how they would feel if I spoke and told them my truth, what I had suffered, but I find that I hardly mind, for at least my life will move forward and not be stuck any more in the mire. I know what happened to my mama now and that she never got justice. This is not justice; this is how the powerful oppress us because we are weak. I will not speak.

Then Tom Olderhall stands up to give evidence. He stands stiffly upright but his body shakes and at first his voice is a whisper and I see how the jury crane to hear him, for it had boomed right enough around the church and the town before. He describes himself as a widower, and archdeacon of the parish of Redenhall. He tells the court that I could not have killed Wypond, for I had been with him, having an interview when it was said that I had landed that fateful blow. He cannot bring himself to tell the whole truth, but he adds that I had been ill used, and Mama too, and begs for leniency. Then he turns towards me and I see how his eyes, once hooded and cruel when they gazed on me, are now the eyes of an old man, watery and faded. "I am sorry for everything that has happened to you." He turns to the judge. "She is more sinned against than sinning."

So after all that I am found guilty, but not of murder. Of assault.

Judge Newman Knowlys looks on me; he knows me from before. I see that he is fumbling and putting something made of black fabric away again, on a convenient shelf. He clears his throat. "You have stood before me once before and this time you will go over the seas and beyond the seas. You will see your friends and relations no more. The friends with whom you are connected will be parted from you forever in this world for though you will be transported for seven years only, it is not likely that at the expiration of that term you will find yourself in a situation to return. You will be in a distant land at the expiration of your sentence. The land that you have disgraced will see you no more. I hope that your fate will warn others."

I cannot help it; I drop Mr Haskin a mocking curtsey as I see the rage on his face. I am taken down and back to Newgate, on to Deptford to wait for the ship to sail. Beyond reach, sailing after Annie.

Chapter Thirty-Three

I arrived on the *Julia* in the evening of the next day. There were women everywhere on deck and below, perhaps fifty altogether. I was sent down to the sleeping quarters and the guard nodded at my hammock, gave me a bundle of items. The lamps flickered and the dialects of the kingdoms slid past my ears. There was one woman who was sobbing, and then talking feverishly in a language that no one else understood. She was picking rotten vegetables off her dress. There were others crying out names that slowly I realised must have been their children. Another woman screamed until she was begged to keep silent. Then sobbed, silently. I felt as if I was the only one who had a purpose in front of her, although how would I find her, in the vast unknown place we were bound for?

I turned back to my bundle. There was a blanket and pillow and clean, well-made clothing. There was a woollen jacket, shifts, stockings and even a cap. I set out my bed, and then, looking around, slid my package underneath my mattress and lay down on top. I wrapped myself in my shawl, pulled the blanket over, and turned my back. I had eaten and drunk nothing for most of the day, woke from time to time with a dry mouth, swallowed, tried to moisten it, slept again.

The next morning we were mustered on deck. A grey day, spitting rain out. In front of us stood the captain, a Mr Irvine, and the surgeon Mr Wilson, who gave us our rules and examined us again, one by one. An older woman, who was coughing and spitting, was to be sent back on shore. She was not fit enough to travel. I saw how the news took her, how she cried out with relief, to be sent back to a prison near home, near her grandchildren. Jennet was examined next, the woman I could not understand. The surgeon muttered to the captain and they both looked her up and down, then passed her for the voyage. She collapsed on my shoulder when she understood that she would sail and Mr Wilson told me to take care of her. "You, Tyrell, will be monitor for your mess. You will be responsible for cleanliness, order and the reading of scriptures. Get this woman cleaned up." He counted six down along the row and the women clustered around me as I was issued with two stout wooden chests, empty and clean. "You will help me take down notes on the women, Tyrell. Explain to them that they may write to their families and the letters will be sent before we leave. Once we have set sail you will be permitted on deck daily, as long as you all observe the rules." Then he took me aside and told me that I would receive a visitor. Mrs Martin would come that morning, when the tides permitted, and he said that we could meet alone in his cabin. A warmth spread in me, for I had missed her and would be glad to see her.

At last she came and we went to the cabin and she held me tight, without any judgement in her face. "I am sorry that I was gone so long, Hannah, and that I meet you here, now." At that I crumpled and cried and at last we sat down and she told me her news until I was calm again.

She had left the penitentiary after it had been cleared and gone to stay with her family in York and meet her new granddaughter. She had returned to collect her belongings and take her leave from her friends at the Ship and what the place had become.

"Once the penitentiary closed Mrs Fletcher's business nearly failed. So she . . ." she hesitated, looked at me and then away, "she branched out. I had no idea she would ask Annie to do what she did. Annie hated it, but it meant both of you could stay."

My mind whirled then, ran over bitter memories, saw them differently. Annie, uncertain, then nodding to Mrs Fletcher as the landlady stroked her head. A down payment, a roof over our heads. Man after man after man while I kept myself apart, polished glasses. Endured men's hands at the weekends, only their hands. Annie, all dressed up every night, ready for them, all of them.

My voice quavered then. "You saw her?" She nodded, then, and opened her bag. Something I had never thought I would see again, a letter in Annie's neat, unformed hand.

"She sailed before you but I saw her before she went." She hesitated. "She endured more than I can say. Whatever kept you apart should do so no longer, because at the end she thought of you and tried to find you. But you had left London and nobody would say where you were."

Her voice trailed away and I undid the letter.

Something heavy is in it, and I take it out: a red love heart, padded. I recognise Annie's neat stitches, as familiar as writing. A handkerchief, with two initials on it, a stitch running between them. I hold these two items tight and start to read.

Dearest Hannah. The words blur before me and I find I am in tears, that the letters are below water and I cannot read them. I hold the letter out to Mrs Martin and she takes it from me, coughs and reads it out.

"Dearest friend and sister, I did not know it but I was pregnant, Hannah, and I did not discover it till you were gone. Mrs Fletcher kept me on even then, for there were men who liked girls who were pregnant. She said that I must give up my room and I was put back into the attic. She reasoned that men with such an unusual fancy could climb an extra flight of stairs."

I feel that Annie is here now, her voice is so clear to me. If only she were, and I could draw her to me. If only. Mrs Martin starts to read again.

"I gave birth on the bed we shared together, that first night. The night I pushed you away. The pain was so intense that Mrs Fletcher burst into the room when I was screaming with it and stuffed a rag into my teeth and told me not to disturb the house, or else she would drag me out herself.

"In the end, after a day of labouring, she slipped out like a fish, a small wiry body, and she wriggled in my arms and cried. I put my daughter on my breast and then her mouth moved and I felt a tugging and it was remarkable, Hannah, I cannot even describe it as my milk came down and fed my baby. Mrs Fletcher brought up the kitchen knife, cut the cord. She was almost gentle, for that moment, as she took the afterbirth away in a bucket, changed my bedding. She reached out a hand and touched her head, almost tenderly. But there was no moving her.

"'You have a night with her, then she goes. You know what we agreed.'"

My poor friend, she had to give up everything to survive. And she was quite alone.

"As dawn came, I saw how she stirred and I put her on my breast again and, Hannah, she was so beautiful. My baby, my darling first born. I swaddled her tightly and then I lay her down and watched her, drank her in as I stuffed rags between my legs. Then I bound her to me, as my mama had bound me, and I left the inn behind me. The river was just there in front of me and I can be honest with you, I thought what it would be like, if we let it take us together. Then I turned away, walked north.

"I had sewn a token for her out of a scrap of fine clothing cut from a cloak that I had made for myself, red velvet on the outside, edged inside with a deep pink silk. I had cut out a heart shape, and then stitched the two together, and I had embroidered my name on one side, and Hannah on the other. I named her for you. Then I sewed another, an exact match of it. To find her later. Every girl giving up a baby knows this, that the orphan hospital will give you your child back, if you have given in a token.

"Hannah. I remember everything I saw that day, as the dawn stained the buildings pink as I walked north, up through Pimlico, then through St Giles and the rookeries, and up to Kings Cross and the orphanage. The rags were soddened by the time I got there. I stood on the steps of a grand building but the door was still closed so I took my child and nursed her. One last time.

"The great oak door opened at nine o'clock. For one moment I held Hannah close, and then I gave her in to the servant. She held her with one hand and with the other took one of my tokens. 'I will come for my daughter. One day,' I said. She looked at me kindly and nodded and then the door thudded shut."

My poor friend, my sister, my Annie.

Mrs Martin held me close, and said, "I should tell you what she told me. What happened next. How she came to sail."

Annie stayed at the inn and worked there. Then Summers came back. He asked for Annie.

"She told me that she could have put up with him, but he mocked you and your mama. And she lost her temper, threw the pot at him and it knocked him down. She was put on trial for assault and nobody spoke up for her, even though she said that Summers had forced her, had torn her clothing from her and at last she had fought back. But she was sentenced all the same because of the previous trial and it was expedited because a ship was sailing."

I speak then, my voice cracking. "She wrote to Miss Clements. Mrs Haskin, now. But the letter was burnt."

Mrs Martin turns the letter over. "I found her on the ship, and she wrote this to you and she told me that she was sorry for everything."

I take the token up at that and hold it between my hands. A fragment of cloth, everything that she has, given in exchange for her baby, and I cannot help her.

Mrs Martin speaks on. "Once she had sailed, I went to the refuge, Hannah, to find out about you, to give you her letter. I asked to see Mr Haskin." Her voice hardens then.

He had admitted her for an interview, told her that there was nothing to be done with the girls, that Tyrell had been an iniquitous influence on Simpkins and that finally they had shown that they could not profit from the work of the refuge.

"He would not tell me where you were, Hannah, but he asked a girl to convey me out. She said nothing at first. But then she held out a package, tied up in paper and string. She spoke right slow, I remember that. She spoke quite clearly, with a gap between each word."

As I had taught her. Sing the words until you can speak them.

" 'Please could you tell her that Maria sends her greetings, and wishes her a safe journey,' she said. 'I am sorry, tell her that, and that I should have been a better friend to her.' "

Mrs Martin bent down and opened up her bag again. A crackle of dry paper, and then the package was in my hand, I knew it straight away, and then I wept again.

"I could write a petition on your behalf, Hannah," Mrs Martin said. "I have done it for others and been successful. My position as the former matron of the penitentiary is helpful. I could petition that you serve out your sentence in England. I would stand surety for you when you are released."

Could she do this – could I then find Annie's girl for her? I looked at her and I saw that she wanted to help but she was fearful that her power had waned, for she had no position any more.

I shook my head. "Please, can you tell Maria that I am grateful, that I am sorry too that I neglected our friendship. I will write to her when I arrive. And to you too."

I gave her back the token. "Please, keep it safe." A silence, then I said, "I hope one day that Annie can send for her girl. Her Hannah. If I find her, or perhaps she writes to you for her." I took the handkerchief and I slid it into my package.

She nodded, put the token away carefully in her bag. Then we both stood up and she took me in her arms again. It struck me only then that I would never see her or Maria again and I cried against her for she had been kind to me and had done everything that she could to help me. Then we left Mr Wilson's room together, and I carried her bag to the rowboat and watched as she was helped down into it. I watched her all the way back to shore and as she landed she waved back to me, one last time. Then I turned away, for Mr Wilson was calling for me to get our chests packed.

Chapter Thirty-Four

Together my mess counted and labelled our belongings and then the women passed their items along so I could pack them in. I looked around at the women and tried to rouse them from their grief with business. "We are to roll up our beds every morning, stow them on the netting on deck and scrub down here. We will be issued with tea and a kettle; we have our lamps already. We will have wine and lemon sherbet."

One woman, a weaver called Grace, from Lancaster, brought two heavy packages of pamphlets and books, which she stowed away carefully so that she could educate other women, she said. Other women brought baby clothes and wedding gowns. Once everything was stowed and safe, I let the women go. Then, only then, did I slide my package out from my apron and slip it right to the bottom of the pile. I heard it crackle. For a moment I wondered if I should open it, and press my face to it, everything that I owned, the dearest gifts I had. But then the sailors came down, and it was too late, and I put the lids down on the chests and they hammered them down in front of me and took them away.

Two sails had been hoisted on deck, and behind it were

two deep tubs of cold, clean salt water. We could wash ourselves in privacy and I took advantage of it first, and then the other women, and then I helped Jennet, with rags, to cleanse herself from the stench of the vegetables. At length she was clean, and all of us shivering from cold, but warmly dressed in a shawl and her woollen jacket wrapped and tied around her. She clung to me then, and kissed my hand.

We would sail soon, the captain had told us, for the winds were with us now and we could lose no time before they changed again. That afternoon we huddled down in our hold with candles lit, for we were permitted to send a letter each and they were to be collected by a boat, and then sent to the four corners of the kingdom. I set to, with Graces's assistance, and we helped the women write; so many came to us that by the end of that afternoon we had written perhaps twenty letters between us and we shook our hands betweentimes for fatigue. I tried to get a sense of what Jennet wanted me to write, in her own language, between sobs, spelling it out as I heard it. My hand trembled by the end. I had written down fears and sadness that I could not even express myself. Another woman, a mama of seven children, wailed that she would never see them in all her born days, and other women feared the voyage, that they would not outlive it, or would go down at sea.

"Such dread and lamentation," said Grace quietly, when all the letters were done and the ink had run out. "But you didn't write a letter for yourself." She looked at me, a question in her face.

I shook my head. I had said everything that was to be said to Maria or to Mrs Martin already, for now at least. "I have no letter to send at this moment. Perhaps when we arrive."

Then, on impulse, I added, "I am sailing in the hopes of

finding someone lost to me. I would have written to her, had I left her behind." She nodded, and for a moment took my hand and clasped it, and wished that I should find her.

That night, as we lay together as a mess, I heard how women wept, and then Grace spoke out, sweet and deep. "We should sing, now and again, as we leave. There is a song I know that the Scotch weavers used to sing, away as they were from their families. It was of two friends, soldiers, and how one was permitted to journey back to Scotland, and the other forced to give up his life. They would meet again, but not in this life."

She sang out low, and then, after a pause, those who knew it joined her and the rest of us hummed, so that the beams of our mess seemed to vibrate with the song.

Oh! ye'll take the high road and I'll take the low road,
And I'll be in Scotland afore ye;
But me and my true love
Will never meet again
On the bonnie, bonnie banks of Loch Lomond.

The wee birdie sang
And the wildflowers spring,
And in sunshine the waters are sleeping,
But the broken heart it kens
Nae second spring again,
Tho' the waeful may cease frae their greeting.

I sang along with the women, a long and sad lament, for none of us knew whether we would ever see those we loved again, whether they were behind us or already over the ocean.

Part Three
Australia, Mid-1820s Onwards

Chapter Thirty-Five

If I close my eyes against the fierce morning light, I can let the thread of time run backwards through my hand, travel back to life on the *Julia*. Those hundred days that hung between the past and the future.

The last day before we sailed, the ladies from Newgate came to say goodbye.

The rain came down in sheets that morning as the rowboat approached, but we were mustered all the same in ragged lines. There were four ladies in the boat, sitting upright as the rain came down. Elizabeth Fry looked white and sick as she was helped onto the ship and then a sailor came running, with a chair that he placed by her, so that she could sit down. Then the rain rolled away and the sailors lifted up tightly packed boxes, placed on deck and then levered open, one by one.

Out came tracts, Bibles, sermon books, books for children, straw for plaiting and material for knitting and sewing. There were aprons, caps, items for sewing, threads of all hues. We all looked at each other and smiled, for we could work now, occupy ourselves. Then came the food and other items – soap, combs, needles, scissors, sugar, tea, meat, lemon juice against the scurvy. There was chocolate, wine, and even black peppercorns, and also goods for the infirmary. Mr Wilson bowed and I saw at last how colour came back into Mrs Fry's cheeks and she rose and gathered her friends together. They went up and down the lines, handing out bed gowns, petticoats, linen, sheets and clothes for children. As she handed out our clothing and Bibles, I could not help myself; I spoke directly to her as she placed my goods in my outstretched hands.

"I was at Newgate. Perhaps you remember me?"

Mrs Fry looked up and studied me minutely, nodded.

"You held my Harry, very gently, when he was just a few weeks old." The feel of him as I held him, warm and kicking. "I never forget those with whom I worship. I gain as much as I give from my visits."

And then she added, "And now, my dear, you are bound for the other side of the world." Mrs Fry put her hand on my head for a moment and closed her eyes. "And your friend?"

How could Mrs Fry remember her, and how had that memory called forth such sorrow in both of us? I shook my head and stepped back, my eyes smarting, into the muster for I found that I could speak no longer.

Mrs Fry then took up her place by the cabin and her Friends gathered around her. I will remember this all my life, how her voice reached across the whole ship for it was powerful but sweet, and all the sailors stopped and listened, quite motionless even up in the rigging; even the gulls seemed to be silent for that first moment. "Before I leave you, before you leave England, I will read you Psalm 107, one for all prisoners who suffer."

A gull shrieked, and I opened my eyes and looked out, to where the river bent, and wondered what life would be like beyond that point, in the water that led beyond England and all that I had ever known for my twenty born years on this earth. I wondered if I would ever be free and if my suffering would end and I would find my Annie in that great land beyond.

Mrs Fry continued her reading, and her voice lifted as the psalm turned, and the chains were broken and the prisoners brought out of the utter darkness. And then she knelt down on the deck and, following her lead, the sailors and the women did likewise. She reminded all present of the parable of the prodigal son, and that whilst he was still far off, the Father saw him and had compassion for him. "The same is true for all of you, as you journey far from all you know," she said as the women wept. "Whatever happens, if you are willing to return to Him, He will be there with you." She continued to pray aloud, and her voice blended with the cries of the seagulls, the slop, slop, slop of the water and stifled sobs from many of the women. A silence settled. My eyes were swimming, but I did not know why as I did not believe the words I heard, yet even I was comforted.

The ladies gathered up their belongings. I saw how one woman, then another, stepped forward, knelt down and offered a convict prayer. Mrs Fry came towards me, one last time. "I hope that you find your friend, and I hope that you make new friends on this voyage, for as women our bonds of friendship are as precious as our husbands."

I opened my wet eyes to find the ladies collecting the letters that the women had written. One by one they climbed down the ladder to the longboat. As Mrs Fry left the ship she looked back, one long look, though whether it was at me or at all of us, I could not tell. Then the sun slid out from behind a cloud, and she was rowed away.

Grace struck up first, and then we took up her song again, and the sailors in the rigging joined in, so that at last the whole boat was ringing with our farewell chorus.

"But the broken heart it kens
Nae second spring again,
Tho' the weaful may cease frae their greeting."

I watched how Mrs Fry grew ever smaller, as the water streamed off the uplifted oars, and danced in the grey sunlight. Then they reached the point where the river bent, the song came to an end and she could be seen no more.

At last, on a cold May morning, New South Wales was in sight. We had talked so many times when we were shut in at night: backwards to the lives we left behind, and forwards, to the lives we might lead when we landed. I remembered one of the few times Annie and I had talked in the Ship, seeing me look at her all dressed up and ready to be taken, paid for in hard-earned money by working men. She looked long back at me and said, we do not have so many choices, women like us. This is for survival, she had said, and I wished that I had not turned away as if I could not see her like that, my mouth twisting. After the silence she had walked away then turned back and said that she hoped she would be forgiven, all the same. This dead feeling in my heart, that last night, as I wondered how much she had done for me, and how little I had cared to ask her.

I am there again, as the candles gutter on that last night. The sailors have carried the chests down to our mess, loosened the lids and clambered back up. I open them, start to pass our items out. So little for each of us, we have so little with which to start over. Just for a moment, right at the end, I hold my paper package to me, feel the familiar crackle, breathe in the scent that is long gone, slide it again underneath my head and lie down for the last time on board.

At dawn we wake and rise together and we wash and dress in our best clothes and silently help each other plait and put up our hair. Everything we have done on this voyage we are doing for the last time as a company of women.

Chapter Thirty-Six

We sail into Sydney Cove on a fine autumn May morning. The world turned upside down, right enough. As we near the quay other boats slide alongside, and there are men in them who look us up and down with hunger in their eyes, although they remain silent and the captain looks down at them with venom.

From deck I wonder if I am dreaming to see these miles and miles of sand and wooded shore and then we are in safe harbour. I look out, and find I am clutching at Jennet and Grace.

The streets are uneven, but the houses have gardens and I can see vegetables and fruit growing in them, and chickens and pigs grubbing for food inside wooden pens. I see a quantity of butchered beasts lying outside a great shop and the men with cleavers and bloody aprons. I look away. The houses are made of stone mostly but there are also huts, higher up where the roads run out between the rocks. There are stores too, and women working in the yards. Others gather water from the public well, or shop, or are even bathing. There is order, but also chaos, for the streets are crooked and unlevel, and the throng immense. Houses perch on the slopes.

We are disembarked and then together we are helped up and onto land. Everything is swaying. We hold onto each other, form a circle of eight as our luggage is heaped up by us. I smell the sea, blood, spices that tickle the nose. London but not London, something else, somewhere else.

The captain comes towards us with papers in his hands. "Jennet will go to the work factory, Grace too. You have farming experience, Hannah?"

"Yes, as a child."

"Wait here."

He gestures for everyone to step aside, except me, but for a moment we huddle together and embrace. We promise to find each other, though how will we do it without addresses? But I tell them, desperately, "I will find you, somehow."

The captain speaks then, seeing our faces. "The newspapers here are full of articles, the names of those assigned often appear in them. It is quite possible to trace somebody, or even place a notice that you are seeking them." I wonder how we will ever pay for such a thing, but it is a sliver of hope.

Then the captain tells them that they must go to the factory and I feel their arms around me, one last time. We have loved each other on this journey and now Grace and Jennet pick up their bundles, their crates are loaded onto a boat and I watch as they embark and are rowed away, upriver, the vision blurs before me and I cannot see them any more. I am completely alone now.

The captain taps me on the shoulder. "You can milk, you said?" I rub at my eyes with my sleeve. The ground stills at last.

Beside him is a tall man, perhaps in his thirties, brown-skinned and with light blue eyes. He carries a leather hat in one hand, a bag in the other.

"I grew up in service, on a farm in the county of Norfolk." I hesitate. "I was born on one, sir, in the east of England. I lived on a farm with my mama, until she died when I was still a child. I used to milk the cows and perform other tasks." Not all of the truth, but enough.

"And could you nurse a little, when I cannot, when I am out, working?" He adds but his voice is jerky, "My wife is ailing."

"Yes, sir. I nursed my mistress. With my mother, as I was just a child." The truth again, measured out. I see the farmer's wife, the spills of opium, and how small her coffin had been, how light. I can bear this.

He turns to the captain, and together they walk over to a table, sign some paperwork and thus I am assigned to work as a servant to Frank Emerson, farmer. I sign my name, and he tells me, "We are sailing to Newcastle, north from here, and then on by river. But first we will eat."

He leads me through the streets and as I look around me, I wonder how it can be that so much is familiar, and yet I am on the other side of the world. The water is crowded with boats and seabirds calling above. He looks down at me.

"It was a speck of a place decades ago, I was told, but inhabited all the same, with people who came and went. We are not the first people here." He points out to the harbour and I look more closely, see that there are canoes amongst the larger boats, with black men and women in them. "You are not shocked to see them?" he asks and I shake my head.

"London is thronged with people from many places. But I did not know that was true here as well. I know nothing of this place." He looks down at me fleetingly, as if he would say more, but then walks on, away from the harbour.

I see long squat buildings that he tells me are barracks for soldiers. There is a stone church with a clock tower and huts and cottages running up the hills away from the waterline. There are even handsome villas, shining in the sun like the houses I had glimpsed walking up west to see Bridget. There are also men, chained together, working on a road.

"The census was taken here in the summer, and the city has nearly 40,000 inhabitants," he says, as we enter the inn. "It has grown fast since I first came here." I put the question aside of when he had come here and from where.

At the inn the bill of fare is short and Emerson selects a dark meat stew for us both. It looks hearty but I hesitate all the same before I take up the spoon, so soft that when I bite on it, I leave marks. It must be tin, I think. "It's an animal called a kangaroo. It's good meat when stewed, but tough. I try not to eat it unless I have to, for it's a fine animal to see, for it is as big as a man, and jumps around. But there is nothing else here today, so we must make do." I thank him and eat and put aside the thoughts of Mama, hiding the rich dark meat under her spoon. I must not think of the past.

We sail with the tides as the day darkens. I am put in a cabin with a pig that squeals all night, along with the mail. I hardly sleep and the weather worsens, and I wake up to see lights guttering in the passageway and sailors walking past, their faces set. Just before dawn Mr Emerson brings me a cup of water.

He takes me up on deck as dawn breaks and I look out on blue skies and silver fish, leaping in and out of the water. I can just see, if I narrow my eyes, that there is a harbour in the distance, and houses glinting in the sun. "The river empties itself out into the harbour, just past Nobby's Island. The harbour narrows between the island

and the point. There is a bar, and the water breaks there, and it cannot be crossed until the water deepens. Tide's turning. We should be able to round Nobby's soon."

The most he has spoken since I met him. We sail into safety and again, as we disembark, I sway. I feel it before I see it, an arm tucked under mine for support, and a shock goes through me, to be touched by a stranger, but not unpleasant. He releases me without a word when I stand steady again. We both look around. "It changes, every time I come here. There are now bakeries, a butcher, carpenters, all tradesmen. I can buy everything here," he says. "Even tea and sugar." There are new houses all around, with flourishing gardens, and at the harbour's edge great quantities of long red logs. He follows my eyes, sees everything. "Cedar," he says. I feel something rise in me, my old curiosity, to see so many strange things around me, familiar at the same time.

He walks on and I look at the sea once more; I see a great grey seabird swoop, catch a fish from the water and fly away with it wriggling in its beak. The silver moving thing glints and flaps and then falls quite still as the bird flies on with it. He speaks.

"A sea eagle. They take fish but I've seen them swoop down and even take a duck." He looks swiftly at me then and adds, "We're going upriver while the tides are with us."

We sit down low in a wide boat, and are rowed on by two silent men. The river is deep and wide and nothing like the shallows of the Waveney, where the water had run clear and the sun had shone on the pebbles at the bottom and the fish had swum, under and over my hands. I can see nothing in the water when I look down, and I shiver for a moment, for the riverbanks are dark with tall trees right down to their edge, silver barks shining.

My master looks at me again.

"We call them gum trees or eucalypts. They can be burned and they give off a scent. I built my first hut with a bark roof, made from trees such as them. It's still weathertight and the men sleep there." He looks out at the landscape, quite content. "If you are lucky, you'll catch sight of koalas. They cling to the trunks, eat the leaves. They are peaceful animals."

I am alone on a river thousands of miles from my home and how could I ever have thought that I could find Annie here? The sadness settles in me, familiar, weighting me down with the old ballast. I feel the heaviness of a bird swoop over me, and I jerk away as it flies on, a flash of blue and black. "Our magpies," Emerson says. He rummages in his bag, brings out a shawl. "Put this over your head and look out over the water. You will see their reflection first; steel yourself. But they are only aggressive in the spring when they are protecting their young. At other times, they sing almost sweetly." I see the magpies I know in my mind's eye, the same blue-black, but a coarse defiant caw.

Then the river bends and the landscape opens up and there are two residences, with the land cleared right down to the river. There are neat fields and a windmill, its sails moving slowly, and then again, we row on, and the gum trees cluster back down by the banks and the sky is darkening. There are rivulets and in one I see two open boats, rowed by dark figures, and they look around and then back and disappear into the landscape. He sees me looking. "This land belonged to them, long before we came." Then he is silent again, and looks away. He is telling me something and I catch at it, want to know more, for whatever it is troubles him.

We glide past another small settlement, with a fine house with brand new sash windows fronting the river, and a verandah that runs the width of it, and on it a lady sitting in a chair, with a shawl tucked around her shoulders. Mr Emerson raises a hand to her and she does likewise. We glide on, past a whole herd of horned cattle, grazing on the meadows.

"We have a herd of thirty-seven, all healthy and quiet too," he says.

The river narrows again and for a moment, I do not know why, I dip my hand into the water, and then I pull it out again, sharpish, for here it runs dark and deep and everything is strange.

Chapter Thirty-Seven

We alight onto a riverbank, just as the sun is leaving the sky. I look around as I take my goods from the boat. The pastureland has been cleared of trees and reaches down to the water. A herd of healthy cows graze quietly in the field and then two men come walking, crying out to the cows. A smaller flock of sheep huddle together nearby.

I close my eyes and listen to the sound of the cows going in for milking, and the years roll away like a carpet up for beating and I am a child again, hearing the farmer touch their flanks, softly saying, "Gooo on in."

In front of me, as I open my eyes, is a small, neat house with a verandah stretching round it. Washing hangs on poles and sticks and the master sees me looking and says, "We can dry clothing at any time of day there, and it protects us from the worst of the sun. I built it after my first harvest came in," and then he strides towards the house, eager to get inside. He points, hastily, to two huts at some distance from the house.

"I lived there when I first landed here. Now the men live there. You will live in the house; I have a room prepared for you."

As we step into the house, he calls out a welcome, and

then a faint sound is heard, and he drops his bag and runs to an open door and closes it behind him.

I look around, at a clean, neat room, with a fireplace stoked up and guarded all around, and with a table set already for tea, with mugs and a quart pot, on a blue and white tablecloth. A silver candlestick stands in the centre, the stub worn down low. He must want tea, as I do. I lift up the kettle and it has been filled already, so I boil the water and make the tea.

He comes out with a closed pail, which he places carefully on the verandah, then goes over to a bucket and washes himself. "I made tea, sir. Should I take some to your wife?"

His words come thickly, although he holds up the tea cup and thanks me.

"Eleanor sleeps now. She can take tea when she wakes. I will take it to her today, introduce you to her tomorrow."

A silence, then he says, as if reluctantly, "She is lingering. It may not be long now."

I do not know what to say, for how should I comfort him, my master? And what does it mean for me – the thought comes quick. He pushes his chair back, clatters the cups together and says that he will show me where to wash the kitchen items the next morning. Then he lights a lamp for me, and shows me my room. It is a clean room and this is something I realise about my master. He keeps everything spick and span by choice. I walk over to the window, and notice that he has tacked up a sheet of sprigged cotton, and I wonder who has sewn the quilt on the bed, for the stitching is delicate. I can hear the river but the birds are silent now. I unpack what I need for the night, and slide Mama's dress underneath the mattress. I fall asleep holding the edge of it, as if it might keep me safe.

I am woken by the birds yelling at dawn, even louder

and more urgent than in Norfolk. I try and distinguish the cries, but I do not recognise the clamour and all of a sudden I feel utterly homesick. I dress hurriedly and wash my face in a pitcher of clean water.

I see him silhouetted, standing by the kitchen window, a clear square of glass looking over the landscape. A morning fog lies over the river so that it has disappeared and it is tinged with pink. It drifts away, slowly, as I join him, but the birds sing on insistently and are joined by other sounds, scraping, a kind of low purring as well as a low clatter. I feel something rise in me, and I remember that this is how I felt when I heard London at dawn, standing on the steps with Jane, looking out. I want to know this place.

He offers me water. "You can drink as much as you wish, for it is clean and plentiful. We will milk the cows, and then after breakfast I will introduce you to my wife."

A pause, then he asks, "The birds woke you?"

I nod, and he says, "I remember that, when I first came, the clamour of it." He points out to a tree. "A quantity of birds roost there and about here. A regular chorus in the morning: magpie morning calls, parakeets, and sometimes a kingfisher. But not the same as in England. They laugh and can kill snakes. Listen."

We stand in silence. I hear a *chip, chip, chip*. "Robin, brown-breasted I think," he says. The chips become a chorus, and the sounds stir something like happiness in me, coming thick and fast and urgent.

I hear a robin that looks like a blue tit, a thrush and even a blackbird. The sound of my childhood, a pigeon. A rasping sound that he tells me is made by a bird called a cockatoo.

We put our cups down and walk outside. He closes the door carefully, stops and listens.

"A choir," he says. I am puzzled. He points up to four

black and white birds. "Pied butcherbirds." I follow their sound as they fluff up their breasts and one calls to another. "A regular choir," he says. The birds distract me. "They can mimic too. But best of all is how they sing a part each."

When we arrive at the barn I sit on one of the two milking stools and lean against the heifer. She moves slightly until I reach my rhythm, one, two, one, two. A faint steam comes from the warm milk, and the smell of the barn takes me way back.

"She loved to do this," the master says, as we finish the milking and he offers me a cup of milk. "She was from the West Country and I bought her these cows as a present, for her birthday last year. Before that we had just sheep and two goats."

But now she was too ill, and the doctor had visited, and shaken his head, for she had a growth in her that could not be taken out. There was nothing that could be done for her, except to relieve her pain, and relieve her of all work. "We had three good years together," he says. "Before the pain came, in her stomach."

He offers me a second cup, seeing how I drink it down fast, and then a flat bread that he tells me is called damper and is eaten here when there is no yeast to be had. When I have finished, we rise and he takes me around the house, showing me my duties.

The first time I see my mistress, I stand by the door awkwardly. She is lying underneath a quantity of blankets, and I see her thin brown hair has been neatly plaited. He beckons me across and she reaches out a hand to take mine, puts it to her cheek. I crouch down, and see how her skin is pale and stretched. I remember this, how at the end the good wife was so thin that I felt as if she was bone only.

Eleanor pats the bed. I look at the master and he nods, drops a kiss on her forehead and leaves.

Her voice is weak but clear and when she speaks, her voice is like Annie's, the same swing of the voice, the burr in her throat. West Country girls, with a stride that suits the hills and the coombes of a green landscape, the gentle drop to a valley, the climb up on the other side.

"Tell me about yourself, Hannah Tyrell."

I sit down. She is looking at me. Her eyes are a startling deep green and I wonder for a moment what she looked like, and how they fitted together, when they were man and wife and she was well.

"I don't know where to start," I tell her, smoothing down the bedclothes. I don't know what to tell her, or what to leave aside.

She points to her water, and I hold her head gently in my hands as she drinks. Her skull, the skin stretched so tightly over it. Even that effort tires her. She whispers, after a moment, "Tell me how you arrived here. Or rather, what brought you here."

Annie brought me here, I think. Annie, but Mama too and my own crimes, committed out of love, because we were poor and saw no other way to rescue ourselves, each other. I cannot help it; tears spring in my eyes and I brush them away.

My voice wavers and shakes, then grows stronger as I speak.

"I was sent into service," I start, and she takes my hand again, and I realise that my stories might help her hold on. More; I want her to hear them, I want to say all of this out loud. I take a breath and then I take the thread of my tale in my hand and follow it back, all the way to Great Yarmouth, and how everything started with my mama and the storm that wrecked her.

Chapter Thirty-Eight

When Frank comes in, exhausted from a day's work, water dripping from his face where he has splashed himself fast to clean the sweat off, he finds me with his wife, feeding her broth. He sits down on a chair on the other side of the bed and he takes the spoon from me, smiling, and I rise and leave. They shouldn't have to leave each other like this.

We do the evening milking together, and he breaks the silence between us as the milk gushes into the buckets. "Thank you for today. My wife liked talking to you."

I think about what I have told her, when she was awake and then when she fell asleep. I wonder, now, how much she heard, and how much she passed on.

The days pass, and I take over her general duties, as well as looking after her as best I can. I will wash clothes, sew, mend, cook and clean. They keep chickens, and we barter the eggs we do not need, and the dairy takes the milk we do not use, rowed upriver promptly to the town each morning. The money we earn from that is used to pay for cloth, tea, sugar. There is ample firewood, and clean water from a lagoon. The four convict men are all from Ireland, and they speak Gaelic, a little English. They keep away from me at first, but I feel their eyes on me. Frank tells me that they were unlucky, that they miss their families and will send for them when they are free men, if they can earn enough for the passage. He tells me this so I am not afraid, I think, so I see them as the men they were and could be again. I learn their names and those of their wives, their children.

In the evening, he takes up sheets of paper and charcoal and sketches, silently. I find that I am watching him, and he looks up and turns one sheet towards me, then another. Sketches of his life here, he explains, of how he and the men log the cedar together, rope it and float it as rafts downriver. Sketches of the animals he sees here, and of a man, young, tall and dark, surrounded by sheep, smiling. "Phillip Williams," he says. "He lives across the river, in the big house. He keeps the biggest flock of sheep for miles around." Another sheet of paper, with details on it, of fencing, bark and farm tools. He has drawn the life he lived alone, and then with his wife, since he came here four years earlier to break the land.

"I heard from other sailors of good country beyond Newcastle, up the coast north from Sydney, and how men had felled timber along the river, and then left spaces open for settlement. I asked again and again, to find out if anyone had a claim on the land. I could find none, and so I applied for a grant."

He gets up for a moment, searches in the drawer and brings me a painting. I see the familiar curve of the river, but there is no sign of the place where we sit now. Instead, it is all trees, so dense that they grow sideways over the river. I shiver. There is a darkness there that frightens me but I cannot put a word to why. His voice breaks through and I follow it, hold fast to the thread. He talks fast and it is comforting, to hear how he came here, how he worked to make this place I see around me, this shelter.

"First, I threw up a hut, where the men live now. I brought two oxen with a slide upriver to the hut, for there was no wheelwright that first year. I cleared twenty-five acres on my own and then the men were assigned to me. We dug out the lagoon first, so we had water, and then month after month things changed. A wheelwright came, so we could have a cart, and he was a blacksmith too. I built a dam so the bullock could fetch me water, and store it. I made a house, wattle and daub, the other place where the men live."

He dug a garden, constructed timber sheds, and made pigsties. They hoed by hand or with the oxen, and then he bought a plough. He planted wheat and barley, tobacco and then an orchard of cherries and peaches. When he arrived here, meat was scarce. He would take his gun and kill wallaby or even a parrot or pigeon to eke out his rations. If he needed company, he would ride on horseback to visit neighbours, or punt across the river to visit other settlers. When he had first come, he had broken the land with a mattock and hoe to sow seed.

One of his men absconded, and was found in Newcastle. The man was sent to the bench and sentenced to flogging. Frank had no part in it.

"I wanted no man whipped on my account." He brushes his arm across his face, as if it pains him to recall it. "Fifty lashes and I was ordered to be present. No one should be flogged; I will never permit it here. He was cut around his throat, under the armpits. We brought him back here, treated him as well as we could. I hope never to see a man cry like that again. I will never forget that when I undressed him his shoes were full of blood." He stops abruptly. Changes tack.

He sent for Eleanor, a year after he had arrived. He had asked again if anyone had a claim on the land he was seeking to clear next, and again, found none. By the time Eleanor had arrived, III days after leaving Plymouth, he had cleared 200 acres.

"Her whole family gathered at the quay to say goodbye and they sang to her as she looked on at them. The only family I had known. They took me in when mine died, entrusted their daughter to me."

My eyes prickle but I do not know if it is for her or for him.

At first, they thought perhaps the child they had longed for had come, for her stomach was swollen. The pain made her gasp and so Frank sent for the doctor from Newcastle. "I think she knew before I did that the pain was not normal. Or rather, we both did, but could not own it to each other until the doctor told us. She might never see another harvest come in, or see her family."

He wipes his eyes on his sleeve. "They thought I could protect her. But I couldn't, not from this."

At the end, she fails quickly. We take turns to sleep in the room next to her bed. I talk to her, all the same. Before she dies, she squeezes my hand and I see tears running down her cheeks, as she looks at a picture of the landscape that he has painted for her. She says, "Stay with him." With another effort she says, "Hannah, promise me that you will write down what you cannot say out loud." I kept both those promises.

She dies in August, three months after I arrived, four years after she had arrived in Sydney. The minister who had married them lays her to rest, and the church is full and all of us shaking from the winter cold. Frank cannot talk, and so Phillip Williams takes his words and speaks for him, of how he had sent for his wife, and how they had dreamed of making a life together here, and having a family to run wild by a river, a flash of kingfisher, a swirl of starlings in their minds. At the end, he pauses, holds up one of Frank's sketches. It is of Eleanor as she was, and I see that Phillip and Frank are both weeping. A pen portrait, on yellowing paper. She sits on the verandah, looking out on the river, laughing up at her husband as he sketches her. A world away from where they had first become sweethearts, walking up and down over the hills of the West Country.

Frank listens, with his head down, and he cannot stop the tears; they flow even when Williams has sat down and the minister takes his place. When the service is done, she is hoisted onto the shoulders of the four Irishmen, Frank and Williams at the front. I see the men draw breath for a moment, as if the burden is lighter than they expected. Our breath steams out in the air. A grave has been dug, and she is lain gently within. First Frank, then Phillip, throw earth, then turn away. Williams puts his arm around Frank, and the master turns, hides his face in his coat.

I linger, wondering what I can do as they separate.

"I can send one of the shepherds over to you, you'll need the help. He knows your men from back home." Frank hesitates, then thanks Williams.

We drink tea together later, for neither of us can eat.

He speaks. "You never knew her as she was. Before the cancer came." And adds, softly, "I am the only one on this continent who knew her truly, for what she was. I sent word to England, to her family." His voice breaks for the pain he could not spare them.

"I'm sorry for your loss, Mr Emerson." The words are not enough, but are all I can say.

He wipes his eyes.

"I have written off for you, Hannah, so that you can apply for your ticket of leave. You should be free to go."

Single men could not have convict women working for them. I will be free, but I cannot return to London.

"But you could stay. I can pay you a wage to work here, the same as any man. But I will need to write to the superintendent and make it right for you."

I stammer then, "Thank you, I will reflect on this." I know my mind already, but it is too soon to tell him.

He rises then, and goes into the bedroom. I have cleaned it since I laid her out, and the linen is fresh. Behind the door I hear him sob, as if his heart has broken. All I can do is stay on. I press hard down on the thought that rises, that I should leave and seek Annie. I wouldn't even know where to start, but it is more than that. I want to be here, with him.

Chapter Thirty-Nine

E very day the weather turns and the light lasts longer, and I take up my sewing again, for I am using rags to make another quilt and Frank sets chairs out on the verandah, sets a lamp by each one, trims it. I sew in silence and Frank sketches. The brush of charcoal, pencil, on paper. Out there, a humming sound from the cicadas, the flow of the water.

"You said you were a mariner," I say, one evening when my back hurts and my eyes are tired, putting aside my sewing. He looks up from his work. I hear frogs, then silence.

He tells me that he came first as a whaler, like other British men, for the call went out to men who knew the sea like him to join the crews. Went up and down sealing and whaling from America to the Cape of Good Hope.

"Everything in between as well. I arrived in Sydney Cove like you. Left Eleanor behind, with her family, and promised I would send for her as soon as I could. I whaled in the bay and in deeper waters too, all around Sydney Cove and down to Van Diemen's Land. Saw the skills of the men and women who lived here first, as I told you."

He was whaling when I was on a hulk in the Thames.

The whole sea in front of him, a free man, and my ship a prison.

He gets up, pulls out an older book of sketches, and puts them on the kitchen table. I walk over and we stand there together, in the lamplight. So close that I feel his warmth, although we do not touch. Instead I watch his hand, brown and strong, as he turns the drawings over, one by one, as he describes what Sydney was like, when he arrived on the south side of the cove, nearby the Rocks. "Tents there, some huts, a few government buildings. Nothing much like what you saw when you came." In a quick hand I see how he has captured what he saw back then. Men in chains and other men and women in open boats, looking on as their world changed forever. For worse. They had no choice either but to watch as things were taken from them, for when they fought they were punished for it.

He goes back to the sea. "It was a young man's game and I liked it well. A change from farming in the West Country. I wanted something more, spent nearly four years at sea, sending letters to Eleanor from wherever we landed up." A catch in his throat and then he talks, rapidly. The past is easier to go to for him; it holds no sorrow except that he realises that he lived all those days apart from her, and for nothing.

"We had a lookout who signalled to us from higher ground, and then we would race to the boats. The cook would run alongside, hand us beef and damper – no time to cook on board. We set off, three boats at a time, and looking up all the time at our lookout, with the headsman steering. I was the harpooner."

"When we were close, I threw the first harpoon, on a long line. Once we hit, we tired the whale out. The pulling hands had to resist for the whale could tow us out further than we could row back easily. I would wait for my moment, finish him with a lance. The easiest were the bay whales, slow swimmers."

He glances at me.

"I grew sick of it, the water full of blood. I found that I wanted to sketch them alive in the water, not spear them and kill them, harvest them. I wanted to be at peace, send for Eleanor, settle up somewhere. We came here."

He steers away from violence, this man. I find my voice.

"It is a peaceful place, this."

He pushes his chair back, carries his sketches and the lamp back into the house. I follow him.

"Goodnight, Hannah," he says. I wish him goodnight. I see him pause briefly, hand on the door jamb, looking in. I wonder what he is thinking. How I had wondered if I could call my mama back by will alone. How I had realised, even as a child, what futility felt like. Then he goes in, and all is silent.

Chapter Forty

The days fall into shape. We rise early, work hard, go to bed early. On occasion he has a newspaper and reads aloud to me. I like his voice. He fetches books from Newcastle and one day a letter about me, which he gives to me with a question on his face. I have my ticket of leave. I can seek a post, paid. I can marry. I cannot go back to England but here I am free. I tell him that I will stay till the spring. I tell myself I want to see the land in four seasons. I push away the thoughts of Annie, where she is, if she survives. I cannot tell him yet; I do not even want to complicate this.

Despite all of this I find myself watching Frank, as though I am under some sort of spell. I see how he shows care, for the animals, his materials, the men, even me. I find that I care too; I have grown to care about him.

One night I am darning clothes that have unravelled, for myself and for him. He offers to read for me, for it is painstaking work and I like to do it well, as Mama would have wanted me to do, her dear papa before her. I take up my yarn and I mend. He reads to me from an old Scottish novel, about clans and battles, honour and love, and I find the story compels me to lay my work down and for a moment, I close my eyes and perhaps I even fall asleep to the sound of his voice. I open my eyes and find that he has stopped reading, and is smiling at me as he looks on.

I rise and so does he; he puts his arms around me and then, as I fall to him, everything seems to whirl around me, even when he has caught me, holds me quite safe. I look at him and into his eyes. I trace his face with my fingers. Rough with hair underneath the skin, pushing through. Not like Annie, a skin like smooth silk. I need to push those thoughts away. I am here now.

"I like how you look, close to me," he says, simply.

I stroke his face again, and feel the square jaw, his fine nose. He takes my fingers away, kisses them one by one and then he holds my hands in his. His fingers are rough from the work. I must rub in ointment, so that they are smooth again, at the end of each working day. I feel a burst of joy and then he lets me go; his eyes cloud over.

"It's too soon," I say. He brings me to him again, hesitates. Then kisses me, light and fleeting, on the forehead.

"Yes, I think so, but the time will come." He takes my hand, walks with me to my room, opens the door. I see how he lingers there for a moment, and then the door is closed and I lie down and I am smiling. I can sweep the past to one side, be here now with him, in this quiet place.

Since that moment we have not spoken of that evening. Eleanor lingers everywhere: in the neat blue crockery from England, her books, a pile of letters, her clothes. I use what she brought with her every day. She is still here. I see him, in the evening, leafing through his sketches and sometimes an indrawn breath and then a sigh. I do not go to him as he presses the pictures to him of how she was. If he could raise the dead from paper, he would, and I would too, for his sake.

I wash and dry and sweep the floor one evening, and hover by the window in the kitchen. A square of blue light in front of me, and the birds wheel; I hear the magpies carol, then come into roost, and all falls silent. From behind I feel him join me, and then his arms go around me and we are one body, resting together, looking out.

He turns me towards him and I am touched by light as the moon slides out over the river and falls on us.

"One day," he says, "perhaps you will marry me."

It cannot be this easy to be happy. I hesitate, and he speaks on.

"I loved her, and she died. I will never stop loving her, but I love you."

He stops, then, and waits for me. To tell my story, all of it.

I move away from him and sit down by the fire. He sits down opposite, and looks at me.

I cannot buy my happiness on a lie, as I did once before. Annie rises up before me, a girl with golden hair, lifting her bonnet. Then she is gone. Not her, not yet. One day, when I can fix her in the past, or find her. Instead, I tell him everything else.

The candles gutter in the soft night air and the moonlight travels across the floor. "I need to tell you something first," and my voice catches on the words, as my memory takes me back to the cold spring evening when my first life ended.

I had only told my story before for people who judged Mama and me: the men in Harleston; the committee members at the refuge; at the Old Bailey; at the penitentiary; at the Ship Jem Summers had ripped my story from me. It had been noted down in minutes. The powerful had described me, judged me, fixed me in their words. Now I find my way through my story and I tell him almost everything, and the years fall away from me and I weep. I feel him rise and come to me and he weeps too, for the child I was, the woman he lost.

He tells me that he must send to Sydney, ask the superintendent of convicts if we might marry. I sit next to him as he writes the letter, and before he sets each sentence down on paper he reads it out loud, and I nod.

"Hannah Tyrell came to work with me when I needed a dairy maid and when my wife Eleanor was dying. She died earlier this year, nursed with real kindness by Miss Tyrell. I have asked Miss Tyrell to be my wife. She is free by servitude and I can earn a comfortable livelihood for a family, if we have one."

The petition is granted, and we are to marry in the church.

Some days before we are to be wed, I unwrap my mama's dress and wash it carefully. As I rub it, I feel how soft and thin the fabric is. Yet the flowers she embroidered are as bright as ever and the stitches she had made sit out proud of the butter-soft muslin and when I slip it on, I find that it fits almost perfectly, outlines the curves I have, inherited from her. I take it off with all due care and wrap it up again, for he cannot see me wear it before the day. I am nearly the same age that my mama was when she died. I will go on past her and leave her behind me, younger than I am.

On the day he brings me a garland of flowers from the valley. The men give me a bouquet to carry and a Gaelic blessing. I thank them, and I wish that their wives were here with them, their children. But still they beam at us, and we walk to the church together.

Williams is there, alone as usual, in his wooden pew halfway down the church. Then we are married and the men burst out in a rhythmic clapping, just for a moment, and Williams joins them and the whole building echoes with it until it is ended.

"I'm glad to see this," he said, slapping Frank's arm and smiling at him, and then at me.

"Will you be next?" Frank asks; he is beaming and so am I.

Williams says, carefully, squeezing our hands, "I think not but I sometimes wonder what it would be like, to have a child in this place."

Then he takes his leave and walks away. I watch him pass, and then he is joined by another man, a tall carpenter, his black dog on a long leash. They talk and then shake hands as the carpenter walks away, down to the ferry, and I notice that both of them look back at each other.

This is our wedding day, yet we still work as normal, although the men milk the cows that day as a gift to us.

We cook and wash like any other day and at last everything is done and I take off my apron and sit down, carefully, in Mama's dress by the fire. Frank sits opposite and then he comes to me, and kneels at my feet. I put my hand to his head and stroke his hair. When I yawn, he turns his head to me, his face in shadow, and then he stands up and pulls me to him, and we walk hand in hand to our bedroom.

I left the quilt Eleanor had stitched on the bed they had shared. She is a presence here, fading into the landscape, into yellowed sketches. The moonlight travels across the floor as we stand together, one entwined shadow. He moves away from me, and I slide my arms upwards so that he can help me take off my dress. The fabric snags and tears. He cries out.

But it doesn't matter. I have carried the dress with me across years and thousands of miles and I married him in it. I take it off and fold it gently and put it on the chair. I turn back to him and I find that I am shivering as I slip my nightgown over my head. He takes my shawl and wraps it tight to me, then pulls me down to the bed.

He is holding out a package to me, done up in paper and string, and we take an end each, pull it loose. He brings the lamp nearer and inside I see a painting, a magical procession of animals that he has seen on all the journeys that brought us to this place. There is a whale, blowing water down by the river; a kangaroo and her child, hopping; the magpies in the trees and koalas eating gum leaves. There are parakeets and robins flying. At the far end of the painting is an oak tree, full of the birds that we left behind us in the valleys and the hills, in Norfolk and the West Country. The light flickers on the painting and it blurs in front of me. He takes my shawl and wipes my face and I tell him it is beautiful and ask him if he can frame it and put it on the wall so I can see it every day. He rises then to place it straight and safe and then he comes to me again and takes my hand.

I have never lain with a man, and for a moment I freeze. I have drawn one person to me. She was like me, so I did not know where each of us began and ended, and now he is here, different and quite strange to me. But then he puts out the lamp, lays his hand on the back of my neck, and draws me to him.

Chapter Forty-One

Another day we are in Newcastle, getting in provisions. Frank takes me by the arm and we walk along the main street, away from the sea. There are other women walking with their menfolk, in much the same way. Something I had carried, for as long as I was sensible, has been lifted from me. I am not an object of any undue attention.

"You're thinking of something," he says, and ties my bonnet on, for the ribbon was coming loose, and adds, smiling at me, "Mrs Emerson." And the name thrills me, to be married to Frank, to be with him as his wife, to live here quietly.

As summer comes, the dawn is earlier, and I wake to the birds yelling, a great clamour of them, shriller and more urgent than before. One morning I wake to find Frank gone already. Some days he leaves me sleeping, creeps out before the light has made its way across the room, milks alone.

I slip my shift over my head and brush my breasts. They feel different, heavier, and I look down and see that my nipples are darker and rounder, like a spill of tea across a table. My stomach rounds gently.

I had seen Mama look down at her body, as I was doing now, and then her mouth had tightened and she had glanced away so that I would not see her face, stricken, panicked. Annie had gone through this alone, and given her baby away. A promise on a piece of cloth, a running stitch between two names.

I walk to the milking parlour. Frank is sitting on a stool, and I can see that the buckets are full already. He sees me in the doorframe.

I sit down next to him and feel how my stomach curves out and my breath is shorter. I take his hand and place it on me and then I tell him, as his other hand rests on the teat of the cow. He is quite still, and then his arms go around me, and his face, unshaven, is next to mine and he covers me with kisses and we are both crying.

I had thought, if I ever had a child, that I would raise it with Annie, that she would be there when I gave birth. And I think of her letter, and how much she lost, and I realise I must tell him more. That night I take a deep breath and take his dear hand in mine and I speak.

"I had a friend at the refuge."

He says nothing, but he takes my hand and holds it to his cheek.

So I start at the beginning, when Annie had arrived in the refuge, all the way to when we parted, angry, and I thought I would never see her ever again in my born days but that she had written to me, and she had sailed before me and given up a child before she left. I tell him so much, but how can I tell him that we had lain together, breast on breast, bone on bone, swaying inside the hammock as the light outside kindled into dawn? That the first time I had kissed her I had felt a wild softness, pushing and yielding but that was so long ago that I can hardly remember the feel of her. That what I thought of as love was weighted and troubled and full of secrets, almost from the start. When I am with him it is nothing like that. I am safe and happy and light in every way. I keep the promise I made to his wife. *Write down what you cannot say out loud.*

I finish my story and I realise that I do not even know what I am asking him for, what I dare ask. I only know that I have put my trust in this man, that I do not believe he will ever do me harm. He draws me close now and I hold my breath.

"We can write to the factories. We can seek to discover where she might be. Someone will know. If we look for her, I believe that we can find her. Bring her here."

I hold him then and thank him, and see no shadow in his face. A thought rises: if he knew her, would he be so kind? I push it away. I will not bring damage into our life; I have to promise him that.

We scour the shipping lists in the newspapers, and read all the news that we can find. We write to all the work factories for women, as far afield as Van Diemen's Land. Frank reads me articles in the evenings. I have started to sew and knit clothes for the baby.

The newspapers say that women like me are full of iniquity and that those still in the factories are the worst. My friends had been sent there. I cannot understand how anyone could think that Jennet or Grace should be punished even more than they were by being transported. I wonder what crime class they have been assigned to and how much Jennet is understood; if Grace speaks out, for she finds it hard to keep quiet when she sees injustice. I wish I could find them all, find work for them, spread my luck out over all of them. But first I must find Annie.

The conditions in the work factories are harsh, for these women are criminals, the newspaper declares. They wash in cold water from a trough in the yard, they are issued with clothing and everything personal is taken away from them. I wonder what happened to those gowns we folded away so carefully and that my friends had put on again for the first morning on shore. Instead they wore brown serge and were issued with other clothes as well, cotton and flannel and one straw bonnet apiece. This was all like the prisons we had ever been in, all over again.

I learn that if they were assigned to First and Second Class, they would be employed in tasks such as oakum picking, wool picking, carding, cleaning and needlework. I could not imagine that they were put in Third Class, for that meant stone breaking. Jennet weeping, Grace organising. I hope they are assigned. It must be better than the factory. I wonder why I am distracting myself with my friends, when underneath pulses this thought: *find Annie.*

Two days later a new paper arrives. I have unravelled a jumper, so that I can knit the yarn up again into bonnets for the baby. Frank holds the yarn for me as I roll it up, and I cast on as he reads out another article. He glances at me as he reads, "A man desiring a wife presents himself to the matron and master at Parramatta, produces a certificate setting forth that he is a proper person and may have a wife given to him."

He pauses. I feel my cheeks burn, but he touches my hand gently, then continues.

"The matron proceeds to the class department with the man, to introduce him to the best behaved, and tells them that those who are willing to be married should step forward. He then speaks to them as they attract his attention till someone is met with who pleases him. It is a most strange and ludicrous scene."

I cannot help it; I burst out laughing and so does he. It should not be funny but I can imagine how the women I knew on board would act with such a man, so that he was befuddled by their charms until at last the matron, quite out of temper, chose for him. I cannot remember what it was like to be like this, light of heart.

He wipes his eyes, reads on that the previous master had been so keen to marry off the women that he had invited a whole body of men to a great welcome feast and the authorities could not ignore such a flagrant act and at last he was dismissed. My laughter falters then, as I think of Annie and the Ship and how she had turned the situation to her advantage, and why I insist on seeking her out. But when Frank offers to write to the matron and superintendent I agree.

He goes further, shows me the newspaper. There are advertisements in it from people seeking others from whom they are separated. I read them all. I do not recognise the names.

The cost to advertise is six shillings. I know what we can buy with that money and I know that he will offer but for now I shake my head, see the relief in him.

Another newspaper comes up on the packet and this time when he reads to me it is about a disturbance, which the newspaper calls a most iniquitous riot, in the Parramatta work factory. The newspaper refers to a number of women who had committed immoral behaviour and then an assault had taken place. One of the women is called Anne Simpkins, and she had been shipped there from Hobart, after perverse behaviour there, to await trial. The women to be punished would have their heads shaved, and be demoted to Third Class, and to solitary confinement. It did not say what she might have done, but the newspaper mused that the women sentenced could have been disorderly, or found in carnal connection, or be drunk or even pregnant. She and other women were due to be shipped onward to Moreton Bay.

A voice cracks on the air. "It could be Annie, although her name is commonplace." I find myself spinning, then falling, and I think I must have fainted, for I wake to find myself in bed.

I whisper, "We must go there, before she is shipped away," and I struggle to move, to find that my limbs do not obey me. The baby kicks me.

"Tomorrow, Hannah, if you are better. We will sail in the morning."

Chapter Forty-Two

I do not sleep that night. My mind is full of memories, sharp and small like gravel. Dawn breaks and I turn on my side, just for a moment, to see Frank sleeping. He breathes quietly, and the baby kicks me hard. I wonder, as the darkness retreats, what it will feel like to see her again, if it is her. It must be her. I feel a flicker within me, dampen it down. I take my clothes and creep out. He does not wake and so I dress and go out to milk. It's a fine clear morning and the fog has lifted.

"You should have let me do it, this morning," Frank says. The doorway shadows him.

"I am well again. You were tired." I do not want to hold my thoughts away from him and so instead I work and we arrive at Newcastle by noon, and all that time I bustle and avoid his gaze. The tides are with us so we sail south, hugging the coastline, on a clear day. Frank coddles me, wrapping me up until I cannot bear it and ask him to stop. I see he looks stricken. I creep into his shoulder, beg his pardon, and close my eyes so I do not have to look at him. I have no right to look for her, to disturb our life together.

I cannot hurt him. I need to find her. I do not know how to reconcile my feelings.

We dock and sleep in Sydney. He goes out while I rest and finds a boat to take us upriver, so we can travel early.

The sounds wake me first, a clatter above. We are nearing a roughhewn jetty and an imposing collection of stone buildings, set back from the bank, walled in. Above us, in the great eucalypts, wings folded, are hundreds of bats. Every few moments perhaps ten wake, call, and fly slowly off to hunt, gather, and then fly back again. "Flying foxes," Frank says, and I see that he is quite awed by the sight, and wonder if he will draw them later. He takes my hand as we alight and we walk together towards the prison door.

I know this foetid smell; it is the same that I was part of, in Newgate, Millbank, even the lock-up. It is unmistakable, it reeks of misery. We are conveyed, in haste, to the offices. Frank takes charge, and asks the superintendent and matron for details about Simpkins, explains that he has written word that we are seeking her. The two of them stand there and I see the disgust in their faces. The matron confirms it is her, that she should face trial.

"It has to be her. She was a maid in London, and came recommended to my wife."

"I cannot recommend her. We were about to send her for hard labour after the disturbance. Then she leaves for Moreton Bay."

Frank stares at her with his sharp blue eyes and takes out his pocket book.

"I am due a servant to be assigned to me. My wife is pregnant."

She shrugs then.

"I will convey you to her class."

I find my voice at last. "I had two friends who arrived here. Could you tell me what has happened to them?"

They look at me as the knowledge I have given them sinks in. I stare back and with a sigh the matron reaches up, takes her books down. They have both been assigned, and she gives me their details.

We are led through more narrow, reeking corridors, and then through a doorway, into the light and an enclosed yard, and the women, slumped against walls, picking oakum apart.

Matron calls out.

"Simpkins?"

The woman looks up. Her hair is growing back in tufts. I notice, with a knot at my heart, that the thin strands are mostly grey. Her eyes flicker, fix on me. This is Annie now, this ruin. How can I take this person with me? I am afraid of her, of what she might bring with her. But how can I tell Frank that I do not want this any more, that this was a mistake?

"What do you want with her?" says another woman, rising up and standing between us, and she reaches out towards me, fiercely, with fingers that clutch. The nails are long and jagged and she is so filthy. Frank steps in front of her, and she falls back.

"You have been assigned. Get your items and you may leave," says the matron flatly.

What Annie was looks at me for a moment. I could say I have changed my mind.

"Do you have belongings?" Frank says.

"Just a bundle." She speaks for the first time. Her voice, hard as stone.

She collects her belongings and I see how she looks back once, long and serious, and nods at the women, the woman who spoke out in particular. I can guess what they mean to each other. Then we walk, in silence, down to the steps and the boat. Above us, the bats fly in, then the boatman casts off and we are in deep water, the centre channel.

I had never thought to find her again, the girl I had

loved for as long as I had known her. But now, looking at that stony face, framed with grey, and the stench of prison coming off her, I wonder why I had to seek her out, and open up the past like a trapdoor. Except that I had to, I had no choice in this, for I had loved her once and owed it to her to rescue her. To her daughter as well. But where was the Annie who wrote me, who had cracked me open again and allowed me to hope?

When we reach our house, I am grey with fatigue. Two days of travelling. But still I open the door to the room I had first slept in, and show it to Annie. She has not said a single word to me since she was assigned. She throws her bundle on the floor, and walks over to the window. I see her looking out as I did when I first came here. I remember looking at John and Elsie all those years ago and wondering what it would be like, to live in a quiet place with Annie, to raise our children together.

I hesitate, then say, "I could help you bathe." I do not want her to miss the sense of what I am saying, so I add, more formally than before, "I can heat water, then leave you alone in the kitchen."

Annie looks around, pushes her hands towards me. I step away, see that they are clean, dry.

"We washed ourselves with rags in prison. We did the best we could," she says, and her voice is cold and the words like pebbles rolling in her mouth.

"I don't doubt that. I remember."

"I will wash myself but you can help me undress. And fetch scissors."

I bring my scissors to her and watch as Annie peels off layer and layer of grimy clothing. I take my scissors; cut the underclothes she has been sewn into. Her shift tears as I cut it. We bring clean water in a tub, I shut off the kitchen for her, to give her privacy, and I tell her that I have new clothes for her, and will burn those she does not need. She nods again.

The burn reaches from her fingers all the way up to her elbow and has puckered, so the skin has healed in creases, and the fingers will not stretch out. I cannot help myself; my eyes fix on it as a terrible pity washes over me. Annie is naked before me now, covers herself with her arms.

"I can wash myself. I don't need you." I nod, bring her clean clothes, cast the others on the fire. They burn up suddenly, and then are gone.

Even when Annie is clean, I cannot help myself, cannot stop looking, transfixed, as that hand claws, red and shiny, around the broom and emerges wet from the washing. I wonder if it hurts, pulls, dare not ask her.

The second night, after all the work is done and Frank goes to bed early, I offer her a glass of peach brandy I have brewed. She hesitates, then nods. I have set out two chairs on the verandah, a lamp by each one with a fat candle in each. At first, she says nothing but drains her brandy dry, tosses it off. I pour her another brandy, as she starts at last to talk.

Chapter Forty-Three

"I left letters for you, Hannah."

Our shadows stretch, separate and long, across the cooling verandah. I nod, speak then.

"I never saw the letter you left at the refuge, Annie. But I was told of it, after Mr Haskin had cast it into the fire. Miss Clements told me that she had promised to obey him, had struggled with the knowledge. But Mrs Martin found me, and gave me your other letter."

She looks at me then and gasps. I am fearful that I did the wrong thing.

"I left the token with her; I thought it was safer with her. I did not even know if I would find you. This way, I thought, was safer for you. For your baby. For Hannah."

A long exhalation from her, and then she stifles a sob. I cannot help myself; I take her rough hand in mine, and bring something out of my pocket.

"I kept this, all the way here." She looks down at the scrap of linen, puts out her thumb and touches her stitching, sewn so long ago. An H, an A, linked together.

I ask her, "What happened next?"

I see how she shivers and pulls her shawl around her. Then she starts.

"I sailed away in the autumn, and our boat was bound for Van Diemen's Land."

I nod. "I've heard of the place. From Frank."

"There were ninety of us, and twenty children. Then I wondered, would they have permitted me to bring my Hannah, but it was too late. She was gone."

The desolation in her voice. The Hannah she had lost. I want to fold my hands over my stomach but I dare not.

"There were just a few of us in Newgate and we were brought on first. The others came days, even weeks, later, from the county prisons. Most were from the county prisons. But then the end came fast, for the winds blew north-west and they hauled us out and we set sail from Woolwich on a fine morning.

"You should have heard them, Hannah, the women from Scotland, as we sailed. They wrapped their babies inside their shawls and we stood on deck in lines. They struck up an old boat song, 'My Bonnie Lies Over the Ocean', and they taught us enough so we could sing along until the whole boat was singing and even some of the men joined in too and we sang until we were down the Thames, and then out to sea."

We had sung too, but this is not the moment to tell her, for she is in full flow and I dare not stop her.

"The surgeon, Superintendent Stewart, asked me to write the indents for him, to describe the women, and so for every woman, as he looked them up and down, I wrote down his words. Just like the penitentiary. Or the refuge." We had shared so much, drifted so far from each other.

"My hand hurt by the end, but I recall some of them. There was one, Sarah Murchison, and she was just fifteen, the same age as you were when I met you. She was sailing towards her sister, Susan. The surgeon asked me to note that she was the fairest lass on board, with her fresh complexion and dark brown eyes."

I wondered what the superintendent had asked Hannah to write down about herself. Always the fairest of them all, wherever we had been together. Until the work factory, and now.

"There was a mother and her daughter, and they had stolen a great quantity of drapery and were sentenced to seven years; they held hands all the time that their indents were written. I hope that they were assigned together."

She holds out her glass now, and I refill it. She has drunk so much that her words slur, but she is easier with it.

"Almost all of us were thieves, Hannah, we were nothing out of the ordinary. We were a ship of thieves, except that I had assaulted a man."

The last shadow of Summers and what Annie had done out of anger. For me.

"Thieves and servants. A few on the town, like me."

I think of how much she had done, without telling me, thinking that she was protecting me. A penance perhaps.

"What were they like, the other women?" I ask. She looks at me then.

"I made friends, Hannah." Defensive, and rightly so, for I had been jealous of her attention. But now I nod and feel nothing for her but pity and gratitude, that she had made friends when she needed them.

"There was Elspeth, who the surgeon told me to write down as having a blond beard and being pockpitted; Lydia, who was described as large and unprepossessing; Eliza, who suffered seizures and now spoke out of one side of her mouth, the right side drooping; the sullen-looking Lucy, dark and with rose-red lips; Margaret, who the surgeon called sinister-looking; and then Mary, who was melancholy, and kept to herself and who seemed to be unable to bring herself to wash her hair, her hands or her feet."

A breath, then she says, "Then there was Frances, from Dundee. She was in next to me, in the mess, and had a child called May. When the child was asleep and the lights out, she shared her whisky with me. She had left her two sons behind with her husband. May died a week out."

I put my hand to my mouth, then over my stomach. Annie has not seen.

"We wrapped her in a sheet and we were summoned to deck for the service. The captain read it out and the body was weighted and we held Frances upright as May was lowered into the ocean."

Unbearable, to imagine what this was like for the woman.

"She drank herself unconscious, Hannah. One day she slipped on the stairs and fell. Her leg was completely twisted beneath her and she was taken to the hospital. It never healed right; she limped after that. I was told to nurse her."

She looks over at me then. "She talked on and on about May and her boys and I listened and said nothing. I thought then that she needed me to hear her, not for me to burden her with my story. But then she was allowed to leave, to come up to deck."

Her voice changed then, angry.

"She leaned out so far over the water that I thought she would cast herself in and wailed May's name, and I could not have held her alone. I shrieked out loud for help. She was carried back down to the bed then, and I screamed at her for what she had done. I told her she was not the only one to lose a child, and that she was selfish, and I know it was cruel but it brought her back to life."

She finished her brandy then, and added more softly,

"You had done the same for me when we first met. Listened so much that we got stuck, and you never talked. I was angry with you first. When Summers spoke. Not later. I understood then."

I do not want the past to come back like this. To hear that name. I get up then, collect the glasses and brandy. She looks up at me then, in the darkness.

All of a sudden, she reaches for me, touches my face. I pull away.

"Please, Hannah, let me mend what I broke."

No, not this. This is not what I meant when I searched her out.

"Annie, I married Frank and I did it freely, out of love. I chose him."

Her hands drop then. I say, gently enough, "I never forgot you or stopped looking for you. And I wish never to be parted from you, as long as we both shall live."

She gets up and stumbles away from me, and I hear the door to her room close behind her with a clap, as the baby kicks me twice over.

Chapter Forty-Four

I feel as if I am betraying my husband. He is the same towards me, but I have curbed my affection toward him, because Annie is here. I should have told him. His life was open to me, and I have kept this part of me secret from him. I weighted and sifted and skated over parts of my life, and dredged up others with my hands until the stones lifted from my heart. But I could not tell him everything, and so I lied by omission, right from the start.

Annie is angry, even to Frank. He is unsure how to behave around her and this is my fault. Her fault too. Even with the men who are assigned, he has found a kind of companionship as they work together. They speak Gaelic together, but English to us, even if it is halting. Frank insists that we must celebrate Harvest Supper with them. A country custom, from thousands of miles away.

When the day comes round, we clear space in the barn, carry out the table, and the men bring up theirs. I shake out a clean sheet to cover them both, set flowers in the middle.

I stand by Annie as she chops vegetables, sharp and angry, for the stew. I have refused to use kangaroo, for I like to see them bound away, not be chopped up. I think back to Mama, the sightless hare, her hands covered in blood. All the same the stew is plentiful and tasty.

At the end of the day the men come walking, hair slicked back and with clean shirts on, up to the barn. We set the dishes on the table, and sit down together. A hush falls over us, as the men close their eyes and pray in Gaelic. I think back to the people who have prayed over me before and used their faith to judge me. This is not the same.

We eat together and make as much conversation as we can. At the end Patrick stands up, the oldest of the men. I wonder what he will say, but instead he takes a breath and he sings. At last he is silent, and I see how all of us have eyes that glisten in the candlelight. We shake his hand and thank him, and then the other men rise, and we do the same, and then they take their table, and walk back to their quarters, one at each leg.

I see how Annie looks at Frank, as he rises and gathers together the dishes. She snatches them from him, a tightness in her lips. She refuses help as she washes, puts dishes away. I whisper to her then, when he has gone back to the barn, "He is your master. You cannot treat him like that." She rewards me with a glare and I crumple, walk away back to Frank. I am failing him; I do not know how to discipline her. How can I be mistress to her?

Frank and I stay in the barn, put it to rights for the morning. He looks at me, and I wonder what he will say. We carry the table back to the house. Annie has finished her work and has disappeared. We undress in silence, and Frank falls asleep. I lie there, my hand on his chest. There is a whistle at the end of his breath, then a pause, before he takes breath again.

I never thought I could love a man, until I met Frank. They had caused me such burning sorrow, the whole awful procession of them. Jem Summers, Tom Olderhall, Wypond, Haskin. Even Harding. But there was Elsie's John, and the pattern he made for me meant that when Frank came and took my bag so I could step next to him, lightly, I could look back and see how I might come together with such a man, make a life with him. Then I took the life we made and I disturbed it, by bringing Annie here. I have to make it better again.

In the morning I rise and find Annie washing the floor. She does not look up. I step carefully to the kitchen table, sit down. I want to reprove her, for she deserves it. Instead, for some reason, I say, hesitantly,

"I have fabric for you." It is a bolt of new pink cotton, which I bought in Newcastle.

"I wear servant clothes," she says. "I'm your servant. You pay me to work for you."

I press on. "You used to love dressing up in fine clothes, choosing which ones to try on, do you not remember?"

I do not expect this, but she takes the water and hurls it against the wall, the open door.

"Other folks choose their life, Hannah. Not people like us. Our lives were chosen long ago and laid out for us. We just follow one of the paths, or another."

Then I hurl back at her all the anger which has built in me since she came, and before. "You have spoiled every-thing. I do not want you here."

She looks at me then, stricken.

"You treat Frank as if he has done you wrong, when he has done nothing to you. Blame me. Not him."

The bitterness in her, it has cankered everything and it is my fault that she is here.

Before I can stop myself, I say, "I can send you back, Annie. I won't let you come between me and Frank."

But then she sits down at the kitchen table and covers

her face and begs my forgiveness, and I listen to her as the wall dries. The stain of the water remains.

"We arrived in the January, Hannah. We had been put below deck before we landed and then they opened the hatches up and brought us out in batches. I could scarcely see at first. The sparkle on the sea."

I remembered that, the first sight of this place. A golden light that I loved.

"The sailors were steering past a small, rocky outcrop as they tacked nearer to land. On the rocks sat a great multitude of seabirds, calling to each other, and the stench of fish, and the tumult, it overwhelmed me. Then I saw a creature, basking on a rock. It looked like a sort of fat leech, lying there, hardly breathing. Then a twitch of its whiskers and it leapt into the water and then out again, the great fat grey body, with a silver fish squirming in its mouth. The sailors were pointing. 'Seals,' they said, and then we were in Hobart town."

I thought of how we had moved into the harbour at Sydney and how we had clung together, we women.

"There was just a bit of water left, and some bread, and then we saw a boat coming towards us and the captain called for us to gather our belongings and we were rowed to shore. We had to hold each other up when we stepped onto dry land."

That sway, in each other's arms.

"We were marched up a road called Macquarie Street. Frances whispered that she had heard a soldier say we were bound for the female factory and we walked until we were out of the town, and there it was, a large building. High walls around it, and the door was unlocked as we approached and we entered, and it was so dark, Hannah."

Her story unfolds and I look at her in a kind of horror,

what she has been through. What she became to survive in a kind of hell.

"The matron of the factory was called Mrs Wilkinson. She sent me to Parramatta, where you found me. She hated me."

There was another register, and Hannah and her friends were recorded again. Frances went before Annie.

"She assigned her, even though she limped, and then she snapped at me because my bonnet had slipped and I saw that she was looking at someone behind me; I glanced back and there was such a tiny man there, Hannah, her husband. He was dressed all in black and stared at me as if he would undress me with his eyes."

She shuddered at the memory of him.

"I did not tell Matron about my condition. I was warned not to. By Molly, the wards woman."

Her voice has changed and I look over at her and her burning face, and want to know more. She adds, quickly, "I let a sailor at me, Hannah. For money. It was over fast but I regretted it for he went too far. I made sure after that that I was never alone, but it was too late. By the time that we were nearing Van Diemen's Land I knew for sure."

She had been a mother, twice over. And has no children.

She changes tack.

"Matron had grown up at the Parramatta, as it was being built. That's why she was sent to Hobart, for her father had been the superintendent there. Her husband was just a helpmeet. She ran the factory. And she hated women with children, Molly told me. She had lost four, buried them in Parramatta, before she sailed to Hobart."

I want to feel sorry for the matron, but everything that Annie tells me about her hardens me against her: how she and her husband reduced the rations down, fed the women skilly morning and night although few of them could stomach the poorly mixed flour and water; how her husband watched the women as they walked past, a hungry look on his greasy face.

"I saw her place two women into crime class, and took her clothes from them. They had to wear letters on their jacket in bright scarlet. She was cruel, Hannah."

Annie was assigned to a house in town, as the matron did not know her condition.

"The Mildenhalls, with their dear son. Mrs Mildenhall was always fussing him and herself, always ill. My duties were light, but I grew lonely in that house. I stole drink."

She talks flatly. I glance at the brandy. It doesn't matter.

"It dampened everything, the brandy. Seeing their child every day, how Mrs Mildenhall fussed over him. She had headaches, and I had the care of him. It brought everything back to me."

Everything came back to the child she had lost and could not forget.

"Mrs Mildenhall called me to her one day and confided that she was with child again. She asked me if I could stay with them. I didn't know what to say or do, and asked leave to go to bed. They could not find me in the morning and so she came in. She saw how I was. So she returned me."

So she had gone back to the factory. Perhaps she would tell me now.

"I packed brandy and tobacco around me, and that night, in the ward, I gave them to Molly, and we celebrated my return. The whole ward of us, dancing in the dark."

I had a vision then, of Annie, taking Molly by the hand, and how they danced together, up and down the ward as we had done. A gaze on each other.

"The matron told me that I was assigned to laundry until the birth, and then when my child was born and

I had nursed them, to crime class. The laundry, Hannah, again."

For a moment we look at each other and we are back in the refuge, in the warm room, the coppers steaming. I see her striding up and down in britches, taking a bow at the end.

"Molly protected me there. She made it tolerable, just about."

Whilst I was nursing Eleanor, in the warm of this place, Annie was enduring such privations. With a child growing inside her.

"The rations were sparse, and Molly took it upon herself to feed us."

There is a story here that I remember Frank telling me about. A riot at the factory, an Irishwoman at its helm, who had said, defiant, when she was tried for the offence, that she would never see another woman hunger in front of her, not again. It had been thrilling to read, but I had not known that Annie was there. That the woman had done it for her. Annie laughs suddenly, her mind miles away, and suddenly radiant.

"You should have seen Molly, when she pulled a great joint of meat out and we passed it from one to another, and the blood ran down our faces."

I feel something like jealousy grip me. I can't, won't say her name.

"I remember reading that the ringleader was put in a cell?"

"She was dragged there. The rest of us were put in other cells together. She was locked inside alone. We were all to go to crime class, but first they took us to cut our hair. They dragged Molly away to cut hers, and she punched the kitchen window out with her bare hand and we were in uproar."

I think of the docile Annie, in the penitentiary, in Newgate. How she had changed.

Her voice shakes, suddenly. "They let her out the next day, and we led her to the ward, for she could hardly see. We washed her and bathed her as best we could. And then we came to stand in front of her and two of the girls went behind her and they wove their own hair into hers, so that she had a plait, and then they showed her how she looked, in a metal mug. I gave her a cap I had made, and we hid her plait below it and I had never seen her cry, but she did then."

The candles have burned down low in the lamps. I take Annie's hand in mine and together we look out into the darkness. There is more sorrow to tell, I can feel it. Annie finishes her glass, her voice thickened.

"Then you found me. There you were, in blue muslin, like a brown bird, head tilted to one side. Your face was beaming, and then I saw a man beside you, and he took your arm. You were pregnant. Still I was happy to see you again, but you looked at me and your face changed. You took a step back, as if you were afraid of me."

I have a sudden impulse to take her in my arms but I cannot. There is a bond I will never break with Frank and now a stab of something like jealousy as well.

I had her assigned to me and now she is my servant and nothing is the same. I sailed thousands of miles to find her, and I did. But it will never be as it was before.

"I was shocked, perhaps. You had changed so much." I cannot stop myself; I glance at her arm and she turns, suddenly.

"I did. But so did you." She rises and leaves me alone. I sit in silence, watching as the sun moves across the floor and creeps up the walls until the windows repeat as shadows in the light.

Chapter Forty-Five

F rank and I lie in bed. It is quite dark and the only movement is his hand on my stomach, as the baby kicks and turns.

"You aren't yourself," he says, as our hands entwine, catch fast, hold tight.

I owe this man everything.

"I find Annie so changed. I should not have brought her here. I have ruined everything; I should never have done this."

He could send her back to the factory if he wanted to. There is a silence. If he did want to, what would I say to him?

"Can we help her?"

Every time he surprises me.

"Perhaps her child lives still, in London?"

We could never afford to seek her, send for her.

He pauses. "I will need to write to the authorities. And her conduct at the factory will tell against her if they inquire. But only if you agree." I think of how he built up this life through quiet hard work, his and Eleanor's. I feel how his grip tightens around me. He is doing this for me.

I am sewing clothes now for the baby, putting by a

stock of garments and at last, without saying a word, Annie joins me. I put a lamp by her, pass her a gown to hem and watch as her fingers tremble, how she fails to thread her needle. I kneel down before her and thread it for her, then sit down again, with an effort. I watch, see how her stitching is looser now, as her hands claw over the fabric.

"I had nothing like this. For either of mine."

I see the tears fall on the clean cotton.

"The second time was in July. Winter in Van Diemen's Land. My waters broke during the service and Molly and the midwife, Sarah, took me to the pregnant women's ward, each on one arm. He was born at dawn and Sarah swaddled him, put him in my arms and told me that the placenta was delivered whole."

The memory came back, unbidden. How I had washed my mama and wrapped my sister, changed the bedding, slopped the afterbirth into the kennel. A child who had no idea of what to do.

"I called him James, after my papa. I had nine months with him there, in the yard."

I waited for it. The saddest part. "I was to be sent away and I begged Mrs Wilkinson to let me become a wards woman in the yard, and stay with him. But she refused."

Her hands still and she looks up and out, then, into the dark. "He had just taken his first steps and he was tired from it. I was nursing him when she came, with a warder on each side. She let me finish at least, and then took him from my breast and I remember how the other breast was completely full but she refused to let me put him on it."

I drop my sewing and kneel by her. This is not to be borne.

"The Mildenhalls came to collect me and she had her own baby in her arms."

The cruelty of that. I know now why she can hardly look at me.

"I kept my milk going by feeding their daughter. They took me to the Sunday service there, a week later. When we descended from the gallery an overseer let me hold him and already he felt like a feather in my arms and I yelled at her as the Mildenhalls jostled behind me. The overseer said he was quite well, being fed pea soup, and I tore my clothes open and latched him on. Wilkinson came running at that, and he had scarcely started feeding before she tore him away from me. I screamed and so did he until at last they took me away."

My poor friend.

"He died."

I feel the shock of her words course through me. I cover my stomach with my hands.

"James died. He never even reached his first birthday."

I feel my baby kick. Alive and strong. I hold Annie's hand, and she tells me that he was buried in the yard there.

The desolation in her. How does anyone ever recover from such a loss? Live on after?

"I wondered about you, even then. I was set to washing again and so my mind was free and I would look up at the mountain and wonder what life would have been like. If we had been there together. Gone through this together. But you weren't there."

The girl who turned on a penny.

"Molly saved me."

It gives her relief, I can see it in her, to talk of something that is not about her children: where Molly had come from, how her husband had beaten her before she fought back, how they had grown closer. Then Annie ceases talking, becomes distracted.

I cannot help it; I snap at her, "You called me unnatural. Vicious even."

It is underneath everything, despite all my pity for her. A raging anger at what she said, all those years ago, and I take up my sewing and leave her alone in the lamplight.

Frank knows nothing of this. He takes me across the river to see Phillip Williams the next day. We embark at his landing stage and walk up through his estate. Away from our house and the perpetual work, from Annie's constant presence, for even if she is not in a room, I know she has been there.

I feel lighter then, leaning on Frank. He looks down at me.

"Let me show you something," he says, and steers me off the path. He comes to a stop in a clearing, a pond in front of us. "Phillip had this dug out, about a year ago. The water runs through it, so it is clean."

He pulls me to the edge and helps me sit down and unlaces my boots, does the same. We put our feet in the water.

"It's warm," I say. He stands up again for a moment, looks around, then removes his clothes, swiftly, until he is quite naked, and then he wades in. It is waist deep on him. He is brown on his neck and face, the rest of him bright white in the light that breaks through the gum trees and then I cannot help myself, I take off my dress and he reaches out to me and pulls me to him in my thin shift until we are both half submerged and cling to each other as our laughter echoes in the clearing.

We dry off on the edge of the pond and eat apples and cheese. Then I lie back against him and doze in the sun. The comfort of being alone with him.

"Before we talk to Williams," he says, breaking the silence, "are you sure that we should send for the child?"

He has given me back the decision to make. I see Annie in our house, gaunt and angry, throwing water against the kitchen wall. Her burn, still livid. A memory of everything that she has lost. She has disturbed everything. But I brought her here. We could send her away, but things would never be the same, anyway. So I turn to look at him and tell him yes.

We walk hand in hand up to the big house and see Phillip Williams. He offers to take Annie's girl on, in the dairy, or even to set her to learn the trade of his new vineyards.

"She will want work," Williams says simply when I thank him. "I will look after her as if she was my own, for your land would not support another mouth to feed." He says he can even loan us money, but Frank reassures him that we can afford it.

Williams offers to send word to Sydney. It is possible, he says, she can be found and brought.

Later that same day, not wanting to waste time, Frank writes two letters and I one. One was to the authorities in Sydney, the other to the orphanage. He writes in glowing terms of Annie Simpkins. He assures the superintendent that "the character of myself and wife will bear the strictest investigation to support the child and her mother, who I wish to be under my protection. Our characters bear the strictest investigation for honesty, sobriety and industry."

He continues: "The girl is destitute and has no friends in London. We are free, both man and wife, and are enabled to support her and her mother and give her education and training. It is her mother's anxious desire to bring the girl here. We will give to her offspring the means to earning their bread." He sends the money that is owed for the girl's board and lodging, a year of our earnings. I write to Mrs Martin, to York. I tell her that we are reunited, Annie and myself, and that I am married, and I send her money too, and ask her if she can take the token to the orphan hospital and help the girl set sail, when all is arranged.

Annie knows nothing of all of this. Since I had left her so abruptly, she keeps to her room, and does her work quietly. I know that I was unkind to her. I do not even want to understand why I was so angry with her, only that it has left a sadness in me, and I want my friend back. She is washing the kitchen again when I come in and stand near her. Her sleeves are rolled up again, her hand clawing. She sees me looking, rolls her sleeve down.

I take the mop from her, and ask her to walk down with me to the river, just for a moment.

"It was an accident," she says.

Her friend, Frances, had been returned from service. Molly had been strange since she arrived, distant. Annie had thought little of it, had enjoyed being with her shipmate.

"Molly was on serving duty, at the tureen, and I was in the queue with Frances, and we had been laughing at something, I can't even remember what. And I am not even sure what happened but all of a sudden, I was burning and there was soup all over me, in clumps. It must have been boiling for there was a keening and then I felt the water on me, and I was carried off, screaming.

"They put her in the dark cell again; they said that she had kicked over the tureen at me. I never saw her again."

She puts her hands out in front of her, turns them over and studies them. "They ache, sometimes. Every day when I wake, I unclaw them, finger by finger. I was in the hospital ward for weeks. By the time I came out Molly had escaped. Sarah, the midwife, told me that she had been put in the band of iron. Around her neck. For seven days."

She gulps for a moment.

"You could not sleep in the band, for the spikes dug into you if you lay down. All the time for a moment of anger. I would have forgiven her in an instant."

I find my voice then. "Where did she go?"

"Molly was never afraid of the bush; she told me that a person could disappear into it, make a life if they needed to. I only know that she was helped to escape. When I was sent to Parramatta, for my place in the attack, I thought I saw her, on the headland. She was dressed as a man, but I knew her, I think. She raised a hand and I did too, and then she was gone."

We are by the river now, and we look at it as the sun catches it and all of a sudden, I shiver. She says, looking straight out, "It was only when she was gone that I realised that I had used my beauty all my life to get what I wanted. Now nobody wanted me and some even shrank from me. Even in crime class, in Parramatta, there was only Emma, the woman you saw, who came near me. I was a ruin and then you came and I saw that even you thought I was destroyed."

I turn to her then and I realise that all my anger is gone. "I sought you as my dearest friend. And I am truly sorry, for everything that I have done too." We stand there for a moment, looking at each other, full face in the sun, and then we walk, arm in arm, back to the house and separate for our daily tasks.

Chapter Forty-Six

It must be over a month later that a letter comes for me. Frank and I sit down together on our bed and I open it with trembling hands. Mrs Martin has written to me, a long letter, and I scan it feverishly and find the name. My name. She writes, "I found the child and she is well. She knew a little about her mother, and is eager to know her and excited that she has a family. We found her just in time, for she was to be sent out to a family, before being trained for service. The sweet child that she is, Hannah, you will love her."

Frank reads as fast as I do and I burst into tears to read Mrs Martin's words. The sweet child, Annie's daughter. Found at last. Frank turns the page, and there she has written, "She sails on the next boat, and all bills are paid. I have spoken to the captain myself, and he has said he will look out for her. The Friends will visit the boat before she sails and impress upon the captain again that she must be looked after as if she was his own daughter."

I hear a clattering outside in the kitchen and glance at Frank. He hoists me up and we walk hand in hand to the kitchen. Annie is cleaning the kitchen table. Everything about her has dulled now. The anger has left her; the grief has come to the surface, the losses no woman should have to bear.

"Annie," I say, and then ask her to sit. She does not look up as she takes her chair.

I slide the letter across the table to her. "I wrote to Mrs Martin," I say. "I asked her to look for Hannah."

She looks up then, a wildness in her eyes. Then my words trip over each other for I cannot torture her like this, "She is alive and well, Mrs Martin says, a sweet child."

I take her reddened hands in mine then, and tell her, "Frank has paid for her to come here."

At last she hears the words, and repeats them, uncertain. "Come here? Hannah?"

And then we both nod and she falls to her knees before him and thanks him again and again and then buries her head in my lap. Frank touches me on the shoulder and leaves us on our own, and I lift up her head and kneel down beside her and take my weeping friend in my arms.

Chapter Forty-Seven

We try and work it out, and calculate that Hannah will arrive after I have given birth. Annie is anxious, counting away the days. But everything is different now between the three of us.

I watch the two of them as they have taken to walking the farm together, once a week. They have this lope, up and down the slopes of this place, and I think that it comes from a landscape they share, thousands of miles away. I see how they talk, businesslike, about the farm, dispensing with my help so I am spared as I grow bigger and more uncomfortable.

I have ordered a present for him, a teapot which he has coveted for months now. It arrives in Newcastle so I refuse all offers of assistance and shop there alone for the teapot and other provisions. I realise I am laying in for my baby, buying everything that we cannot sew or knit, as well as salted meat and dry goods.

I return in the evening, cradling the teapot in my arms, anticipating his happiness when I lay the tea tray out, pour tea for him. He will reprove me for spending money on him, and thank me with kisses.

I walk towards the house, packages in my arms. Annie

comes out of the house and towards me. She puts her hand on my arm. "Frank," she says, and her voice cracks and breaks.

My packages, his teapot, slide from my hands.

I run inside. He cannot be dead. I run to our room.

"Hannah," I hear, but I speed on, and there is my Frank, lying quite still in bed. He is warm, not dead, and then I see the doctor is there, looking at me with an awful sympathy.

"His heart," the doctor says. He is talking but I cannot hear anything as Annie comes in.

How could his heart give out, this man who was so strong, who could chop wood all day and still lift me up and carry me with him? How could his heart fail on him, so that he stood stock still, as the men had told Annie, then fell like a stone in front of them?

He lies in the bed like a statue, but his chest is rising still.

"Don't leave, not now," I weep, and the tears flow onto him, as he lies there, felled.

I have only had two years with him. I have had two years of happiness, and other people have a lifetime with the person they love. Where does this anger come from towards the man I love best in the world, when none of this is his fault? I take my anger with me to the barn and punch the wood with my knuckles until they bleed and then I run to the house and cradle his head in my arms as the pillow slip turns red.

But Annie is there now. She helps me to lift him and dress him, and as she is taller than me, she walks with him to recover his strength. They start by the house, walking to and fro with a stick. When he stumbles, she catches him, holds him tight with her good arm. His strides get longer, day by day, week by long week, until the Sunday comes at last when they walk the farm together, for the first time since he fell ill. I see them walk into the distance together, talking, arm in arm.

He tells her what tasks need to be done, in what order. She has taken to wearing britches again, like the girl I knew long ago, and a wide-brimmed hat. I see how she comes in sweating at the end of a working day, brown and tired. Happier.

Three months pass and he recovers slowly. I am enormous with child by the time he is dressing himself, walking without assistance. He comes to me in the kitchen, slowly, and I weep into his chest, and feel his heart beating steadily against my hand. At night I lie with my arms around him, the baby between us until he falls asleep, and I slip a bolster underneath my belly and try to sleep.

The dreams return, Mama returns. That night my sleep is unquiet, and I wake with salt on my cheeks. Frank stirs and takes my hand, swims back though his fatigue to find me.

"I saw my mama. She was walking towards me as she did when she met me at the school gates, and she was smiling. And then I woke and she had gone."

Then everything in me seems to break apart and I cry out loud and shake. There is the sound of running footsteps, a dim light as Annie knocks and walks in. She hesitates, but I struggle up, stretch out my arms. Through my tears I see her look at Frank and he nods. She sits down on the bed and strokes my hair. She shivers. Frank offers her a blanket, and she huddles beside me, so I am safe between them. I have to speak now. Everything that I can say out loud.

There is a silence, when I tell them that I dream of my mama, my sister. That it must have been my fault that my sister died. For rocking her cradle, for wishing the trouble she had brought gone.

Annie first. "My baby died, Hannah. He died too. Women like us, like your mama, our babies die young."

"Not always," Frank says then. Thinking, no doubt, of my condition. "But all too often." Then he reaches out a hand and feels how the baby kicks. "Not this one."

I must have slept, for I wake in peace to hear the birds sing.

My birthday comes before our baby is born. On that day I sit down at the breakfast table and watch as Annie set the teapot down and pour us each out tea, the steam rising. There is a thin package tied up with a red thread. "From us both," Frank says, as he kisses me. I take one end of the thread, Frank the other, and we pull as Annie looks on.

I understand now why they had both asked me about my mama and papa, how they both looked. Frank must have done this, fighting against the tiredness that captured him at night and in the morning. He had taken the little time he had each day and poured it into this sketch, the best of what he had to give. My parents, together, by the river Waveney. He has captured her and he has raised my father George from Mama's memories and brought them over the sea to me. My parents are smiling in the Waveney water meadows, bursting with cornflowers and poppies.

Frank fights for every step of his recovery. But he is not too proud to ask for help. One fine morning, he gathers the men together, before the working day has started. Annie stands beside him and I lean against the door jamb, looking at them all. The men stand there, twisting their hats in their hands as he talks.

"We've all worked here, on the farm, together. You know that I have been ill. Miss Annie has taken my place, and works as hard as any man. She is your master when I cannot be."

305

And then, with difficulty, he shakes each of them by the hand, and promises that he will write for their tickets of leave, and recommend them most heartily. Annie steps forward to talk to them, and they go off together.

"Come to the river with me," he says, and we walk down to the bank. The sun catches the water so that every movement glitters, then is gone. We stand together, looking out, and then he points with a stick at a group of stones.

"Promise me that if there is a claim on the land, you will honour it." I look at him. I know what this is about. The grinding stones. They suggest a life before we were here. That we may have displaced, however hard he had looked for those who had the claim, those who came before, who have a right to this land.

"Yes. But where would we go?"

"I was sent money from whaling and I put it by. In case you need to leave. And for the men too, if they want to stay, and send for their families. There is enough."

The word hangs in the air. You, not we. I shake it off. It must be a mistake.

Night after night Mama and my sister visit me and drag me by my hair backwards towards a valley and into the river and down where the weeds go. The baby and I kick and set ourselves free, come up for air as they hold me. Every morning I am exhausted and they watch me with such compassion. How can I be a mother when I brought a baby into the world that set off so much sadness? Mama was cursed, and so am I, I think, wildly, until I wake to Frank, the farm, and everything I have been given. Blessed, not cursed; blessed, but still weighed down with guilt.

At last the day comes, and there is fire and water and blood, soiling and a clean and whetted knife. Frank is stronger and so they hold me together as I labour, work and at last free my baby from me, cut the cord that bound us together, throw my afterbirth in a bucket. At last, my baby cries out, and I close my eyes and see how my mama is flying high and I am sure that she looks down at me, one last time, and is smiling before she is gone from view.

We have a son. I hear his voice, a thin new voice that cries out, and when he cries, I feel the milk let down in my breasts. The pain has thrown me onto a new shore. "Frankie," I say, faintly, and Frank takes him in his arms and calls him by his name and his face, his lovely face, is quite naked with love.

Chapter Forty-Eight

F rank sets our baby down on paper; the three of us together. A life in charcoal, pencil, paint. Puts his things down to cradle his son and sing to him, the old songs from the West Country, the folk songs that conjure up the countryside, the sea shanties and the whaling songs. The song I sang to my sister, long ago. My son kicks as I sing, his eyes following me all the while.

I want to remember every moment that we spend together. One morning, when the baby is at my breast, Annie asks me if she can take my wedding dress.

"I think I can mend it for you," she says, hesitantly, and takes the poor ragged garment away with her. She must have worked on it every evening for a week; she brings it back to me one morning, as I sit at the kitchen table with Frank.

"I could not repair it completely," she says, and passes the folded garment to me. I shake it out and gasp. She has cut the good fabric clear from the rot, and sewn a gown for the baby.

"I thought he could be christened in it," she says, hesitantly, as Frank and I look at what she has made, a gown sprinkled at the hem with poppies. I see how she has saved my mama's stitching, where she can, and then woven vines around her cornflowers.

"Thank you, Annie," Frank says, simply. "I wonder, would you be his godmother?"

Her hands go to her mouth and then she cries out, "Yes, a thousand times."

On a clear Sunday morning we dress him and the three of us go to the church to christen him. Francis George Phillip, and Phillip Williams was his godfather, and Annie his godmother.

Frankie was not yet weaned when his papa is stricken again. He fights for every breath and he loses. One early morning, as the sun creeps across our room the breath leaves him and the blood retreats from his fingers, his hands, and as if I am outside myself, I marvel, just for a moment, at how quickly his warm brown skin grows white. I kiss him for that last time and lay myself next to him while he is still warm. He didn't want to leave us, he will never see his son run across the farm he created, and there is nothing to be done or said.

He mended me once but now I am beyond repair. Phillip Williams takes us to the church to bury him, and this time he speaks for me, and what Frank meant to me, to the baby I cradle, as Annie holds us close to her. We bury him near to Eleanor and I put my hand on the stone and weep for them both. Williams stands to one side, but when it is all over, he takes Annie's hand.

"Look after her," he says, his voice shaking. "Frank entrusted her to you."

They stand there, holding hands, looking straight into each other's eyes. She nods. "Always, and our godchild too."

When Phillip comes to me, he takes me by the hand and he cries without shame. "Send for me, for whatever assistance you need."

"Be his godfather, because he needs you," I say and he takes the boy from me, and holds him protectively.

He moves back to Annie, then, holding my son, and together they settle on what is required for now, the men he will send over to assist with the work. They part with a handshake and he hands her my son.

Periwinkles push up where Frank lies, as bright as if I had taken a duster to them to raise a sheen. The spring crops are sown, the cows milked, the sheep dagged, and later sheared. Phillip Williams sends help whenever we need it, but nobody can restore what I have lost. Again. He is quite simply all around me, for nobody comes this time to take me away from the place I lived when I lost a person I loved. He is there in the fields he sowed, the cows he milked, his teapot, and every drawing. This is a haunting that he went through too, but how can I live without him, and raise his son without a father?

I cry, night after night, and then there is a night when Annie comes to me, carrying a candle and sits on the bed. The silence spreads all around us and she puts out a hand, strokes my hair. She shivers. The baby stirs, then sleeps again. She blows out the candle and then lies on the bed, and pulls me to her, and holds me, so we are as tight as spoons, curled into each other in a kitchen drawer.

I wake in the early morning, as the birds sing, full-throated, outside and Frankie stirs, those first small bleats of his morning. I open my eyes and turn around. Annie is looking at me.

"I loved the girl you were, the woman you became and the mother you now are."

The sun comes up and creeps across the room towards us, the bed, my sleeping baby.

We had lain together last when we had been young

girls, thin and pinched, with small breasts and waists that we had encircled with each other's hands and laughed. I could still remember how Annie's hair had flowed like a river as she brushed it, and how it had felt, new-washed, like three skeins of the finest silk, as I plaited it.

Between us we have given birth to three children. Annie's hair has bleached in this sun and now her hair is like wool and, here and there, even touched with grey. When we hold each other now, we are substantial, matronly. But when I look into her eyes, the years unwind and I arrive back to where we started. A scent of lavender and sage. A breath. We were there together, and now we are here, and that is enough to be going on with.

Frankie gives out his few notes, and I sit up and take him onto my breast, and I take Annie's hand and smile, faintly, and hold on.

I am finished now with the past; I have written it down and spoke it out loud. One day, when my son is of the right age, I will take this soft leather book down from the shelf that Frank made for me to sit opposite our bed below his wedding painting. One day I will wipe the dust from this book and watch how the motes dance in the golden air and fall to the swept floor and then put it in his hands. When he is ready.

I open the door and there is my family, waiting for me, for the work of the day is done, and the baby's face has been washed and his fine hair combed. I see how his darling face cracks open and how he reaches out his arms towards me, his mama. I take him and hold him, wriggling and alive and laughing out loud, and we walk away from our house, and down the river. I look overhead for the birds are circling, and then, in a swift movement they swirl and come in to roost. The great magpies strike out last, one final defiant carol they give us, and then they settle and fall quite silent. Until tomorrow then.

I crook Frankie tighter into my arm and then Annie's arm goes around my shoulder, and we stand there, in the darkening. "We should go in," she says, and then, as if the words have only now become real, as she speaks them out loud, "We should sleep, for Hannah arrives tomorrow." How it sounds, to hear how she speaks out her daughter's name. My name, shared.

We stand for a moment longer, and the sun dips down and then we turn as one, and walk back towards the house. The lamp flickers in the window, for the wind has got itself up, and it brushes the landscape and the cows merge into the meadows, standing stock still. One day we may leave this place, give it back, if it is claimed. If we do go, it will be together.

For now, the gum trees glimmer white, as the light fades and then the wind rouses itself again in the leaves and it whispers to me, "You go on now, girl." And so we do.

Acknowledgements

I came across the story of *The Low Road* in Harleston, in South Norfolk's Waveney valley, where my family settled when I was seven. Thank you to local friends and historians for their sense of the lay of the land, including Kath Wallace, whose paintings of the landscape capture it so well; the Harleston and District Historical Society for old maps and tips, with particular thanks to local historians Margaret Griffiths, Michael Clark and Kate Chennour, and to the Reverend Nigel Tuffnell, who told me about the Redenhall churchyard and the unbaptised babies buried without headstones.

I traced the real-life journeys and experiences of my characters through UK archives, including the Norfolk Record Office, the Hackney Archives in London, the National Archives in Kew and the Old Bailey Proceedings Online. Local and national museums were also helpful, in terms of imagining places and dress from a time before photographs, including True's Yard Fisherfolk Museum in King's Lynn, the Time and Tide Museum in Great Yarmouth and the Norwich Castle Museum for its fine collection of the Norwich School of Artists. In London, I visited the Foundling Museum and went on historical walks to trace some of the key journeys that young women caught up in criminality would have taken. Ken Titmuss led me and others on some of those walks, which helped me to reimagine the Vauxhall Pleasure Gardens, as well as seeing the only surviving galleried stagecoach inn in London, the George, where we drank hot cider on a cold day. To put a hand on one of the walls of what once was the Millbank Penitentiary, behind Tate Britain, was strangely moving, as was seeing the trenches still visible around its former boundaries, now full of washing lines and raised beds. Friends at Hampstead Quaker meeting have been unfailingly knowledgeable about the history of Friends and Elizabeth Fry in particular, as well as being, at all times, so supportive. Thanks also to Ian Bruce, Justin More and Susan Doe, from the Friends of Hackney Archives, Hackney History and The Terrier.

The Royal Literary Fund Fellowship I held for two years at the LSE whilst writing gave me time to research the history behind *The Low Road* more deeply, and an Authors' Foundation grant, which Emma Darwin kindly encouraged me to apply for, financed a trip to Australia.

For the lay of the land in New South Wales, I am indebted to the hospitality and knowledge of Dr Cameron Archer and Mrs Jean Archer for the opportunity to visit colonial era properties, including Tocal Homestead, Paterson, Rouse Hill House, Rouse Hill, and Belgenny Farm, Camden. I also had the opportunity to visit Camden Park House, courtesy of Mr John and Mrs Edwina Macarthur Stanham. Dr Brian Walsh provided invaluable background information on convict life on rural estates.

In and around Sydney, I am grateful to the Parramatta Female Factory Friends, who look after the legacy of the Female Factory there so well – one of 13 such factories for women who arrived from the UK as convicts. Attending the bicentenary events at Parramatta in July 2018 shed light on the hard lives women endured – and on the setting of the factory by the river. In Tasmania, I could have had no better guide to the Cascades Female Factory there and other convict era institutions than Dr Alison Alexander, president of the Convict Women's Press, with thanks also to James Alexander and Reannan Rottier.

Anyone who has British ancestry should be painfully aware of the legacy of the Empire and its devastating effects on Indigenous people and the injustice of our shared history. I have read and honoured the Australian Society of Authors guidelines. I acknowledge the cultures of the Indigenous people and their place as Australia's first storytellers.

Historical fiction couldn't be written without the help of historians and experts – with a novel that spans three locations and two countries even more so. This includes the late Dr Robert Lee, for his book, *Unquiet Country*, about the rural poor in Norfolk, Professor Peter King, for his research on the Refuge for the Destitute, including on same-sex relationships there, as well as the work of Dr Megan Webber. I am indebted to the work of Dr Helen Rogers, who writes on prisons in the UK in the nineteenth century, as well as Associate Professor Tony Moore and Drs Isabel Fangyi Lu and Monika Schwarz from the Conviction Politics project led by Monash University who helped me understand the legacy of colonialism and unfree labour, along with other members, Dr Tim Causer (University College London's Bentham Project), Professor Hamish Maxwell-Stuart (University of New England) and Professor Michael Quinlan (University of NSW) and Steve Thomas from Roar Film.

Although *The Low Road* is based on a true story from my hometown, I have taken some liberties with the geography of the Waveney valley, the architecture of Redenhall church and drawn on a mosaic of real women's lives in the Refuge for the Destitute and before, during and after transportation.

Thank you to editorial consultant Andrew Wille, who gave me the gift of playing with my writing, and to writing friends Kate Beales, Tom Shakespeare and Anne Koch. The Words Away writing salon, run by Kellie Jackson, provided a warm space and a convivial writing community. Thanks also to Melanie Abrahams and Kath Melbourne from the This Is Who We Are programme and Renaissance One for support.

Unbound staff were supportive, right from the early stages, when Katy Guest encouraged me to place *The Low Road* with her, as well as Eve Seymour, Alex Eccles, Imogen Denny, Cassie Waters, Rina Gill, John Mitchinson, Mark Ecob, Sophie Griffiths and Hayley Shepherd. Fellow Unbound authors Alice Jolly and Caroline Sanderson gave valuable advice about the processes involved. Many thanks to the Unbound readers who put their faith in me. I couldn't have done this without you.

Thanks to all my readers – friends at the Islington Writers for Children group, including our much-loved Judy Cumberbatch, who read an edit not long before she died, – and Emma Hindley, Jess Leigh, Jane Mistry, Nicolette David, Lydia Syson, Caroline Preller, Brendan O'Keeffe, Vicky Gayle, Meirion Jones, Cal Park, Abi Hardwick and Catriona Oliphant. Mary Quarmby and Alice Bloch were kind enough to read and discuss a number of edits.

Most of all, thank you to my family – Josie, Raffy, Mary, Paul, Margaret, Chris, Jane, Tom, Alice, Rachel, Sarah, John and Tiffany, and to my friends, for everything.

A Note on the Author

Katharine Quarmby has written non-fiction, short stories and books for children. *The Low Road* is her first novel. Her non-fiction works include *Scapegoat: Why We Are Failing Disabled People* and *No Place to Call Home: Inside the Real Lives of Gypsies and Travellers*. She is also an investigative journalist and editor with particular interests in inequalities, the care system and the environment. Her reporting has appeared in outlets including the *Guardian*, *The Economist*, *The Atlantic*, *The Times*, the *Telegraph*, *New Statesman* and *The Spectator*. Katharine lives in London.

Unbound is the world's first crowdfunding publisher, established in 2011.

We believe that wonderful things can happen when you clear a path for people who share a passion. That's why we've built a platform that brings together readers and authors to crowdfund books they believe in – and give fresh ideas that don't fit the traditional mould the chance they deserve.

This book is in your hands because readers made it possible. Everyone who pledged their support is listed below. Join them by visiting unbound.com and supporting a book today.

Janice Acquah
Savannah Acquah Storey
Claire Adams
Judith Aldridge
Zara Aldwych
Alison Alexander
Claire Alexander
Suki Ali

Alison Allen-Gray
Angus Andrew
Nina Ansary
Cameron Archer
Clive Attwood
Liz Bailey
Caroline Bald
Vasileah Antigone Bassel

David Bausor
Kate Beales
Angharad Beckett
Julie Belanger
Emilia Benjamin
Tom Fortune Benskin
Ben Bergonzi
Sheila Bielby
Nikki Bielinski
Alice Bloch
Mathew Bloch
Paul Bloch
Rachel Bloch
Wendy Bottero
Victoria Boydell
Tim Brady
Deborah Brower
Su Brown
Sam Burgess
Kirsty C
Kirsten Campbell
Carter
Barbara Challender
Oliver Charles
Thalia Charles
Kate Chenneour
Katherine Clanchy
Michael Clark
Martha Clements
Mary Clunes
Dan Cochran
Allan Cochrane
Richard Coleman
Grace Conway

Rachel Cooper
The Cosmetatos Family
Elizabeth Coulter
Virginia Crompton
Carmen David
Caroline David
Frederick David
Gabriel David
Nicolette David
Leonora Davies
ADW Decorators
    (Lancaster)
Julie A Dexter
Susan Doe
Giorgia Dona
Kate Donoughue
Anna Eagar
Robert Eardley
Carole Elliott
Odette Elliott
Andrew Ellson
Michele Emerson
Robyn Fairman
Sara Feilden
Amanda Fine
Jane French
Sarah Fussell-Quarmby
Elizabeth Gardiner
Lucy Gaster
Vicky Gayle
Maggie Gee
Malcolm Gibson
Frances Ginn
Ruth Gladwin

Deirdre Godfray
Tom Green
Margaret Greenfields
Joanne Greenway
Lucia Grun
Samantha Gruskin
Katy Guest
Abi Hardwick
Jane Harris
Neil Harrison
Clare Hemmings
Margot K. Herstad
Emma Hindley
Jane Hindley
Katherine Hindley
Tony Histed
Madeleine Holt
Antonia Honeywell
Valerie Hooley
Izzy Hopwood
Emma Howey
Allison Hulmes
Kellie Jackson
Mike James
Mike Jempson
Jet
Alice Jolly
Anatole Jolly
Bill Jones
Meirion Jones
Nicolette Jones
Mary Jordan-Smith
Annabel Judd
Diana Kader

Frances Keeton
Ella "Kind" Kennedy
Dan Kieran
Delagh King
Clare Kinsella
Judith Kleinman
Anne Koch
Emma Krasinska
Helene Kreysa
Carmen Kukuljevic-David
Kinneret Lahad
Dawn Le-Gros
Ciara Leeming
Jessica Leigh
Camille Lofters
Mac Logan
Kari Long
Audrey Ludwig
Cas Macdonald
Kate Maguire
Mel Massey
Tracey Matthews
Natasha Maw
Catriona May
Pete May
Sadie McClelland
Linda McDougall
Ebony McKenzie
Alison Mcnaught
Jane Mcroberts
Sheila Melzak
Tim Minogue
Alisha Miranda
Jane Mistry

Elen Mitchell Reid
John Mitchinson
Nathaly Molle
Yann Monnet
Tony Moore
Sahar Moussavi
Jessica Moxham Lynch
Kate Nash
Carlo Navato
Sarah Neal
Dorothy Newton
Julia Newton
Megg Nicol
Sian Norris
Gem Novis
B O'Keeffe
Brendan O'Keeffe
John O'Leary
Lindsay O'Leary
Karen O'Sullivan
Julia Oakley
Andrea Oates
Catriona Oliphant
Renaissance One
Diana Osborne
Rachel P
Cal Park
Steph Parker
Hugh Pearson
Margaret Pearson
Katrina Phillips
Mark Phillips
Oliver Phillips
Justin Pollard

Caroline Preller
Faziah Prentice
Siân Prime
John Pring
Eeva-Maria Puska
Jane Quarmby
Paul Quarmby
Raphael Quarmby
Tony Quinn
Susannah Radstone
Caroline Reid
Naomi Renek
Richie
Sean Risdale
Rob Ritchie
Nick Robinson
Helen Rogers
Marion Rose
Jonathan Rosenthal
Reannan Rottier
Adrienne Rowe
Katherine Runswick-Cole
Donald Russell
Louise Russell
Angus Saer
Saba Salman
Caroline Sanderson
Joanna Sargent
Naomi Schillinger
Liza Schuster
Tom Shakespeare
GIll Shepherd
Candy Sheridan
Tiffany Sibthorp

Gabriel Sibthorp-Quarmby
Saranjit Sihota
Rebecca Simor
Ruth Slade Walker
Michelle Smart
Hanisha Solomon
John Solomos
Kathleen Stock
Mike Storey
Helen Sumbler
Carrie Supple
Lydia Syson
Carrie T
Natasha Tahta
Jacqui Timberlake
Josie Tindale
Raffy Tindale
Penny Tinkler
To my lovely daughter
    Anushree Uma
    Gupta-Smith
Sarah Toner
Frances Traynor
Mary Turbin

Matthew Turbin
Imogen Tyler
Sophie Tyson
Stephen Unwin
Dawn van den Berg-Hider
Priya Vansia
Katharine Wallace
Brian Walsh
Jessica Warren
Lynda Waterhouse
Andy Way
Ruth Wayte
Wahab Weli
Wahab Weli and Judy
    Cumberbatch
Allie Wharf
Francis Wheen
Alex White
Andrew Wille
Adam Williamson
Dawn Williamson
Philip Womack
Alicia Wood
Leah Y